Charlotte turned her head to find Ben watching her with amused speculation. Sometimes it seemed to her as if the wretched man had been regarding her so since they first met.

"I am here as a chaperon, sir, not an idle guest with nothing on her mind but flirtation and gossip," she said tartly, hoping he wouldn't realize she'd been covertly watching him flirt mildly with a lovely blonde widow for most of the evening.

"I really don't think it would be a good idea for me to indulge in an amour with you tonight, Miss Wells," he murmured silkily, revealing that he was as conscious of her uneasy disapproval as she was of feeling it.

He gave a soft chuckle when she sent him a look that should have turned him to stone. He sat on as serene and content as an alderman at the Lord Mayor's banquet.

"I have no wish to indulge in such wanton behavior at any time, sir, and least of all with you."

Oh, how she wished that last caveat were entirely true!

* * *

Rebellious Rake, Innocent Governess
Harlequin® Historical #267—September 2009

ELIZABETH BEACON

lives in the beautiful English west country, and is finally putting her insatiable curiosity about the past to good use. Over the years Elizabeth has worked in her family's horticultural business, become a mature student, qualified as an English teacher, worked as a secretary and, briefly, tried to be a civil servant. She is now happily ensconced behind her computer, when not trying to exhaust her bouncy rescue dog with as many walks as the Inexhaustible Lurcher can finagle. Elizabeth can't bring herself to call researching the wonderfully diverse, scandalous Regency period and creating charismatic heroes and feisty heroines work, and she is waiting for someone to find out how much fun she is having and tell her to stop it.

Rebellious Rake,
Innocent Governess

ELIZABETH BEACON

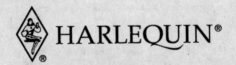

HARLEQUIN®

TORONTO • NEW YORK • LONDON
AMSTERDAM • PARIS • SYDNEY • HAMBURG
STOCKHOLM • ATHENS • TOKYO • MILAN • MADRID
PRAGUE • WARSAW • BUDAPEST • AUCKLAND

Recycling programs
for this product may
not exist in your area.

ISBN-13: 978-0-373-30576-6

REBELLIOUS RAKE, INNOCENT GOVERNESS

Copyright © 2009 by Elizabeth Beacon

www.eHarlequin.com

Printed in U.S.A.

Chapter One

It had been a mistake to come. In fact, Charlotte decided crossly, it would have been better if she had never left her post at Miss Thibett's select academy for young ladies in Bath in the first place. She'd been perfectly content with life as an ordinary teacher until the new Countess of Carnwood had offered her the position of governess to her younger sisters. How she wished now that she'd refused to listen to Miranda Alstone's persuasion and was still a humble schoolteacher. As a schoolgirl herself, she'd been in awe of the lovely and vivacious Miranda, a year older than she was and a world away in looks and confidence. When Miranda had turned up at Miss Thibett's two years ago, married to her late grandfather's scapegrace heir and very distant cousin, Charlotte should have recalled that spoilt young miss Miranda had once been and hardened her heart against this much more likeable Miranda Alstone and refused point blank to leave her job and her sanctuary.

Charlotte had enjoyed teaching her classes more than she had expected when she had become a schoolmistress out of dire necessity seven years ago. Miranda's little sisters, Katherine and Isabella Alstone, were delightful young women of course and her lot was much happier than that of the average governess, but she had her future to consider and even the youngest Miss Alstone was now fifteen. Already they were in town for Kate's début and that fact alone might prove Charlotte's undoing.

She surveyed the overheated ballroom and tried not to wish for delicate muslins or a mere satin slip with a light gauze over-gown, instead of the acres of suffocating grey crepe she now wore. How much better off she would have been marking essays and contriving next day's lessons in her last employment, she thought disgustedly. Instead here she was, reluctantly accompanying the Honourable Katherine Alstone, granddaughter of the last Earl of Carnwood and sister-in-law to the current one, to this society crush in the Countess of Carnwood's stead and enduring the company of the most infuriating male she had ever had the misfortune to encounter, which only added to her miseries.

When Mr Ben Shaw joined herself and Kate in the carriage tonight he had looked at her as if she were akin to a piece of furniture astray from its rightful place. A side table, suddenly putting itself forward in the centre of the room perhaps, she decided crossly, or more likely a plain deal kitchen table trying to pass itself off as something far more elegant in a lady's drawing room. Well, she certainly hadn't asked to come, and if he didn't like her company he should never have forced her into the role of chaperon for the night. Doubtless he'd only remembered her existence once he had exhausted every other possibility and it wasn't her fault if she looked more like an antiquated quiz than a lady a man like Ben Shaw would be proud to accompany to a ball. After all, she *was* an antiquated quiz and perfectly content with her lot. Yes, of course she was; the sort of ladies Mr Shaw normally accompanied had very different ambitions from hers, and she had no wish whatsoever to end the evening in his bed, thank you very much.

They might not have been more than nodding acquaintances at school all those years ago, but she and Miranda had become good friends over the last two years and she knew that, while Ben Shaw was rich and astonishingly successful now, he'd grown up on the same squalid streets as the new Earl, but without the benefit of legitimacy to protect him from some of the slings and arrows thrown his way. Even Charlotte had to secretly admit he was a powerful and handsome man who gathered beautiful women like bees did honey, but, Miranda had cautioned unnecessarily, he'd long ago forsworn marriage and regarded the idea of fatherhood of any sort with unswerving revulsion. Yet despite all that tonight, as he handed her up into the carriage she'd felt a ridiculous flutter in her usually cynical breast and briefly longed to be beautiful, so she could at least wipe the bland, condescending smile off his handsome face and make him take notice. Not that she would know what to do with it if he centred that formidable will and intellect on her, but it would have been satisfying to see him rocked back on his heels by admiration and desire for someone he couldn't have for once, instead of the mild surprise she had detected behind that social smile that such a plain and spinsterish female was about to share his exotic company for an entire evening.

To soothe her ridiculous agitation over such a masculine and utterly maddening irritation as Mr Shaw, Charlotte let nostalgia for her former quiet existence overtake her for a moment, if only to blot out the discomfort of sitting in this noisy ballroom, trying desperately hard not to be noticed. After all, she had been content over the last two years to be invisible to the world outside the schoolroom and Mr Ben Shaw, so why should tonight be any different? No reason at all, she reassured herself and went back to reviewing her career as a schoolmarm. It had begun with awe at the task ahead and sheer hard work, as she learnt her trade from a mistress of the art. Not for Miss Thibett the perfunctory education and insipid accomplishments most establishments for the education of young ladies insisted upon. No, a young lady who graduated from her elegant academy in Queen's Square would have an unusual grasp of mathematics, literature and the world around them, as well as more ladylike skills such as water-colour painting, music and fine needlework. Not that many people here tonight would appreciate such a breadth of knowledge, Charlotte mused cynically.

She observed the *haut ton* at play and concluded that they took their amusement as seriously as those less fortunate did the hard work needed to keep the wolf from the door. At least she had escaped the chaperons' benches for this quiet niche, she decided, trying hard to see a silver lining to her current cloud, and she wondered how many of the duennas present tonight understood they were as wrapped up in commerce as a Lord Mayor's banquet. Instead of silks, perfumes and spices, or raw materials to feed the voracious manufactories in the north, they were the purveyors of delicately brought up young ladies of course. Even so, it was a commercial transaction and Charlotte sat a little further back in her alcove as she tried to reassure herself that her particular young lady was very much her own person and would have something very pungent to say to anyone who suggested she sold herself in return for a fine house and a title.

The idea was laughable. Charlotte considered Miranda's appalling misadventures after such a charmed beginning, and her husband Kit's early life at the mercy of a drunken, spendthrift father living precariously in the meanest part of town. They had both been forged into something more than they might have been if the fates had been kinder to them, and overcome their troubles magnificently, so forcing Miranda's sisters into marriage for the usual dynastic reasons was unthinkable. The Earl and Countess of Carnwood would never do that, even if they lost every penny of their vast fortunes, Charlotte thought wistfully, and tried not to wish her happiness had been of such crucial importance to her own relatives. No, she refused to sit about repining about the past, or she would do if there was only something better to do, she thought crossly, and wiped the frown off her face and tried to look inconspicuous as possible in this ill-lit corner of the ballroom.

It wasn't easy to efface yourself when you were about as tall as a lady could get without being publicly displayed as a curiosity, but she managed it more often than not nowadays. Charlotte fiddled with her snowy cap and adjusted a strategic piece of lace to conceal the suggestion of a curl that she pushed back into hiding with exasperated efficiency. She had a job keeping her rebellious locks in place at the best of times, but if they showed themselves here the results could be disastrous. It would never do for some sharp-eyed dowager to detect even a hint of the gangling débutante who had once sat out so many dances at her chaperon's side beneath the guise of a humble duenna.

'Ah, so there you are, Miss Wells,' a deep voice rumbled at her side and made her jump at least six inches. Charlotte shivered in the stuffy air of Lady Wintergreen's elegant ballroom with an infuriating mix of apprehension and excitement. How could such a very large man move so silently that she had no idea he was anywhere near her until he spoke? And where else did he think she would be when this entire fiasco was his fault in the first place?

'Go away!' she ordered rudely, even as she strained her neck to meet Mr Benedict Shaw's altogether too intelligent grey eyes challengingly.

He just laughed at her as usual, and gave her the

quizzical smile that usually swept all feminine opposition before him so effortlessly, despite *his* dubious credentials as cavalier to an innocent young débutante. She had a very long way to look, she decided absently, and put a hand to the back of her head to make sure her cap stayed securely in place. Unused to being towered over by anyone and recalling the humiliation of looking down on nearly all her dance partners during her ill-fated Season, she firmly squashed the idea that to waltz with the very tall and broad-shouldered Mr Shaw could quite possibly feel a little too wonderful.

'May I not sit beside you for even a short time while I rest my weary bones then, Miss Wells?' he asked mildly and she wondered what he was about this time, for in her opinion Mr Shaw had never been meek or mild in his entire life and probably only slept when he could spare a few moments from his busy schedule to do so.

'What a ludicrous idea,' she dismissed tartly.

'Ludicrous?' he echoed contemplatively. 'I have been called many things during the course of my chequered career, Miss Wells, but so far that's not one of them. If you can tell me why my sitting beside Miss Alstone's very respectable chaperon whilst I politely await my dance with her charge could be construed as ludicrous by anyone but yourself, I might even oblige you and take myself off.'

'For the very reason that I am her chaperon and about as dull a female as you could find if you scoured every ballroom in Mayfair,' she parried crossly as he sat anyway, despite her embargo.

'Nonsense, you are very far from dull, Miss Wells, although it's plain to me, if to nobody else, that you study very hard to appear so,' he observed coolly and watched her steadily, trying to look as if butter wouldn't melt in his mouth and not succeeding at all well. 'I have the misfortune to be very tall, you see,' he said with a look of quite spurious innocence as she continued to glare back at him in a most unladylike fashion. 'You would have got a crick in your swanlike neck had I continued to stand, Miss Wells, and no doubt that would have been my fault as well.'

'Well, of course it would,' she answered and made herself look away from the suppressed laughter in his apparently guileless grey eyes.

Finding nothing fascinating enough to engage her attention, she shot him an even more irate glare and wondered how he knew everything about tonight's débâcle was to be laid at his door.

'You should never have sought me out in the first place,' she informed him grumpily and turned her head to find him watching her with amused speculation. Sometimes it seemed to her as if the wretched man had been regarding her so since they first met, and she was heartily sick of being the butt of some private joke. 'I am here as a chaperon, sir, not an idle guest with nothing on her mind but flirtation and gossip,' she added tartly, hoping he wouldn't realise she'd been covertly watching him flirt mildly with a lovely blonde widow for most of the evening.

'I really don't think it would be a good idea for me

to indulge in an *amour* with you tonight, Miss Wells,' he murmured silkily, revealing that he was as conscious of her uneasy disapproval as she was of feeling it.

He gave a soft chuckle when she gave him a look that should have turned him to stone and sat on, as serene and content as an alderman at the Lord Mayor's banquet. No wonder her palm itched to slap that parody of a gentleman's politely interested smile in the face of small talk off his handsome face.

'I have no wish to indulge in such wanton behaviour at any time, sir, and least of all with you,' she said sharply and wished that last *caveat* were entirely true.

There was a silly, and usually firmly suppressed, side to Charlotte's nature that had never quite relinquished the romantic rebellion of her youth. That Charlotte had stood to attention the moment Ben Shaw hoved into view two years ago, and had annoyed her everyday self at the most inconvenient moments ever since. Now the silly idiot clearly yearned to become the sort of female who could exchange languishing glances with a gentleman in search of more sophisticated amusements, and lure him to heaven knew what wanton and forbidden rendezvous that a true lady shouldn't even know about, let alone consider in her wildest fantasies. She was rather foggy about how a *femme fatale* behaved once she had lured her quarry into her perfumed lair, of course, but that other Charlotte was quite willing to improvise, at least if the shortness of breath she suddenly suffered at the very idea was anything to go by. It was all utter nonsense, of course, sensible Miss Wells informed her fiery secret self, and met Mr Shaw's eyes with chilly resolution.

'I, sir, am a chaperon. It is my duty to watch over Miss Alstone and make sure nobody can level the accusation that she was so laxly chaperoned that her reputation might be in danger. That is my purpose and my destiny,' she finished rather wistfully and quite spoilt the effect of her first chilly statement.

'Now *you* are being ludicrous, Miss Wells. Those young cubs wouldn't even blink the wrong way with your stern eye on them, even if they were intent on mischief, which I doubt as they're clearly besotted with the little minx and have sickeningly honourable intentions. Besides that, I dare say young Shuttleworth is so upright and respectable he could chaperon Kate himself, if you weren't here to play the watchdog so determinedly, and nobody would raise an eyebrow,' he asserted outrageously.

Such a foolish notion appealed to the sense of humour she usually managed to conceal in mixed company and she couldn't help smiling at such a revolutionary notion. Lord Shuttleworth was indeed a very virtuous and earnest young man, but he would look very odd indeed sitting with the dowagers, frowning at Kate's many admirers and shaking his head over the more rakish of their number. Come to think of it, he would probably perform the role far too diligently, and make sure Kate only danced with himself.

'You are most certainly mistaken in that notion, sir, and I still wish you would go away,' she informed him forthrightly, having long ago discovered there was no point in wrapping up her meaning in the polite conventions where Mr Shaw was concerned—and almost as useless as trying to carve rock with embroidery scissors, in her experience.

'And there I was hoping you'd take pity on me and grant me a dance. You must admit it's a confounded nuisance for a tall man to stoop over his partner like a grazing crane every time he's fool enough to take to the floor with the usual run of female,' he teased, doing his best to look as if he needed her sympathy when he was the least deserving case she had come across.

Despite his lowly upbringing, or maybe even because of it, Mr Benedict Shaw had succeeded in cutting a swathe through the more sophisticated beauties of the *ton*, and Charlotte suspected his great wealth had very little to do with that success. He was very much a man among the shallow youths who usually clustered about Kate, and even those gentlemen who were his equal in years faded to insignificance in his vibrant company. She couldn't currently recall another single gentleman who matched him in either height or presence herself, which was very annoying of them now she came to think of it. No, hardship and sheer bull-headed stubbornness had honed him from an illegitimate waif from the slums into a subtle and dangerous man of power, and only a fool would underestimate Mr Shaw.

If she had ever been among their number, the ease with which he moved among the finicky *ton* would have opened her eyes to his dubious talents. And he had even done his best to conceal rather than reveal the fact that some very aristocratic blood indeed came to him on one side of the wrong blanket he was born under. He cheerfully admitted to being the son of a seamstress on the other, and still the rigid rules of society had first bent and then broken under the impact of his peculiar brand of charm, and the weight of his lifelong friendship with the current Earl of Carnwood, of course.

Charlotte surveyed Ben Shaw surreptitiously, while pretending to watch the dancers as if utterly absorbed in the figures of the dance. He made few concessions to the outward conventions, she decided, with a sniff of disapproval she hoped would be drowned out by the music. In this day and age, a gentleman did not go abroad with his unruly blond hair allowed to grow so overlong that he had to tie it back in an old-fashioned queue, which she absently noted was tied with black velvet rather than leather tonight, and really rather becoming. Giant that he was, he cut a magnificent figure in a superbly cut black tailcoat and restrained grey silk waistcoat. To herself, she could admit to feeling incredulity that he had donned the meticulously correct knee breeches and stockings of a gentleman's evening dress as well.

He must be very fond of Kate to have forced himself into such a concession for her sake, she conceded, as Charlotte could never recall seeing him in such garb before. Mr Shaw usually claimed to be far too big for such refinement, but secretly she thought he looked magnificent. It was a demanding fashion to carry off, and some of the dandy set padded their puny calves to make them look shapelier, but he certainly had no need for such artifice. Long, strong and muscular, his limbs were honed to perfection by his energetic lifestyle and, if she secretly compared every gentleman she had seen tonight to his mighty form and found them not only wanting but almost invisible, there was no reason on earth why anyone should know it, least of all Ben Shaw himself.

Charlotte allowed her silly heart to flutter just the tiniest bit as she forced her gaze back up to his perfectly tied cravat, and told herself she should have the experience to hide her thoughts and feelings from him and the rest of the world by now. His face was rather memorable as well, she decided distractedly, trying hard to disapprove of the ridiculous hairstyle he habitually adopted and failing as she finally met his amused grey gaze and realised he had known exactly what she was thinking all along.

'Am I to have an answer at all, Miss Wells, or do you consider me unworthy of one?' he asked brusquely and she thought she caught a lightning glimpse of a much younger and surprisingly sensitive Ben Shaw under that pose of indifference to the world and his wife.

'I thought you merely jesting, Mr Shaw, for you know as well as I that chaperons don't dance,' she informed him flatly, even as her heartbeat increased at the very thought of doing so with him, because it would expose her to far too many interested eyes, of course.

'Nor do cits,' he replied with a rueful grimace she refused to even countenance—he was far too much at ease in company, of whatever kind, for her to feel the least need to bolster his self-esteem. 'And I really don't think Mrs Ramsden agrees with you,' he added with an expression of such dowagerly shock that she had to suppress a silly urge to laugh with him at the follies of mature society beauties who ought to know much better than to openly pursue rather *risqué* gentlemen, while supposedly chaperoning her innocent young daughter.

'Miss Ramsden has my sympathy,' she said truthfully and shot the still lushly beautiful Mrs Ramsden a covert glance as that lady danced airily past with another admirer and received a furious glare in return. 'Maybe you should dance with Mrs Ramsden again if you really want to set the dovecotes fluttering,' she added cynically. Without even trying to, she had won herself at least one enemy tonight, and how right she had been to wish herself a hundred miles away.

'I'm told the lady has extensive gambling debts and is in search of a new husband with limitless credit and an accommodating nature. As my chief detractor, you must surely admit that she is very much mistaken in thinking I might be that man, Miss Wells,' he told her with an ironic smile.

'You would have me save you from fortune hunters, sir?' she said lightly, in an attempt to avoid the thought that she could indeed pity him just a little after all.

Never to know if the slavish feminine attention he received was the product of lust, or lust *and* avarice, must be a severe trial to a proud man, and something told her Ben Shaw was a very proud man indeed. Some of the so-called gentlemen she had encountered would no doubt pour scorn on the notion that a dressmaker's by-blow had anything to be proud of, although probably not to his face, but she thought they erred rather mightily.

'Or at the very least from a female I overtop by at least a foot and a half and must always make ridiculous, Miss Wells,' he returned lightly enough, but suddenly she could see something more in those fascinating grey eyes. It was almost as if he could read her thoughts, she decided, resolving to stop them being on show to a shrewd man like Ben Shaw a little more determinedly in future.

'As ludicrous as you must make a governess by such attentions,' she told him steadily enough, as she looked coolly away and saw with relief that the quadrille was over at last and Kate was making her way towards them with her very correct young swain.

'That appears to be a favourite word of yours tonight, Miss Wells, but I have no desire to make you so, whatever you may think. One day, my dear Miss Wells, I'll have that dance with you and you'll be forced to agree that we complement each other to the finest degree, or prove yourself a liar to both of us,' he threatened as he rose to his feet and towered over her once more.

For a moment even she felt a little intimidated by his mighty presence, and Lord Shuttleworth looked as flustered as he might if a mountain suddenly uprooted itself and walked towards him. Profoundly annoyed with her unwanted companion for making all four of them conspicuous against her express wishes, Charlotte forced herself to breathe deeply and evenly as she also rose to greet the newcomers. For a moment there had seemed to be a promise in that complex gaze of his that she dare not read, but surely she was mistaken?

Gentlemen who towered over the general run of their kind with no effort or noticeable gratification didn't flirt with plain and virtually penniless governesses, who had long ago given up on their last prayers. It simply didn't happen, not to her and not to any other sensible female in her position who valued her peace of mind. Charlotte ordered her thudding heartbeat to resume some semblance of its usual smooth rhythm, and tried to ignore the disturbing fact that she felt so stupidly at home standing at Mr Shaw's side. It took an assured gentleman to ignore her inches and, just for once, she felt like most women must as he towered over her. Fragile she most certainly was not, but she felt so for a reckless moment.

Reminding herself it was her declared aim in life to be the most quiet and mouse-like of duennas, despite her natural disadvantages, she forced her shoulders to slump and adjusted the eyeglasses on her nose so she could peer at the world as if quite lost without them. Fortunately for her that was another lie, but there was no sensible reason to waive an extra layer of camouflage in such dangerous company.

'What a squeeze,' Kate observed wearily as soon as she had got her breath back, and Charlotte hid a smile at the weary sophistication of the young lady standing in front of her.

Not six weeks ago Kate had begged to be excused her début, on the grounds that she could never learn to comport herself properly in the drawing rooms of the *ton*, even if she wanted to. As Charlotte eyed her flame-haired former pupil with wry amusement, she knew Kate had grown up at last and told herself to be glad. Even so, she couldn't help but eye her former charge anxiously. Rich and aristocratic young women had a harder furrow to plough through life than most people thought, and Kate had more brains than were probably good for her. A sillier young miss might be content with a marriage of convenience and quietly bearing the future lords of England, but what would Kate make of the marriage mart and all the pitfalls it contained for a young lady of spirit?

The Honourable Miss Alstone was tall for a lady, although not on her own unfortunate scale, as well as being a beauty of rare distinction. In fact, her former pupil showed every sign of becoming the belle of the Season, and Charlotte silently predicted a procession of smitten hopefuls clogging up Lord Carnwood's busy schedule when he returned from Ireland. Not that Charlotte had seen any sign of partiality when Kate's deep blue gaze rested on any of her court. If anything, she thought Kate rather amused by their antics and thought them no more than boys. She was right of course, Charlotte decided, at least for the most part. Young Lord Shuttleworth was sincerely attached to her friend and a warning not to trample too heavily on his dreams might not go amiss when she found the right moment.

'Would you care for refreshments, Miss Alstone?' he asked earnestly now with a look of rapt worship.

'Heavens, no, I feel as if I'm awash with lemonade already,' Kate replied carelessly, 'but Miss Wells has not indulged quite as often as I have, so perhaps she is thirsty?'

Lord Shuttleworth bowed politely and tried to look as if he could think of no greater honour than fetching orgeat for a dowd. He really had the most exquisite manners, Charlotte concluded and wondered if he'd truly thought about Kate's suitability as the wife of such a serious young peer. No doubt Kate would lead him about by the nose if she ever succumbed to his serious air, ancient title and rumoured fortune.

Charlotte sincerely hoped her eldest protégée would wait for a gentleman who would challenge and stimulate her excellent mind, as well as doing the same for the more sensual side that almost certainly lay under her innocent impulsiveness and fiery temper. And when had Miss Charlotte Wells become an expert on love and marriage? She refused to answer that question, even in the privacy of her own mind, and obligingly declined Lord Shuttleworth's polite offer of refreshment. Obviously feeling towered over by Mr Shaw and humiliatingly overtopped by Kate's chaperon, that young gentleman bowed and took himself off.

'Never mind, Miss Wells,' Mr Shaw consoled outrageously, 'I'm made of far sterner stuff and shall bring you a glass of champagne after I've done my duty and danced with this irritating little chit.'

Charlotte contented herself with raising her chin in

the air and enjoying looking down her nose at a very disobliging gentleman for once.

'How dare you call me so in public?' Kate flamed back at him.

'Because you're an appalling brat, and likely to become completely intolerable if these silly young pups convince you you're a cross between a goddess and an angel come down from heaven to dazzle them, which is very far from the truth, I'm pleased to say,' he said with a grimace of distaste.

'Oh, I pay no attention to them,' Kate dismissed with an airy wave of her hand and Charlotte thought she was telling the truth, even if Mr Shaw doubted her from the frown pleating his unfairly dark brows together.

'Have a care, princess,' he cautioned, 'they're just whelps and quite unused to dealing with feisty little monkeys like you. You'll break their silly hearts if you don't watch out. I don't want you branded a heartless flirt, for all you're a confounded nuisance.'

'No, for you're as soft hearted as Kit's favourite mastiff under all that "to the devil with you all" air of yours, aren't you, Mr Shaw?' Kate taunted softly.

'Don't forget how fearsomely Spartacus barks and growls at anyone he doesn't like, minx, and have a care for my skin. I make far too large a target to be called out for thumping one of the young idiots when they try to force what they can't get with your consent.'

'I don't see what business it is of yours,' Kate responded rather sulkily. 'Anyone would think you were my chaperon, not Miss Wells.'

This last was said with a reproachful glance at Charlotte, who was trying hard to look both innocent and sympathetic, while secretly agreeing with Mr Shaw for once.

'I'd rather have half my teeth pulled,' he responded amiably enough and Kate laughed, her temper forgotten as soon as it fired.

'You really are the most disobliging gentleman I ever came across. I've half a mind to marry *you* and make both our lives a misery, just to serve you with your own sauce,' she told him, her bluest of blue eyes sparkling with mischief and Charlotte thought not one gentleman in a thousand could fail to be charmed.

'I'll manage without any teeth at all to be spared that,' he responded, giving Kate a straight look to discourage any more experiments in flirtation.

'Don't worry, the other half of my mind is the sensible one and couldn't tolerate a domestic tyrant like you, Ben Shaw,' Kate replied.

'Good, you need a stern critic to keep you in line, miss, but it won't be me. Now, if we don't make haste they'll start the dance without us and I'm conspicuous enough on the dance floor without insinuating us on to it after the music starts.'

'It would give the faster ladies of your acquaintance more chance to admire your manly form,' Kate teased relentlessly and Charlotte wondered at her courage, but all he did was shake his head sadly, as if despairing of her former charge.

'Behave yourself, brat,' he ordered not very seriously, and with one last, complex look at Charlotte that made her feel more confused than ever, he led his partner on to the dance floor.

Satisfied Kate was intending to behave herself, Charlotte could resume her anonymity and brood in peace. She should be profoundly grateful to be spared Ben Shaw's infuriating company, she decided, but somehow she wasn't and sat back on her uncomfortable sofa feeling out of sorts with herself and the rest of the world. Watching them dance so harmoniously caused her a pang she had a terrible suspicion might be jealousy. Heartburn, she assured herself prosaically, and considered the idea that Mr Shaw could be the man of sufficient character, humour and humanity to become Kate's husband.

Some remnant of the silly romantic girl she'd once been rebelled at the notion of that match for the girl she'd come to love over the last two years. And while she was about it, that part of her seemed to hate the notion of Mr Shaw becoming permanently unavailable to plague and infuriate *her*. Reminding herself never to eat apricot fool again, she tried to divert herself with the company, but failed rather badly as her eyes were drawn to that well-matched pair gliding about the floor in such harmony.

Charlotte suspected she was not the only one speculating that their partnership might become more permanent in time. It would be a splendid match in material terms, she supposed. Kate was very well dowered and of ancient lineage and Ben Shaw was so fabulously wealthy his irregular birth was largely ignored, except in the most finicky circles where she doubted Kate had the least wish to shine. He could be charming as well as amiable when he chose to be, and apparently he could take his pick among the high-flyers against some very aristocratic competition. She really shouldn't know about that side of his life, she told herself sternly, and must stop pricking up her ears whenever his name was mentioned by the Alstones' footmen and they thought she wasn't listening. Then there was his avowed intention of never marrying anyone. Given that he would have to be so deeply in love with Kate as not to be able to stop himself offering for her, why did the very idea of a marriage between Ben Shaw and Kate seem an abomination?

Was it because he must be about three and thirty and Kate was just eighteen, perhaps? A significant gap, but hardly insurmountable. Nobody with the slightest intention of being fair-minded could accuse Ben Shaw of being anything but in his prime, and Kate had wit and a keen intelligence to add to her youthful glowing beauty. When she matured, she would be a rare creature indeed, and Charlotte thought her former pupil would become a real force for good if she wed the right man. So was the right man the infuriating giant dancing so lightly with the vibrant young creature who absorbed the attention of most young gentlemen in the room one way and another? No, the bone-deep certainty of that answer surprised her, and sent Miss Wells, governess, home with a very thoughtful frown on her shadowed face as all three sat silent in the Earl of Carnwood's comfortable town coach later that night.

Chapter Two

Ben lay back against the luxurious squabs, considering a curiously unsatisfactory evening. He'd gone to Lady Wintergreen's ball to keep an eye on Miss Kate Alstone in his best friend's absence and, with Miss Wells's reluctant help, had successfully done so. Yet something crucial had been missing and he tried to reassure himself it wasn't the lack of a dance with the disapproving dragon seated opposite.

He wondered idly if she concealed an elegant little tail under the acres of grey crepe that she used to conceal her figure from the eyes of the world. There was no doubt she breathed fire, he decided ruefully, as he recalled some of the barbs she had shot at him tonight. Yet there was something about Miss Charlotte Wells that made him eager to know what lay under all that disapproval. Under her formidable exterior no doubt there was a formidable woman, but, whoever she was, she fascinated him, and he'd never been one to shirk a challenge. The question was, a challenge to what?

He wasn't rake enough to make a dead set at a lady in impoverished circumstances. He frowned as he contemplated the careless actions of such men, for hadn't his father seduced his mother, then denied her and his bastard as if they were strangers he might pass in the street? Ben admired his late mother more than any woman he'd ever known, but he was certain her life would have been far better if he'd never been born. He could never inflict such suffering on a woman and he'd made sure no woman he was involved with risked carrying his child. So, if he didn't intend to storm the stoutly defended Fortress Wells, why on earth had he been trying to flirt with her in the middle of Lady Wintergreen's overcrowded ball?

Because trying was all he would ever manage, the uneasy answer occurred to him as he stared broodingly into the darkness. Had she just become a challenge he couldn't quite resist? He shook his head and hoped not and his stern expression softened as he watched Kate asleep on her dragon's shoulder, as if it was far more comfortable than it appeared. Then they passed a lamppost and he saw Miss Wells's face momentarily through the gloom and it looked curiously softened. She'd removed those ugly spectacles and the clear-cut lines of her finely made features were momentarily visible, both illuminated and shadowed by the soft glow.

He recalled the first occasion he'd met the Alstone girls and their fearsome governess, almost two years ago now, and he'd keenly enjoyed the clash of arms between them on the rare occasions he'd met her since then. Kit Alstone had been his best friend ever since they could both walk, and Ben had agreed to escort the carriage from Bath to Derbyshire, despite the fact he had a hundred things to do and a dozen other places to do them in. He'd been a little impatient of the whole business, but knew his very presence riding by the Earl of Carnwood's travelling carriage would stop most highwaymen in their tracks. After all, there was every reason to guard three unprotected females allied to his friend, when they'd made too many enemies for comfort in the rise to success.

In a spirit of resignation, he'd set out to escort two no doubt timorous young girls and their superannuated governess and found the artlessly outgoing Misses Alstone and their young dragon instead. No doubt one glare from the formidable Miss Wells and the most enterprising villain would instantly have turned to stone, or hastily dropped his pistols and run home to his mother, but they'd met with no reckless challenges on that memorable journey. Ben just managed to hide a grin as lamplight now splayed over him instead of his own particular dragon. Ever since he laid eyes on the very correct Miss Wells, he'd struggled with the urge to kiss her until she was breathless and bemused, and finally giving the lie to her rigidly severe exterior. So far he'd stopped himself, just, but if she went on producing those comedy spectacles at every opportunity his self-restraint might not last.

Yet in the two years since he had first set eyes on her, he'd managed to learn almost nothing about the elusive Miss Wells, which was a mystery in itself. He could usually discover whatever he needed to know about a person within two days of setting eyes on them, so either Miss Wells had lived a life of such tedious respectability that she had rendered herself thoroughly unmemorable, or she wasn't exactly who she seemed. Up until now he'd been content to trust his judgement that the woman was harmless, at least to her charges and his friends, and she even seemed quite fond of them and unbent noticeably whenever she thought he wasn't about. Yet lately he'd been experiencing a familiar tension that warned him trouble was too close, and anything out of kilter must now be considered a threat.

He frowned thoughtfully and shot the stately figure of the governess a sidelong glance. What was it about the wretched female that goaded him into being less kind than he should be, he wondered? He wouldn't be surprised if it wasn't that aloof air of superiority; or perhaps her disapproving sniff; or maybe even the hideous cap that hid her scraped-back hair. He wondered what colour it was under that monstrosity and considered her dark brows and eyelashes with what he told himself was purely a spirit of scientific inquiry.

The latter were extraordinarily lush and even curled in enchanting crescents when they rested on her creamy cheeks, he remembered with a jolt. He'd seen her so undefended on that memorable trip to Wychwood; one day she had slept in the carriage and as he rode closer to check on his charges and saw her face all soft and un-guarded and wondered if she was much younger than she pretended. Not that he had been allowed so much as a glimpse of such sweet vulnerability since that day, nor had those oddly enchanting eyelashes swept down over eyes heavy with sleep in his presence ever again. He found he regretted that lack and supposed that, when all else was covered and battened down, even the most ridiculous detail became intriguing.

Tonight he'd been forced to exert every ounce of willpower he possessed not to rip off that ridiculous dowager's cap and sweep prim Miss Wells up into the dance. A waltz for preference, he thought with a wicked smile, as darkness engulfed him once more. Although come to think of it that dance was quite circumspect by the standards of the poor. Nights at Kate Long's when the girls swung from one partner to the other with joyful abandon would undoubtedly shock Miss Wells to the soles of her proper feet, he concluded wryly.

Perhaps, his imagination persisted, she would have brushed against him even in such select company as they were forced together by others on that overcrowded dance floor. Or maybe she would feel drawn to engineer such closeness of her own accord. Yes, and pigs might fly. He was quite certain Miss Wells would consider such rakish liberties repulsive, and tell him so in no un-certain terms if he ever ventured one. Yet the idea of any other gentleman stealing a kiss from her lips, which he noted were very well shaped and surprisingly full as they went past another lamp, made him feel strangely discomfited. He frowned so fiercely at her the next time they passed a streetlight that she looked startled.

His gaze softened and he had to suppress a surprisingly strong urge to reach across and pull her to him, so he could reassure her, of course. Enough! He didn't want her to realise the ridiculous state even the thought of holding her got him in and avoid him even more assiduously in future. Ben spent the rest of their brief journey back to Alstone House in Cavendish Square watching a largely uninteresting view of shadowy streets and thinking of cold and barren wastes to get himself back under strict control, before he must step out of the carriage and escort them inside.

Even he was shocked to find the Countess of Carnwood waiting up for them when he escorted Kate and Miss Wells up the steps and into the marble hall. From the expression on the latter's face, she disapproved of her employer's over-protective attitude to her sister nearly as much as Ben did, so at least for once they were in accord.

'I know what you'll say,' Miranda Alstone claimed with a disarming smile her lord was quite unable to resist, but it had no noticeable effect on the trio facing her. Her ladyship sighed. 'I can't help myself,' she admitted. 'With Kit away so long I can't convince myself all is well with the world.'

Since he shared her apprehension, Ben allowed himself to be pacified and gave her an encouraging smile as he urged her upstairs and back into the cosy sitting room she had made there, despite the strict Palladian style that made the rest of the house a little too sternly elegant for his taste.

'Tea, if you please, Coppice,' he requested the stately butler with a manly exchange of glances that admitted there was no point in trying to send her ladyship off to bed to worry away the little hours alone.

'All will certainly not be well if Kit comes home and finds you have fretted yourself into a decline, particularly in the present circumstances,' he then told his friend's wife as gently as he could, as he manoeuvred her towards the fire. After the hothouse atmosphere of Lady Wintergreen's ballroom, even a mild night felt frosty to the partygoers and the warmth was welcome.

'True, his lordship will be very put out if all is not as serene as he left it, but I fail to see why he should blame you for my folly,' Miranda told him with a return of her usual spirit.

'Because I happen to be handy, I expect,' he said with a rueful grin she returned weakly, as she obediently sat on the nearest sofa in response to Miss Wells's urging and even consented to put her feet up.

'And at least you're big enough to mill him down if he loses his temper,' Miranda admitted with a fondly exasperated smile as she considered her sometimes fiery lord.

Kit's lady knew her husband all too well, but Ben suspected she also knew they only sparred when nobody else was brave enough to enter the ring with them at Jackson's Boxing Saloon. Neither had much taste for gratuitous violence, having witnessed the dire effect a selfish and violent drunkard could have on his unfortunate family during their boyhood. Ben's mother had been one of the Alstones' lodgers in the shabby house in St Giles that Mrs Alstone somehow contrived to keep, in the face of all her husband's efforts to drink it down the River Tick along with everything else they had ever owned. There Ben and the Alstone children had learnt far too much about the bitter realities of life with a man who made no effort to control his temper or his fists.

'My shoulders are broad enough to take whatever fate throws at them, even with the help of my lord the Earl of Carnwood,' Ben said lightly.

'True, but I shall not demand of you the sacrifice of taking tea with me at this unearthly hour of the night,' Miranda observed, and Ben was relieved to see her resume her usual self-command and order her protesting sister off to bed, before she fell asleep in her chair. 'Oh, and bring brandy for Mr Shaw, if you please, Coppice,' she asked, then smiled her approval as another footman followed on the heels of the first one with the required decanter and a fine glass. 'Why did I ever expect otherwise?' she asked ruefully as the doors closed behind the butler and his cohorts.

'I have no idea. Especially considering Coppice adores you just as foolishly as the rest of your staff,' he informed her with a smile and watched Miss Wells pour tea with her usual stern disapproval.

Miranda flushed with pleasure at the thought that those around her actually liked her and, if Ben needed a reminder of why his friend had fallen so hard for her in the first place, that would have provided it. As the

Countess carefully sipped at her fragrant China tea, Ben thought she looked considerably better now that two of her chicks were back under her roof unscathed. He fleetingly wished he could find such a wife, then dismissed the thought as paltry—there was only one Miranda Alstone, and an even bigger rogue than himself had already captured her. For himself, he enjoyed his state of single blessedness too well to give it up for married life.

He dismissed such ridiculous ideas as seeking a bride for himself among the belles of the Season, whilst he kept his eye on Miranda's sister whenever Kit was unavailable. Instead he wondered why on earth her ladyship should consider the self-contained and dauntless Miss Wells in need of her protection. It was beyond Ben, but he sipped his brandy and watched them thoughtfully while they chatted of nothing in particular, as if to soothe each other's ruffled feathers. There seemed to him to be a sincere friendship between countess and governess, and he was suddenly intrigued by the idea that Miss Wells must be a very different creature whenever he was not by.

Perhaps feeling his speculative gaze on her, she turned and shot him a fierce look of either suspicion or condemnation, and suddenly he felt very tempted to live down to her expectations. Good behaviour or bad seemed to cut no ice with the haughty dragon. Next time he was in the position to do so, he might just snatch a kiss to see if her lips were as cold as her eyes, which were once again glinting so disapprovingly at him that she didn't even need those wretched eyeglasses to emphasise her aloof dislike.

Thank goodness Miranda had never provoked him to turn her upside down and shake her to see if there was a real warm and breathing woman under all the hairpins, caps and spectacles Miss Wells came armoured in. It was perfectly obvious from looking at his friend's beautiful wife that she was all of those things, and a few more into the bargain. As he didn't have the least wish to meet his best friend early one morning on Paddington Green for a very unfriendly encounter, it was very lucky Ben needed no proof of the Countess of Carnwood's humanity.

'Why are you flying in the face of experience and worrying about your husband, my lady?' he turned and asked Miranda in an attempt to get at the truth, and distract himself from the remarkably sweet notion of finding out if Miss Wells's rather lush mouth would yield under his and give the lie to her fearsome appearance.

If anything it was even more disapproving now, as if she could somehow read his errant thoughts. Anyway, how did she think they could soothe Miranda's fears when they had no idea what they were? He sent her a fiercely repressive glance and then regarded his friend's wife with gentle enquiry, having no idea that the contrast in his gaze when resting on the two women in front of him could have hurt the formidable governess.

'Because I hate being apart from him, I suppose,' Miranda admitted slowly, then seemed to come to a decision to confide more deeply. 'And I have received a letter from Cousin Celia,' she finally added.

Now he would happily have taken a joint share in Miss Wells's most icy look of disdain if the wretched

Celia were actually here to receive the full benefit of it. No wonder the poor girl was fretting herself into a headache if that murderous bitch had been stirring up the Alstone pond once more.

'Not at all the sort of letter I would expect of her,' Miranda added hastily as she observed his thunderous frown. 'Indeed, I suspect that Celia has discovered actually living with Nevin is even more of a punishment than we all intended. Maybe she's trying to soften Kit's heart by warning me, in the hope he'll allow her return to England without her husband.'

'She has mistaken her man then. Kester will never forgive her for what she did to you, both before and after you met him. Even if he didn't love you quite ridiculously, how could he forget her wanton cruelty to a vulnerable young girl who happened to be her own cousin into the bargain? But besides bringing up that mare's nest again and upsetting you, what does the vixen have to say? If you're able to tell me the details, of course,' he said with a cautionary glance at Miss Wells.

'Oh, there's no need to hide any of it from Charlotte,' Miranda said blithely, 'she knows all about my past. Kit and I decided it was necessary that we told her, in order to make sure neither Nevin nor Celia could approach the girls in our absence.'

And it had been an understandable relief to unburden herself to a sympathetic female, Ben concluded, rather surprised at his sudden conviction that the suffocatingly correct Miss Wells would make a stalwart and very partisan ally.

'I wonder she dared set pen to paper after she had done her best to ruin your life by urging her secret husband to elope with a seventeen-year-old girl, then bigamously wed you, as well as the pair of them doing their best to kill you when you returned to Wychwood and threatened her supremacy. So what on earth *has* the repulsive female got to say?' he asked impatiently, trying to ignore the fleeting thought that he would quite like to meet a friendly dragon, rather than the condemning one he knew all too well.

'That we're in danger,' Miranda finally admitted. 'She says the crime you and Kit have been investigating for so long is about to be exposed, along with a good many others, and someone very rich and powerful is furious about the threat to his income and position.'

'The devil he is!' he exclaimed and began pacing up and down the fine Aubusson carpet as he considered the implications of such an attack. 'How much does she know?' he rapped out.

'I would remind you that you are inhabiting a lady's drawing room and not a board meeting in the City, Mr Shaw,' Miss Wells rebuked him, 'and, come to think of it, you must speak a little more politely to those gentlemen if you wish to retain their good will.'

'Much you know about it,' he told her with an unrepentant grin, even as he was secretly grateful to her for checking the temper his anxiety threatened to spark into formidable life.

He might as well store that up for the enemy who had stolen one of their ships and murdered far too many good men for him to think about too deeply and stay sane. She was quite right, though; he needed a cool head if he wasn't to let the villain behind it all slip through his fingers once again.

'I beg your pardon, Lady Carnwood,' he said with a nicely judged bow and exquisite irony, 'would you inform me of any further details you might have gathered from this missive? Just so we might guard ourselves against any harm, you understand?'

'Of course I do, but my cousin was very vague. The one thing I can tell is that she's terrified of the man. Too terrified to give me more than the most obscure clues as to his identity, I'm afraid.'

'Which probably explains why Mrs Braxton sent her warning in the first place—so that you and his lordship would defeat him for her, Mr Shaw,' Miss Wells put in shrewdly.

Ben was impressed by her acute grasp of the situation. There was no false optimism, no impulse to think the best of a woman who so far as he could tell had neither heart nor soul under all that chilly blonde beauty. Which, he decided, argued that Miss Wells had been forged in a very fiery furnace indeed, and he was astonished by the powerful wave of protectiveness that suddenly swept over him at the thought of her so vulnerable that she had been forced to armour herself against the world so sternly.

'Very likely you're right,' he agreed absently.

'How astonishing of me,' she replied sweetly.

'If I ever feel myself growing self-satisfied, I'll rely

on you to depress my pretensions, Miss Wells,' he parried with a rueful smile.

'Then it will be my pleasure to oblige you, Mr Shaw,' she replied pertly and he was once more overtaken by a strange compulsion to kiss her soundly, if only to stop her wicked tongue for a few moments.

He turned and caught Miranda's thoughtful gaze on them both and cursed himself for a fool. His friend's wife was loyal to a fault and capable of going to the most ridiculous lengths to secure the happiness of those she loved. The last thing he needed was the Countess of Carnwood matchmaking between him and the governess. So respectable a bride might increase his standing with the more cautious of his investors, but it would do very little for his personal comfort, he suspected. Having his fiercest critic on hand on such a permanent basis might even sap his adamantine will.

'To get back to our sheep, exactly when's his lordship due home?' he asked, partly because he wanted to know and partly to divert Miranda's attention from his determination never to wed anyone, let alone Miss Wells.

'Last night,' Miranda said mournfully and he could have kicked himself for reminding her, then his friend for giving her so precise a date for his return.

'I'd best go and find the rogue for you then, hadn't I?' he said and immediately felt better on making that decision, so he must be more worried about Kester's thick hide than he'd let himself know.

Then he glanced at Miranda's intent face and decided Kit hadn't stood a chance against those brave blue eyes of hers. No, he amended, his friend hadn't a hope in hell of resisting his true love, and that was just how it should be, he supposed. Suddenly the lure of such a love was strong after all—to be loved and to love so deeply seemed like a wonder to a boy brought up on the harsh reality of one of the poorest neighbourhoods in London. Yet it had also forged him into a man suspicious of all human weakness, and he really had no idea that he was now regarding Miss Wells with a stern frown that even made her shiver briefly under its frosty reproach.

'If only I could come with you,' Miranda said wistfully and Ben reminded himself he'd cause to deal with her gently and wiped the glower off his face.

'The best thing you can do for him is stay safe and keep close,' he said, horrified by the idea of taking any pregnant woman on such a quest, let alone his best friend's precious countess.

'Indeed,' Miss Wells backed him up, which must go sadly against the grain, 'nothing would worry his lordship more than knowing you were abroad and vulnerable and, given the vagaries of the weather, let's hope the sea crossing was calm. Not even Lord Carnwood could swim the Irish Sea if the captains won't leave port,' she added shrewdly and he nearly cheered.

'That's true,' Miranda conceded, relief taking some of the tension out of her braced shoulders at last. 'And I'm being a terrible widgeon, am I not?'

'You always look more like a swan than a duck to me, my lady,' Ben teased lightly.

'Say that again in a few months' time and I'll very

likely hug you, if I can reach you,' Miranda said with a rueful smile and he sensed the worst of her megrims were fading at last.

'And as I've no wish to be challenged to a duel by my best friend, I beg you'll contain your transports, my lady,' he observed with mock terror and even got a laugh out of her at that very unlikely idea.

'I hope Kit knows he's no need to be jealous of any other man on this good earth of ours,' Miranda said cheerfully enough, reminded of the passionate love that existed between herself and the man Ben had once thought too damaged by his early life to let himself love so completely.

Again he felt the tug of feeling that sort of love, then dismissed the notion as impossible even if it did make him feel at odds with himself. Seeing Kit happy in the midst of so much domesticity must be turning him soft, for suddenly he longed not to be forever guarded and aloof from the wider world. If there was some special she he could lay aside his omnipotence in front of, he felt as if some gap in him might feel complete. The idiocy of being able to set the man he had made of himself aside for a space occurred to him at the same time as he frowned formidably at the coal scuttle. It would take an exceptional kind of woman to love him once she knew who he really was, deep inside. And he could never be innocent or unguarded enough to let them find out, he reflected bitterly, nor could he lay himself open to the danger of such hurt if he ever dared do so.

The truth was that he had outgrown the wenches of

the streets, both honest and otherwise, and would never be admitted far enough into the *ton* to win himself an aristocratic wife brought up to expect a marriage of convenience. He wasn't fish, or flesh, or good red herring, and he could hardly search for some pale imitation of his friend's countess, even if he wanted to. A picture of a certain stern and very respectable female who would certainly never approve of him slipped into his mind and he did his best to dismiss her, for even the idea seemed absurd.

Miss Wells would obviously rather eat nails than marry a *parvenu* like himself, then he forced himself to be a little fairer to the formidable governess. Somehow he doubted his low beginnings made her look at him as if he had just emerged from under a stone. He'd seen her look icily severe in the presence of any unattached male, from the third footman to the septuagenarian Duke of Denley, when he visited Wychwood and was reckless enough to ogle any female under the age of fifty. It occurred to him that perhaps Miss Wells was a man-hater, but she would never have an easy friendship with Kit if so, or the young vicar of Wychwood village, who was almost as happily married as Kit himself. So the lady was wary and perhaps that was just as well, but what if she could be persuaded out of her formidable shell and he discovered the real Charlotte under all that starch?

He eyed the stately figure seated across the room from him and considered that prospect with surprising pleasure. He'd long ago decided those truly awful gowns and 'you can't see me' caps were a disguise.

And she *was* the one female he knew who didn't make him feel like an awkward and ungainly bear in her company, considering she easily reached as high as his chin. If her slender, long-fingered hands were any indication, under all the acres of grey shroud there could be a very different female. He forbade himself to dwell on that incendiary subject in mixed company and coolly examined the idea that a lady in her circumstances might be persuaded to accept a less-than-perfect suitor.

He was certainly wealthy enough to turn even the most resistant female's thoughts to marriage, if money was her overriding concern. He knew that without vanity, especially since one or two of the grand ladies of the *ton* had hinted they would welcome such a rich lover even if, regrettably, he wasn't noble enough to pay court to their daughters and become their rich son-in-law. So maybe he was handsome enough as well, as even for the pleasure of plundering his deep pockets he doubted such *grande dames* could get the smell of the shop out of their delicate noses without a healthy seasoning of desire. His smile was cynical as he met Miss Wells's eyes with some of his thoughts in his clear grey eyes and, when he saw her shiver, immediately regretted it. She was different, he assured himself with a certainty that almost shocked him, even if he didn't know quite why.

Glaring at the very annoying Mr Shaw, Charlotte wondered for perhaps the hundredth time since she had first met him why he made her either want to prickle like a rolled-up hedgehog, or itch to be the sort of blonde pocket Venus he seemed to admire. It was almost as if he regarded her as he might some odd curio he had spied in a museum and came back to inspect now and again, in the mistaken belief that one day he would work out her mechanism and remove all mystery from the conundrum.

Little did he know that there was far more to the curio he sometimes eyed like a botanical specimen than he, or anyone else, suspected, she thought, and smiled rather secretively. If he ever had an inkling that she was other than what she seemed, he would never give her a moment's peace until he had her worked out and suitably recorded. Not having the least wish to be considered an intellectual challenge by the famously astute Mr Shaw, she told herself it was almost her duty to be as tediously predictable as possible and took a certain joy in fulfilling his low expectations. In his presence she became a parody of the correct governess, and, remembering that fact now, she dug about in her reticule and triumphantly pulled out her spectacles. Perching them on her nose, she felt as if she had assumed a latter-day version of a shield before going into battle and dared him to comment.

It proved to be a wasted gesture, as he was listening intently to some sound so indistinct that she had yet to hear it, and she might as well have been wearing a wig and a false beard for all the notice he took. Then she heard the faint noise of a carriage in the square herself, followed by the subdued fuss of an arrival who knew this was a ridiculous hour to turn up in a respectable neighbourhood. She looked questioningly at Mr Shaw, who gave a very slight nod and casually got to his feet.

'I dare say Coppice is wishing me at the devil, so it's probably high time I relieved you of my presence, your ladyship, Miss Wells,' he said with rather mocking formality and a bow to each, then he raised his eyebrows at Charlotte as if to inform her she shouldn't intrude on a private reunion.

'I believe I shall retire,' she informed him regally and, bidding her employer a hasty goodnight, allowed Mr Shaw to hurry her out of the room before Miranda had even fully taken in that they were going.

No doubt she soon forgot about them, considering the Earl of Carnwood rushed up the stairs and into her ladyship's sitting room, without even seeing them, as far as Charlotte could tell. She sighed audibly, then ordered herself back to battle order as Mr Shaw met her unguarded look with a rueful acknowledgement that, yes, it was a very unusual marriage, and yet a very desirable one, even in his cynical view. Their eyes stayed locked as if they were united in longing for the forbidden for once, but she made herself look away and told herself she was imagining it. Somehow it made him seem oddly vulnerable to want such an impossibility, especially when they were both too chastened by life to believe it could exist, either separately or, heady, forbidden thought, together.

'There's no need to fret about his lordship's health from the speed of his run upstairs,' Mr Shaw remarked ruefully.

'Yet he was carrying his arm rather awkwardly, don't

you think?' she asked anxiously. She might not want to believe her employers were truly under threat, but there was no point fooling herself it didn't exist after such a warning, and from such a source.

'It would take more than a strained arm to keep him from his lady, but I dare say Coppice will know what's been going on, he knows everything.'

'So I long ago concluded,' she agreed with rare amity and surprised him by accompanying him downstairs to satisfy her curiosity.

Somehow tonight had proved such an upheaval of her usual steady world that she couldn't bring herself to poker up and retreat into stately solitude just yet. Ben Shaw's presence at her side made her feel oddly safe anyway, a notion that could hardly be more dangerous, she chided herself, as they descended the elegant stairs at a far more reasonable pace than their owner had just run up them. Coppice was in the act of closing the door on the Earl of Carnwood's travelling equipage and turned to face them with his usual calm omnipotence, yet for some reason Charlotte thought it concealed his true feelings on this occasion.

'Your hat and cane, Mr Shaw?' the butler asked blandly.

'No, an explanation if you please,' Ben demanded impatiently, 'and don't pretend you've no idea what I'm alluding to, you old fox.'

Coppice shook his head as if about to reproach a cheeky young boy and then one look at the giant, and very adult, figure seemed to remind him that Ben Shaw was a force to be reckoned with on any man's terms. 'I understand his lordship met with a slight accident,' he finally admitted.

'How and where?' Ben snapped, evidently too pre-occupied with worrying about his friend to modify his abrupt tone.

Coppice met Charlotte's gaze with a shrug as if to say 'ah well, boys will be boys', ushered them into his pantry and shut the door against any listening ears. Awed by being admitted into his very private quarters, Charlotte allowed herself a quick look around this holy of holies and told herself she shouldn't be surprised to see it was unusually comfortable, as well as rigidly tidy. The earl and countess took their servants' comfort very seriously and she knew how well the governess was lodged, so of course they would see to the well-being of so crucial a person as Coppice.

'Reuben informed me that his lordship was waylaid by thieves when riding about Miss Kate's estate. He seems to think that, if he had not been following Lord Carnwood at a discreet distance, the day might have gone rather ill with his lordship. As it is, he had his hat shot off and took a blow to his right arm that would have kept anyone else from travelling for a sennight, or so Reuben seems to think, but his lordship insists we make light of the matter for her ladyship's sake.'

'And you think they were not common thieves?' Mr Shaw asked.

'Most unlikely from the sound of it,' Coppice assured him, with a significant look at Charlotte she supposed she was not meant to see.

'If her ladyship's peace of mind is to be guarded, you might just as well tell me, because the more of us who are close to her know the truth, the better she'll be protected,' she informed them both with what she thought exemplary patience on her part.

'Very well, ma'am,' Coppice admitted rather stiffly, as if she was at least twice her actual age, Charlotte decided very impatiently.

'So who were they really?' she demanded.

'I have no idea, madam, but Reuben said they wore silk masks and appeared very prosperous for common thieves, as well as carrying the very latest in firearms. When they were turned over to the local magistrate they refused to say anything, preferring to take their punishment rather than betray even their names, which you must admit, sir, is highly suspicious.'

Ben nodded sagely and they exchanged manly looks as Charlotte was torn between fuming at Coppice, for addressing only what he obviously considered the important part of his audience, and terror for her friends. Added to the letter Miranda had received, it seemed something deeply sinister was coming to a head, and who knew what hurt might befall those she'd come to love in the process? When she had time and privacy, she might take herself to task for letting herself care for her employers so much, but now there were more important considerations than icy self-sufficiency.

'I wonder just what the magistrate made of that,' Ben mused.

'Not a great deal, sir, he sentenced them to be transported for life.'

'And they still said nothing?'

'Yes, sir—quite significant, don't you think?'

'Indeed, most criminals would name their own grandmother an accessory to avoid such a sentence.'

Charlotte thought of Celia Braxton's letter, where she too refused to name the man who was threatening the Earl and his family as well as Ben Shaw and shivered. An implacable will lay behind such a depth of fear, and she wondered what he had done in the past to make his tools prefer the penal colony at Botany Bay to his vengeance. He was obviously more than just another common criminal, and tracking such a Machiavellian mind to his lair would be a task fit for Hercules himself. Her gaze turned inevitably to the giant at her side and she became even more thoughtful. If there was a man capable of the quest, it was surely Mr Benedict Shaw and she thought him capable of being every bit as subtle and unrelenting as his quarry, in the pursuit of those out to harm the man he considered a brother. For some reason that notion warmed rather than chilled her as it should have done. Such single-minded pursuit of his enemy should have made her shudder with revulsion, instead of feeling his protection was cast about her as well as her friends. Something else she must chide herself over later, along with the chill that dissipated that warmth as soon as it occurred to her that he would be in acute danger while pursuing a seemingly invisible, untouchable enemy.

'Her ladyship will soon have the story out of him,' she insisted in the face of two sceptical males.

'All the more reason for Miranda to be away from here and safe at Wychwood,' Ben Shaw said grimly and for once Charlotte agreed with him wholeheartedly.

Indeed she could think of no better scheme than them all returning to Derbyshire post haste and staying there for the foreseeable future. Then the unpalatable truth of such a hasty withdrawal occurred to her.

'The gossips will say Kate has committed some grand misdemeanour and had to be taken home,' she warned.

'Which is why she will have to stay here, with a suitably responsible female to bear her company, of course,' Mr Shaw said with a significant look that Charlotte distrusted intensely.

'I'm a governess, not a chaperon, Mr Shaw,' she informed him sternly.

'What's the difference?' he asked with an interested expression that had her clenching her gloved hands at her sides.

'I should think that quite plain,' she said repressively.

'Then pray consider me just a stupid male and explain it to me,' he replied with spurious meekness.

She shot him a furious look, but in front of Coppice she couldn't give way to a strong urge to inform him what she truly thought of him.

'A governess is an educator of young ladies, and sometimes of even younger gentlemen, Mr Shaw. A chaperon is a lady who has the entrée into the *ton* that will help secure her charge a marriage suitable to one of her lofty station in life,' she said blandly, hoping it was very clear to both of them that she was the former and not the latter.

'Are you telling me that you weren't born a lady, Miss Wells?' the wretch replied with a mock deference that made her long to slap him.

'Let us say I possess no turn for matchmaking,' she informed him with what she hoped was a superior smile.

All the same, she felt profoundly uncomfortable discussing such a role under the interested gaze of Coppice, who seemed secretly amused by their discussion for some reason. Ben Shaw was either unaware of the butler's feelings or indifferent to them, for he continued to look at her as if she was some odd curiosity he currently found fascinating.

'Surely that makes you uniquely qualified for the position?' he said and, when she haughtily raised her brows in question of that statement, added, 'Being a cynic of the worst sort, you would see through the fortune hunters and shady characters and find your charge a paragon among men.'

'I'm far too stern a critic to manage that, I'm afraid,' she explained shortly and treated both men to one of her best icy looks before turning to make a fighting retreat. 'If I might suggest someone writes to the Countess's godmama and offers Lady Rhys the role? From all I have seen of her, she would be highly entertained by the notion of chaperoning Kate in polite society, and might prove a shrewder matchmaker than any doting mama. I know she offered to take up the task weeks ago, but her ladyship was so eager to present her sister to the *ton* that I suspect she overestimated her own strength under the present circumstances.'

In front of Coppice she couldn't refer directly to Miranda's pregnancy and Charlotte felt distinctly impatient with the ridiculous conventions of a society that refused to refer to the very natural process of pregnancy and birth openly in mixed company.

'Yes, it took Kit weeks to persuade her ladyship she wouldn't blight her sisters' prospects with unfounded gossip about her own past if she did bring them out, but I dare say he's wishing he hadn't made such a good job of it now. Nevertheless, that's an excellent notion of yours and I'll suggest it to him in the morning,' Mr Shaw informed her rather pompously and she spared a little impatience from her general supply of it.

'How do you know that he'll consult you about any of this?' she weakened enough to ask, as she stood with one hand suggestively on the doorknob, but couldn't quite turn it and escape his infuriating presence.

'And how could you think he wouldn't, ma'am, especially as he doesn't share your low opinion of my abilities, or lack thereof?'

'I really couldn't say,' she replied snippily and opened the door and went through it with a frigid goodnight, before she said something she might truly regret.

Chapter Three

'Kindly pay attention, Miss Wells,' Miss Isabella Alstone ordered her governess the following morning.

'I should probably make you stand in the corner for that piece of impudence,' Charlotte returned placidly.

'Well, you might as well actually be in the Americas for all the attention you're paying to your lesson about them,' Isabella replied with the warm smile that would have the young gentlemen of the *ton* lining up in fervent hope of winning another in a few years' time.

'I certainly seem to have failed dismally in my task of turning you and your sister into well-behaved young ladies, so perhaps I might just as well go there,' Charlotte admitted ruefully.

'Who wants to be a milk-and-water miss? I certainly don't and I doubt Miranda and Kit would thank you if I suddenly became one. There are far too many of *them* about already, at least if the girls at Kate's waltzing parties are any indication of things.'

'I agree that they can seem a little giddy, but I dare say it's all the excitement,' Charlotte managed to defend those silly young ladies half-heartedly in the face of her own doubts about their common sense.

'In a watering place full of senile octogenarians they would still contrive to be the most foolish creatures imaginable, but when are you going to tell me what happened last night, dear Miss Wells?'

'Since you avow contempt of the fashionable throng, I really can't imagine why you're interested in their sayings and doings,' Charlotte observed slyly, 'and in any case there are the Americas to consider.'

'Yes, and you obviously need to do so, as you can't seem to concentrate on either their geography or history this morning.'

'I have the excuse of having been from home and out of my bed until the early hours of the morning and you do not, miss.'

'Then why not tell me everything that went on at the Wintergreen ball instead and get it over with? After that I would have no excuse not to take a proper interest in geography, now would I?'

'I'm quite sure there's something wrong with the grammar of that sentence as well as its intent, Isabella.'

'I dare say, now cut line and tell all, Miss Wells, before one of us falls asleep.'

'You really are a shocking minx, Isabella Alstone,' Mr Shaw's distinctive deep voice informed her from the doorway.

'Ben!' Isabella screamed in a manner that had Charlotte shuddering to the depths of her governessly soul.

'Hoyden,' he greeted her, laughing as his youngest adopted sister jumped into his mighty arms and he swung her round as easily and unselfconsciously as if she had been five instead of fifteen.

Charlotte was forced to admit that, while there were any number of gentlemen she wouldn't trust with a young girl's open adoration, Ben Shaw was not one of them. When it came to her charges, or any other female he considered himself bound to by ties far stronger than blood, there was an absolute integrity about him. She'd seen enough of the relationship between Lord Carnwood and his oldest friend to know they were more like brothers than most men born in the same bed. What was more, that kinship extended to his lordship's true sisters, who were as easy with Mr Shaw as their brother was. It was those outside that magic circle who needed to be wary of him, and Charlotte was conscious she was excluded and should be very cautious of letting her thoughts linger on his very large person and subtle mind.

Now where on earth had that odd idea come from? And why did her exclusion suddenly seem so chilling? She must be more tired than she realised, she decided with an impatient sigh, and did her best to dismiss such ridiculous thoughts. She hadn't the least desire for Ben Shaw to act like a brother towards her and refused to countenance the shocking fantasy of any attentions he might pay her instead. Since last night a stupid fantasy of being gowned and groomed as finely as the beauties of the *ton*, and dancing the night away in the arms of a man ideally suited to enchant a very tall lady, had troubled her as never before. Charlotte wondered if tiredness and terror of being recognised had relaxed her usual iron grip on her traitorous emotions and reminded herself who and what she was. A governess, she informed herself flatly, a woman unfortunate enough to be forced to make her own way in the world and relying on an unblemished reputation to secure every post that came her way.

'Miss Wells won't tell me what happened at the ball last night and Kate was still asleep last time I looked, so what was it like, Ben? Did she dance every dance and slay a legion of suitors with just one blink of her beautiful blue eyes?'

'Something like that, minx, and isn't it bloodthirsty to wish so many youthful hearts trampled on?'

'Not in the least, they'll recover soon enough,' Isabella replied cynically and Charlotte felt herself frown even as she ordered the crease from between her brows and did her best to banish all expression from her face as she became conscious of Mr Shaw's acute gaze.

Did he think she was responsible for such cynical observations from one so young? She sincerely hoped not. While anything other than a distant acquaintance was clearly impossible between them, somehow she didn't want him to think she'd foist her own views of the world Isabella must move in sooner or later on her pupil. She suspected he would need to look closer to home for that, to Celia Braxton and her stony-hearted mama, who

seemed to have had too free a hand in the education, or
lack of it, provided to the younger Miss Alstones before
their grandfather finally realised it and sent them both to
school. When Charlotte first met them there, she had been
shocked by both girls' ignorance of so much that seemed
essential to a well-adjusted young lady, especially considering the acute minds concealed by their often careless
behaviour. Four years on she was fairly confident they'd
realised more of their potential, and would make fine
wives and mothers as their destiny surely dictated. She
sincerely hoped, however, that they would wait to feel
something more than the bare tolerance that seemed to
Charlotte to constitute most society marriages.

She wondered what Mr Shaw would expect from
marriage and felt herself blush, as the combination of
his speculative gaze and her improper fantasies blos-
somed into something downright outrageous. Still, a
cat could look at a queen, or a king. Some instinct told
her he would be a magnificent lover and she tried to
meet his gaze with an indignant question in her own,
even as her mind skittered over the mental picture she
suddenly had of Ben Shaw naked and superb and very
masculine indeed. Building a picture of what he might
look like under that finely cut coat and all that pristine
linen ought to be far harder for a respectable spinster
lady than it actually was. She could imagine hard
muscle rippling under a sweat slicked, satin supple skin,
and really those breeches and his very highly polished
boots left far too little to her fertile imagination!

Shaking her head sadly at her own folly, she looked

up again and encountered laughter and what looked suspiciously like a reflection of her own state of unwilling arousal in his eyes, which she did her level best to return with her best governess look. Perverse creature that he was, her formidable frown seemed to encourage rather than reproach him and his firm mouth actually had the cheek to tip into an open grin as she fought off her ludicrous state of confusion, made even worse by that inviting, too-understanding smile.

'What think you, Miss Wells?' he asked mockingly and she had to fight hard to keep her own expression serene as he openly challenged her.

'That hearts aren't quite so easily broken, and that Isabella needs to learn some compassion toward vulnerable young gentlemen before she makes her own come-out,' she managed to say calmly enough; at least formulating a reply gave her something to do other than speculating about Mr Shaw's masculine attributes.

'How very well done of you, Miss Wells,' he returned softly and still she could read secrets in his eyes no governess could afford to look for and stay sternly respectable, and therefore in employment.

'It seems to me that young ladies require protection against the gentlemen rather than the other way about,' Isabella put in and Charlotte finally managed to give more of her attention to her pupil than their visitor, and saw there was more than just youthful scepticism behind her attitude toward Kate's suitors.

'That is always a consideration, of course,' she replied carefully, 'but your sister is a beautiful young woman with plenty of native wit and a great deal of family influence at her back. It would be a very reckless, or downright foolish, man who would risk bringing all that to bear against him.'

'Why? It didn't stop that worm of a Braxton creature Cousin Celia married from deceiving Miranda into eloping with him and then treating her abominably, and I don't want to lose Kate from my life for five years as I did my other sister, thank you very much.'

As Isabella stuck out her chin and looked determinedly defiant after making that pronouncement, Charlotte knew they had finally got to the crux of her pupil's restless moods and uncharacteristic irritability of late. She had thought it came from taking her lessons alone and being bound to the schoolroom while Kate shopped, danced and was driven round the park, and, yes, slayed gangling young gentlemen through the heart with just one limpid look from her famous dark-blue Alstone eyes. Really she should have known there was more to it than that, and it wasn't Mr Shaw's fault she had failed to look deeper, so why she was scowling at him instead of thanking him for bringing the whole matter into the open, even she could not have said.

'Ah, but Braxton didn't have Kit Alstone to deal with now, did he?' Mr Shaw asked with apparently academic interest. 'And can you honestly see Kate falling for some plausible rogue with such an example before her? I'd say she's got too much common sense to do anything of the sort, but if you think otherwise I suppose I must bow to your superior knowledge.'

Isabella looked thoughtful and Charlotte could see her testing his words against her experience of both her sisters and some of the tension went out of her young shoulders and a smile began to dawn. 'Miranda always was a dreamer,' she finally admitted ruefully. 'Kate is much more practical.'

'You can't be too practical when your future happiness is at stake,' Charlotte said impulsively, then immediately regretted it when Mr Shaw's attention centred on her once more. What a fool she was to give him so much to speculate on, she condemned herself, and risk revealing painful decisions she had made when no older than Kate.

'I suspect there's a happy medium between being a dreamer and Miss Practical,' Mr Shaw drawled with a sidelong glance at Charlotte that she was quite sure was intended to provoke her. 'Perhaps we can rely on you to find it one day, minx,' he challenged her pupil on just the right note of affection and speculation to set Isabella a task she would find irresistibly challenging.

With an internal groan as she dreaded Isabella practising it on every susceptible young gentleman in Derbyshire, Charlotte cast Mr Shaw an impatient look, but at least he'd diverted Isabella from Kate's future.

'Whichever you plan to be, Isabella, a sound education is going to stand you in good stead, so perhaps it's time I got on with providing it?' she suggested and won a moan of protest from Isabella and another of those speculative, sensual looks from Mr Shaw.

'Trying to get rid of me, Miss Wells?' he asked inexcusably and perched himself on the corner of a map table she was certain would bow under the pressure, but even that piece of inanimate oak failed her and remained as stout as ever.

'Not with notable success,' she managed to say coolly, as his wicked grey eyes met hers with an open invitation to look her fill, as he had so obligingly put himself on her eye level.

Well, she wouldn't! That way lay the ruin of many a good governess's future and one she would have thought him all too conscious of. Shooting him a hostile look, she pulled the book she'd found on the lives and customs of the Native American tribes toward her and tried hard to focus on it, only to find it might as well be written in one of their languages.

'Please stay, Ben,' Isabella urged him traitorously and Charlotte found herself quite unable to insist he went away and left them in peace in the face of his innocent look and Isabella's pleading one.

'Then you may take over the lesson, Mr Shaw. After all your voyages, doubtless you know the customs and habits of our American cousins much better than I do, or the author of this book,' she informed him briskly and met his eyes with a certain triumph in her own.

Unfortunately he confounded her by returning her gaze with one that answered her challenge and returned it with utterly wicked intent. Part of her was fascinated by the prospect of being teased and maybe even seduced by a master, but another was horrified. She retired to a usually comfortable corner of the room and delved in her bag for her spectacles, fully intending to pick up her embroidery and pretend she wasn't here and neither was he. He soon put paid to that idea by coming far too close, so that her heart beat so loudly she barely took in his words.

'Put those ridiculous things away, Miss Wells,' he warned with the hint of a driven growl in his gruff whisper, 'you don't need them any more than I do, and every time you put them on in my presence from now I shall claim a forfeit.'

'I'll do as I like,' she sparked back, but Charlotte knew he could almost see the shiver of delighted apprehension sliding languorously down her spine at the very thought of what such defiance might cost her.

'Oh, I guarantee that you will like, Miss Wells, but I'm not at all sure it would be proper for such a correct governess as you are to like it so much.'

'Which is one very good reason why you should leave me alone,' she pointed out rather breathlessly and cast a warning look at him, then at Isabella, who was eagerly paying attention to all she could catch of this highly improper conversation.

'For now,' he half-threatened and half-promised and Charlotte sat back in her chair with what must be relief as he finally swung away from her and her world could expand again.

Ben did his best to consider the book Miss Wells had set on her neat schoolmistress's desk and finally decided she had completely shot his concentration, and that she was right and it wasn't a very good book to start with.

Sweeping it aside, he perched on her usual desk instead and tried to muster a description of his first meeting with the inhabitants of that young country, both native and more recently arrived. He must have succeeded, for Isabella hung on his every word and even Miss Wells stayed silent in her corner and didn't interrupt once. The very thought of her there, quiet and sceptical and far more of a woman than she had ever let the world see, was in danger of distracting him, but luckily Isabella had a keen interest in the world and kept him busy with questions and challenges.

His respect for governesses grew, although he suspected Miss Wells was far more learned and genuinely accomplished than most and he could see why Miranda valued her so highly. And nobody could accuse her of being encroaching with any justice, since she was so determined to efface herself in company that at first he used to quiz himself on whether she had actually been in a room while he was in it or not. But that blessed state of oblivion now felt as if it had happened years ago and he knew exactly where and when she was there now, however hard she pretended to be invisible. Just by the reaction of his rebellious body he was all too aware of every look and movement she made. He was sincerely glad she didn't know it, or how infuriating he found his ridiculous susceptibility. Just thinking of her reaction if he gave in to his baser instincts and kissed her passionately, to prove she wasn't the icily correct governess she wanted to believe, made him feel like grinning like an idiot and moaning like a soul in torment at the same time.

He was a damned fool to stir up a hornet's nest that didn't need stirring, he decided, and did his best to answer Isabella's questions. No, more than that, the hornet might win and it only took the quiet, elusive scent of Miss Wells, the sight of her pretending to be obliviously stitching, to let him know he was in danger of being stirred up more than she would think at all proper. Last night he'd tossed and turned in his very comfortable bed in his comfortable house and told himself he had everything he needed in life. It had taken until the dawn was threatening for him to acknowledge that, no, he didn't have one very significant thing and stood very little chance of ever securing it. That he should suddenly be afflicted with the desire to lie with Miss Vinegar and Propriety in his arms in that grand feather bed all night was anathema to him, and would certainly be to her if she ever found out! He'd come here, after assuring himself that Kit Alstone was as indestructible as ever, with the noble object of curing himself of Miss Wells with as large a dose of disapproval and uninterest as a man could physick himself with.

And she'd let him down! Even now he almost refused to believe it, but while Miss Charlotte Wells might hate him for it, she would kiss him right back if he were ever fool enough to risk it and why did that make him more confused, instead of re-armoured against her? Over in her isolation corner, he could tell she was as conscious of his every move and mood as he was, and he felt her sensitivity like a fever running over his skin. She would never admit it, of course; he could imagine her fighting the attraction between them with every fibre of her being and with a slightly bitter twist in his gut he couldn't blame her. No doubt she'd been born a lady, and remained one despite her dependent situation. She might be impoverished, but his Miss Wells would never weaken and seek the primrose path to damnation by accepting a rich man's protection and, as he hadn't the slightest intention of getting married, now or ever, there could be nothing else between them. He should avoid her as if she had the plague and see as little as possible of his adoptive family until Kate was safely settled, and Izzie firmly closeted in her schoolroom and keeping her governess too busy to disturb him.

'Really, Ben, you're as bad as Miss Wells for wandering off into dreamland this morning,' Isabella informed him disgustedly and watched him artlessly with those astounding Alstone eyes he wondered idly how Kit had missed. He needed to take care in the face of the sparkling intelligence he knew lay behind them, and gave Isabella a mock frown to try and distract her from considering the cause of such mutual distraction.

'However much your sister pays Miss Wells, she needs a raise,' he told her with a sternness that wasn't entirely assumed. 'You'd drive me to distraction in half a day.'

'Miss Wells is made of sterner stuff, or we'd have parted company years ago,' she informed him, unimpressed with his attempt to distract her and bringing him back to the subject of her personal dragon instead.

'I am here, you know?' she told them mildly, looking

up for a moment from her infernal stitchery with a slight smile that jarred at something inside him and reminded him he was in no danger of forgetting.

'My admiration for that fact is growing by the moment, ma'am,' he informed her with a slightly mocking bow. 'I'd have departed for the Americas myself rather than endure two weeks of trying to instruct this ungrateful urchin alone—two years of it must be considered heroic.'

'Oh, it's not so very bad when you get into the way of it,' she told him mildly and he knew she was informing him that she was perfectly content with her lot and had no intention of seeking another—particularly not one that might end with her spending each and every night rendering his rest disturbed for a very different reason than she had last night.

He shot Izzie a condemning look, as if he had turned stern educator instead of Miss Wells, and wondered if he really had seen a speculative glint in those fine eyes of hers when they rested on himself and her governess. With an internal groan he decided it was sheer self-preservation and not cowardice to escape immediately and resolved to stay away from both of them until Isabella had forgotten any Machiavellian schemes to throw Miss Wells into his unwilling arms. And of course they *would* be unwilling to receive such a prickly bundle of contradictions, wouldn't they?

'Anyway,' he declared, stoutly shelving that particular conundrum until he had time to consider it properly, which would be never with any luck at all, 'that's enough of my amateur efforts, Miss Curiosity; you can get back to the skilled attentions of your true teacher and I must get back to work.'

'If it's so urgent, why did you leave it in the first place then, Ben?' Izzie asked cunningly and he might strangle the little devil, if he didn't love her for some odd reason that escaped him at the moment.

'I have business with Kit,' he informed her shortly.

'Well, he rarely spends his mornings in the schoolroom, so I can't imagine why you looked for him here,' she replied pertly.

Ben found himself blushing under her frank gaze and just resisted the temptation to shift his feet like a chastened schoolboy. Miss Isabella Alstone was going to be a formidable young lady in a few years' time, and was in danger of being a little too precocious right now.

'He's still abed,' he replied shortly.

'There's a lot of that about,' she said sagely and Ben just resisted the urge to send Miss Wells a look pleading for rescue, before he talked himself into a deeper quagmire.

'And none of our business, miss,' she rebuked her pupil, so no wonder he sent her a grateful smile, or at least that's how it started.

Miss Wells had an enchanting smile, he decided dazedly as she returned it. When she forgot to be formidable, Charlotte's velvety brown eyes lit with mischief and warmth and he could have sworn she had a dimple, although without a repeat performance how could he be sure? Resolved to make certain he was right in the very near future, Ben somehow got himself out of the schoolroom without providing any further grist for Isabella's mill, and lectured himself on the consequences of seeking out dependent females all the way down the stairs and into his quest to discover if his friend had finally deigned to quit the marital bed after six weeks away from it.

Under the shell of correctness and cool severity there was a lively and dangerously fascinating creature, one he sensed might be the exact opposite of the woman she forced herself to portray to the world. Two years on from first setting eyes on her, and taking her too much at face value, he was closer to plumbing the hidden depths under that formidable exterior, yet still torn between a need to know who and what she really was, and one to leave her to her privacy and protect himself in the process. Notwithstanding his growing fascination with the wretched woman, he told himself he'd prefer her to keep her secrets and her privacy, but that shadow of awareness between them, and the vague sense of danger he'd grown familiar with of late, forbade it. Along with this infernal itch he had to see her eyes laugh up at him with complete confidence, to return his teasing with those subtle barbs of hers blunted by affection and familiarity, until they became the endearments of lovers rather than the sharp defences of a vulnerable young woman.

Lovers! How had he got from his perfectly excusable curiosity about a member of Kit's household who chose to mask her real personality to that? He paused on the stairs and explored the notion more deeply and found it all too easy to begin thinking of Miss Wells as an impersonal problem, then progress to Charlotte—the vibrant life of her, the warmth and vitality she concealed under all that careful restraint and deliberate coolness—and become very personal indeed. The contrast of sweet and sour, soft and hard might prove infinitely fascinating if he wasn't very careful, and he'd no excuse for the hardening of his wretched body at the very thought of that other Charlotte, the one she guarded so carefully from prying eyes.

Perhaps he should admit his problem to Kit and let him delve for the truth about the governess's past life instead, except he would want to know why, and that would give too much away about the ridiculous state she got him into without even trying. Opening the door to the nearest sitting room and seeing it had ample room for him to pace—quite a considerable undertaking considering his size—he duly did so and silently cursed this ridiculous attraction and all its consequences.

Ever since Kit had found his unconventional, incomparable Miranda and annexed her as determinedly as Bonaparte would an exotic territory, his friend had been thoroughly unsound on the subject of love. Indeed, since he'd found the love of his life, Kit seemed to think it a very fine idea if Ben did the same. Admitting this nagging, quite incomprehensible yearning for the dragon Wells to himself was quite impossible, so how on earth could he tell Kit he was afraid to investigate his sister-in-law's governess, for fear of falling on her and hopelessly compromising himself and the sternly ladylike creature?

'And it's not as if she's the least bit pretty either!' he muttered under his breath, then looked about him guiltily, as if Charlotte might have somehow heard him from a floor up and through two closed mahogany doors and been hurt by his careless words. 'Well, she might be for all I know, but there's no chance of her ever letting it show,' he went on as if addressing a gathering of sceptical shareholders contemplating a dubious investment he was determined to persuade them against. 'Dratted female could be a stunner under all that bombazine and she wouldn't reveal it under torture.'

Only silence met that statement, of course, and he glared moodily at a very prim portrait of one of Kit's starchier ancestors, dressed in the odd fashions of the previous century, who obligingly glared back. 'Don't know why I'm asking you,' he told her rudely, 'it's not as if you'd so much as a drop of red blood in you, even when you were alive.'

'Oh, I think you'd be surprised,' a very amused masculine voice informed him from behind the substantial writing desk Ben had somehow failed to see in his haste to establish his true feelings about the troublesome Miss Wells. More significantly, he'd completely missed his best friend lodged behind it and engrossed in all the business of his estates that wouldn't wait. Or at least, Ben surmised bitterly, Kit *had* been engrossed, before he blundered into the room and gave his thoughts a more interesting turn.

'There you are!' he rumbled gruffly. 'Took you long enough to get out of bed this morning, didn't it?'

'Indeed,' Kit said with an unrepentant smirk and Ben wished he were in Jackson's ring with him so he could at least try to wipe it off and make himself feel better. 'But at least I got out the right side when I finally did leave it,' he went on to add quite unforgivably, in Ben's opinion, as pictures of his own restless night and the unconscious cause of it flickered through his mind.

'Meaning?' Ben grated dangerously, or at least it might have been dangerous to any other man on earth who chose to challenge him in one of his rare dark moods.

'Meaning that you either have a black dog on your shoulders this morning, old friend, or you're in love.'

'Heaven forbid!' Ben heard himself say with deep revulsion and wondered why he hadn't laughed off the very idea, before Kit got a head full of wrongheaded ideas.

The very thought was utterly ridiculous, of course; he didn't believe in love, and even if he did he wasn't stupid enough to lay his heart at Miss Wells's feet and risk having it firmly kicked back at him. He shot Kit a disgusted look and amended that statement—he didn't believe in love for himself. He acknowledged the possibility it existed for others—no, the certainty of it existed in Kit and Miranda's case—but that didn't mean it was for him. Love, he silently confirmed in his deepest, darkest thoughts, was the very devil's work and could stay in hell along with its master.

Not for him the helpless, heedless passion that had destroyed his mother's life and nearly led them both down the road to damnation. His mouth twisted into a caricature of his usual lazy smile as he contemplated his own beginnings. Anyone sentimental enough to cling to the term 'love child' should walk in the shoes of one for a few days, and find out how loving the world was to bastards. He glowered at the very thought of the heartless, self-serving worm of a human being who had fathered him on an innocent girl and then walked away with his hands in his pockets, whistling carelessly. He forced his own clenched hands to straighten and his temper to respond to the curb he carefully kept it under nowadays. Hobson's choice, he told himself ruefully, when even Kit was nowhere near up to his weight and he couldn't often find a fair fight even if he wanted one.

'Feeling better, Lothario?' Kit questioned and that misnomer was in danger of re-igniting his temper all over again, but he reined it in and reminded himself that he and Kit had long since given up treading on eggshells around each other's sensibilities. Anyway, Kit knew his views too well to have called him that in anything but jest.

'Feeling hungry, Romeo?' he quipped lightly back and luckily his friend took the hint and rang the bell for the refreshments gentlemen were not supposed to need in the middle of the day.

'Although how on earth a man like me is supposed to maintain a healthy weight on what the ladies consider a meal is beyond me, so perhaps it's just as well they think we live on air.'

'Aye, trust Coppice to know differently,' Kit observed lazily as they waited for that domestic magician to produce something more substantial than was probably being consumed in the dining parlour by the ladies.

'Trust Coppice to know everything,' Ben replied

with satisfaction as the door opened on two laden-down footmen.

'Cook likes you,' Kit said indistinctly as he fell on a beef sandwich as if he hadn't eaten for a week.

'It's mutual,' Ben assured him and felt something disturbing settle and drift away for a moment, as he set himself to satisfy one appetite that could be allowed free rein without bringing down disaster on himself or anyone else.

Of course love was impossible, as was anything else between him and Isabella's prim and proper governess. He would find out all about Charlotte Wells's past from a suitable distance and that would be the end of the matter. She was probably just a bad-tempered prude, given to disapproving of most of her employer's friends and acquaintances, irrespective of birth and circumstances. She was quite a democratic misanthropist when you considered her, he decided with a wry quirk of his busy mouth and shook his head in the face of Kit's interrogating look.

'Just thinking about dragons, Kester, which you must admit don't exist.'

'Oh, that depends on the circumstances, I've come across one or two in my time, I assure you. Miranda's one-time maid still looks at me as if she might reduce me to a small heap of smoking ashes if I put so much as a foot wrong in my dealings with my own wife.'

'Ah, well, that's because she knows you always wanted to put a good deal more than a foot wrong with her before you wed her. Sensible female, if you ask me.'

'You wouldn't say that if she was breathing fire down

your neck at every second step,' Kit said with feeling and Ben wondered where the cold-as-iron man of business he had once feared his old friend was turning into had got off to.

'She'll have other things to think of when her second babe's born,' Ben assured him with a not-very-understanding smile, for part of him secretly envied Kit the morass of domesticity he and his cohorts seemed to have fallen into so eagerly. Another part assured him such ties were the very last thing any self-respecting man would bind himself with and, on the whole, he preferred that part and his freedom.

'Not she, having the first did nothing to stop Leah interfering in every pie she could get a finger into, so another is hardly like to stop her.'

'Should be in the army.'

'Aye, Boney would be beat a damn sight sooner if she was.'

'But Miranda would miss her,' Ben qualified and tried his best to feel nauseated by Kit's besotted smile as he contemplated the wife he'd been parted from for what must be nearly an hour by now.

'And that I utterly refuse to contemplate, so Wellington will have to do without her,' Kit said with what was almost a sheepish look as he met his friend's sceptical gaze.

'I dare say he'll manage,' Ben said laconically and eyed the array of pickles included by the thoughtful Cook and considered which ones to add to the mountain of food still on his plate.

'Never mind that, though,' Kit said, serious all of a sudden, and Ben nodded as if acknowledging it was time to talk about the subject at the forefront of both their minds. 'The fate of our nation seems to be in safe enough hands now Boney's on the run, but what of our own? Although I refuse to let some fly-by-night rogue dictate mine, I'll admit he's looming a little too large for comfort just now, whoever he is.'

'And how on earth he's contriving to stay hidden from us is beyond me, but I'm not abandoning my search for him, Kit, not even for your sake.'

'And I'm not asking you to. Marriage has yet to make a coward of me.' Since Kit sounded both haughty and hurt, Ben concluded he'd blundered by implying his friend might want to relinquish the search for their bitter enemy, now he had the happy ending neither of them had ever expected.

'I know it,' Ben replied very seriously, meeting Kit's suddenly hard dark eyes with unusual seriousness in his own silver-grey ones.

Kit sighed and sat back in his chair to contemplate Cook's apple tarts and the thick cream sent up from his Devon estate. 'Of course you do,' he acknowledged with a fleeting grin. 'But it's high time we put our minds to catching him, before he does any more damage.'

'Aye, but how? He's eluded every hound we've set on him so far, and got his own men so terrified they'd die rather than risk his vengeance *and* he's got a powerful protector who's determined to safeguard a lucrative connection.'

'Yet the fact that we know from my less-than-lovely cousin that there's someone important guarding him takes us a step forwards. As well as the fact they've got desperate enough to send their tools after me to scare us off, so at least he's on the defensive.'

'How very reassuring, considering he knows who and what we are, and we haven't an inkling who either of them might be,' Ben replied sarcastically and gloomily helped himself to a syllabub.

'He has to deal with two of us and I warrant he won't trust his backer as far as he can throw him.'

'Something makes me think neither of them attended as hard a school as either of us,' Ben replied, musing over whether or not he could consider their tough beginnings an advantage in this murky business. There were places even his wealth and whispered-at origins would not take him and, if Kit was to remain in Derbyshire, he could hardly get into them either.

'The man behind it all is clever and devious and we're fools if we underestimate him. From my recent experiences, we might be dead if we do that,' Kit said and rubbed his arm ruefully as they both considered where he might be today, but for Miranda's insistence that Reuben follow him as closely as he could get away with while they were in Ireland.

Even Kit would have a hard time fighting off two professional assassins alone, and Ben beat back the very thought of grieving a man who couldn't be more his brother if they were tied by blood.

'We've got to go on the offensive,' he mused out

loud. 'If only we knew who we were dealing with, at least we could set a trap for him.'

'Greed seems to be the most likely bait to lead the active partner to damnation, and I want every last one of his evil gang, Ben, as well as all those other devils who prey on the innocent,' Kit replied grimly.

Thoughts of the good men who had died among the crew they lost to their deadly, dangerous enemy, and even the odd rogues who'd let themselves be corrupted, haunted them both. Ben considered how close that loss had taken them to utter ruin and an ignominious slide back into the mire they had crawled out of and looked grimmer than ever. What if that was exactly what someone had wanted? Yet although they'd made enemies enough during their rise, none were powerful enough to try to snuff their fledgling empire out before it was properly built, as they had proved by recouping their losses and carving their place in the world afterwards. And if the attack on their ship had been personal, why had the cold-hearted fiend stopped his antics when it failed to ruin them the first time?

They had only possessed three ships then and the loss of another would have crippled their fledgling company before it was hardly afloat. Now they had more than thirty, and Stone & Shaw carried cargoes from all corners of the known world, but so far their ships had gone unmolested by the rogues pirating cargoes and stealing ships by putting out reports they had sunk. For a while Lloyds had refused to insure them after the sinking of the *Marie Louise*, obviously thinking the young owners had found a lucrative method of keeping their profits and pocketing the insurance money as well. The damage to their reputations had hurt nearly as much as the loss of a spectacular cargo, Ben recalled now, but they had recovered, by sailing the ships they had left themselves so successfully that they could outrun or hide from pirates and the Royal Navy, intent on pressing their carefully built crews. Yet despite their employment of the most cunning captains and system of the crew taking a share of the profits for every year of loyal service, he doubted that was the entire reason they hadn't been targeted since.

'Who hates us so much that he tried to ruin us, Kit? And what's stopping him from trying to do it again?' he asked in frustration, not for the first time over the years, but they failed to come up with an answer yet again.

'Braxton certainly loathes me,' Kit admitted with a smile that Ben thought boded very ill for the man who'd almost brought about Miranda's journey into hell, if his friend laid hands on the obnoxious sot twice.

'But he's not got the power to hurt you, especially considering he's in danger of hanging if his misdeeds come out, as well as being a few thousand miles off. He might hate you, Kester, but he can't actually hurt you.'

'He could hurt my wife,' Kit admitted painfully and Ben once more resolved never to give his heart away and put it in such jeopardy.

Kit looked passionately protective, deeply disturbed and furiously angry at the very thought of the man who had done his best to ruin a seventeen-year-old girl, then callously tried to sell her into sexual slavery. Part of Ben was awed at such love taking over what he once thought as stony a heart as his own, another dreaded the vulnerability his friend revealed by it and wondered if he should take this hunt alone. To be so engaged with any woman was to divide your heart, render yourself open to so much potential pain that it might threaten the very cause Kit was so determined to fight for.

'All the more reason why you should take her home and guard her among folk who know and love her best,' he assured Kit seriously.

'You think me a fool, Ben,' Kit told him with a steady look and a grim determination about his expression that warned Ben he was about to be stubborn as only Kit knew how.

'No, but I do think you're far too clever to risk our whole enterprise at this stage of the game by putting your queen at risk,' Ben countered, meeting that dark gaze steadily and refusing to be moved by the fiery Alstone temper Kit usually kept under such strict control.

'I don't think the devil behind all this plays by any rules, let alone those of the chessboard,' Kit admitted at last. 'But you win, Ben. I can't play a cool hand, knowing he could harm my wife and family while my back's turned.'

'Knowing you have her safe will free me to do it for both of us, then,' Ben promised. 'Then I can have a proper look at all my enemies,' he added with a grim look Kit obviously recognised.

'You're wrong, you know,' his friend informed him.

'Wrong about what?'

'Your father,' Kit told him, treading on to ground no other man on earth could stand on without igniting Ben's fury.

'I hardly think so,' he parried. 'Actions speak louder than all the fine words his lordship spouts in the Lords to fool the world he's a good man with a soft heart for a deserving case.'

Against his will Ben felt his fists clench at his sides and his whole body stiffen in rejection of the so-called nobleman who had fathered him. To his way of thinking, a two-faced rogue who could seduce and then cynically abandon an innocent young girl and her unborn child to the mercies of a merciless world was capable of any sin in the calendar. Years ago he had resolved never to let his sire's betrayal hurt him again, yet here he was knotted up with fury and, yes, he had to admit it if only to himself, pain, at what the damnable Lord Pemberley had done to him and his.

'And what I have discovered of his actions since he forsook you and your mother speaks of a man wearing a hairshirt. Try as I might, I have found nothing to connect him to the criminals and corrupted officials our enemies' backer must deal with to move against us and others in such a fashion,' Kit informed him sincerely and Ben had to make himself pause and consider such a hard-won opinion.

He trusted Kit as he would no other man on earth, so if his friend thought the great Marquis of Pemberley innocent, should he not at least consider letting the notion go that his own father was behind the attempt to scout him back into the slum from which he came? Despite all he had ever done to armour himself against hope, it seemed as if a huge weight was about to lift from his broad shoulders and he cursed himself for being such a fool.

'Never mind, Ben, you can't help being human, however hard you seem to try to avoid it at times,' his friend mocked him gently.

'Who said I was?' he replied lightly enough, for not even in front of Kit would he admit how heavily that suspicion had lain on him.

'My sisters, along with my wife and sisters-in-law, and all the others you strive to protect, and I must join their ranks and admit you're the brother of my heart, Ben. Despite your reluctance to love anyone, you still do so, my friend.'

'Don't tell anyone, will you?' Ben parried lightly and Kit grinned back at him with a little too much understanding in his dark eyes, but he let the subject drop all the same.

'So what do you intend to do to flush out our enemies this time, then?' he asked and looked as serious and determined about the task as Ben could ever have wished.

'First of all I need information,' he added with a straight look and watched Kit's dark eyes go hard as obsidian when his meaning went home.

'No!' he insisted shortly.

'Yes, Kit! I need your brother-in-law and he'll be the

first one to admit it when he realises how close this villain is capable of getting to those we love.'

'Hugh Kenton has a new life with my sister,' Kit said flatly and Ben felt himself butt up against his friend's strong protective interests and regretted the fact that he must push through them to gain his ends.

'Which is now as much at risk as yours,' he made himself say, although he wanted to pretend they could do this without calling in Kit's brother-in-law, and every other advantage he could muster along the way. 'I need an advantage, some sort of lever to use against those who would act against us, and Hugh is the man to get it for me.'

'Was the man—he hasn't carried out such work for years.' Ben eyed his friend steadily and waited wordlessly for him to acknowledge he kept some secrets even from his best friend. 'All right, he hasn't immersed himself in the underworld for years,' Kit admitted ruefully. 'The odd small job he can carry out at arm's length, so to speak, but no more, and I refuse to ask him to go back into that hell he crawled out of to chase my enemies for me.'

'Then I'll do it for you. I need to know not only who our enemies are, but who stands between them and us and stop them trying to snuff out our company again. Without that knowledge, it's like being asked to run with my legs tied at the ankles.' There was a heavy silence in the quiet room for long moments. 'You might be a gentlemen, Kester, but I lack your breeding and your scruples,' Ben added, 'and surely you don't expect

me to dig about in the mire myself? I'm not exactly unmemorable, you know.'

'No, with your height and breadth I'm not daft
enough to think you could be aught but what you appear,
Ben,' Kit returned and Ben knew he had won, despite
his own reluctance to use Hugh Kenton's unique skills
to break the stalemate shadowing all their lives.

Chapter Four

'So, what do you really think of Ben Shaw?' Isabella asked her governess just as Charlotte was about to take a bite of chicken pie. Glad Isabella hadn't waited until she had her mouth full, Charlotte lowered her fork and considered the delicious morsel on it as if it was poisoned.

'What a question, Izzie,' Kate condemned her sister across the dining table, but looked at Charlotte as if she fully expected an answer.

'I'm in pursuit of knowledge, sister dear, which I'm sure you know can never be taken lightly.'

The wicked parody of her own most solemn pronouncements would normally have made Charlotte laugh and resolve not to be so pompous in future, but this time it failed to work that magic.

'My feelings one way or another about a gentleman who is very close to your brother-in-law and almost a member of your family are private and will remain so, Isabella, so eat your luncheon and at least pretend to show me some respect,' she said with what she hoped was dignified authority.

'Oh, I don't need to pretend, I do respect you, dear Miss Wells, but I should still like to know why you poker up so stiffly whenever Ben is present. He really has a most distorted view of you and, as you say, he's almost a member of the family, and your dislike makes me uncomfortable.'

Meeting Kate's eyes with a similar mix of exasperation and reluctant admiration in her own, Charlotte shook her head and smiled reluctantly. Her remaining pupil was bidding fair to become a very outspoken young lady indeed. Charlotte wasn't sure whether to regard that as a crushing failure or a spectacular success, and hoped she would be safely established in her new employment when the time came for Miss Isabella Alstone to be brought out. Having tutored such an outspoken young lady for so long might reflect less than gloriously on her one-time mentor. Something of her own rebellious nature must still linger, for part of her rejoiced in sending her charges into the world questioning what society considered set in stone and maybe even rejecting some of its sillier notions. In her opinion ladies shouldn't be brought up to be seen and not heard, or be so silly that their prattle could be dismissed as the effervescence of an empty mind. Women made up half the world, and surely only fools would consider it sensible to discard their thoughts and beliefs when they bore and nurtured the next generation?

Just as well that those censorious dowagers who

looked down their noses at a mere governess accompanying her erstwhile pupil to a ball last night had no idea what revolutionary thoughts buzzed in her head, she decided ruefully. At least she had the sense to know her convictions would get any girl who set her path through life by them ostracised and a burden to her friends and family, so she never discussed them with either Kate or Isabella, but she had the uneasy feeling she would be blamed if either of them came up with them of their own accord. Maybe the reactionaries were right and educating females led to trouble, but considering she intended to go on doing so as long as there were parents enlightened enough to want girls to be more than barely literate, she very much hoped they were not.

As they ate their luncheon in thoughtful silence for a few minutes, Charlotte hoped the topic of Mr Shaw had at least been abandoned for now, but was rapidly disappointed.

'Ben likes you,' Isabella announced as she hesitated between gooseberry tart and junket. Charlotte sought the benefit of silence, hoping her pupil would give up and move on to an easier topic. 'He doesn't like any of the society ladies he's come across very much, except us of course, and we're family so we don't count.'

'He liked Mrs Ramsden well enough last night,' Kate put in and Charlotte felt her appetite seize up altogether for some odd reason and pushed her half-finished meal aside as if it revolted her.

'At last, somebody is going to tell me something about last night,' Isabella said and leaned forward eagerly, which Charlotte felt entitled to rebuke her for, considering doing so for anything else would make her ridiculous assertion seem important.

'But I want to know, Miss Wells,' Isabella said with a smile even Charlotte wasn't altogether proof against and just shook her head in reply.

'Can you imagine anything undertaken before the eyes of the *ton* staying secret for five seconds?' Kate replied caustically and this time Charlotte's frown was serious. She wanted her charges armed against the sillier and more dangerous occupations of the *ton*, not turned into cynics.

'A great many of them are good and worthy people,' she said and tried hard to believe it herself. Most doting mothers and even their semi-detached husbands were genuinely concerned their offspring should make good marriages and lead secure and happy lives. If they enjoyed the pleasures and extravagancies of high society while they were doing so, who was she to criticise? Yet she had never felt comfortable among them, even though she'd been born to a higher station than most would consider she held now.

'Then they can be very silly indeed,' Kate condemned.

'Did anyone make unwelcome advances to you last night, my dear?' Charlotte asked anxiously.

'Of course not, they wouldn't dare do so with you and Ben looming like watchful giants,' she replied with a mischievous smile.

'Then why have you suddenly become jaded with your triumphs? You seemed happy enough to be declared a belle of the Season these last few weeks, even after your initial reluctance to come to town.'

'Oh, I don't know,' Kate said with a sigh, 'it's just that I don't want to wed a boy who's more interested in the cut of his coat and the knot in his cravat than the fate of nations and their peoples.'

'I suspect most of them are more concerned about weightier matters than they care to admit in mixed company.'

'Which is precisely why I don't want to marry any of them. Can you imagine what it must be like to be told not to worry your pretty head over such unfeminine problems, Miss Wells? I fear I can and I don't like the idea one little bit.'

'The Earl doesn't treat you so, now does he?' Charlotte asked.

'No,' Kate replied rather mulishly, as if she could see where their conversation was leading and didn't intend to agree with anything else.

'Nor Mr Shaw?'

'No, but Ben's not—'

'Mr Shaw is gentleman enough to look out for your welfare and ensure your suitors don't treat you in lightly, my girl, so I suggest you remember that fact and amend your thoughts and your manners.'

Kate looked hurt and temper sparked in her fine blue eyes for a moment, before she analysed her governess's hasty speech a little more deeply and sat back in her chair, looking rather pleased with herself instead. 'I was going to say Ben's not demonstrated the least intention of ever getting wed, Miss Wells, and I've always wondered just what sort of woman it might take to change his mind,' she said innocently and Isabella was nearly halfway over the table in her eagerness to hear Charlotte's response.

A picture of the rather obvious charms of the shapely, beautiful and obviously very willing Mrs Ramsden slotted annoyingly into Charlotte's mind and smirked tauntingly. 'I suppose time will tell,' she said flatly and laid her knife and fork together before rising from the table. 'I will give you another ten minutes to finish your meal and interrogate your sister, Isabella, but after that I require your presence in the schoolroom,' she said and swept out of the room.

Who cared if Mr Benedict Shaw was as susceptible to the obvious, if elegantly displayed, charms of Mrs Ramsden as the next man? Not Charlotte Wells, she assured herself and retreated to her room to re-pin her hair into its severe style and re-settle her deplorable snuff-brown skirts, then face her own rather formidable reflection in the mirror. Item: one governess, she mocked herself with a frown, as she caught the secrets in her own eyes and dared them to spill out anywhere else but here. Exceptionally learned for a gently reared lady, useful with all the globes and accomplished in both the French and Italian tongues, able to instruct young ladies in sketching and watercolour and almost guaranteed to fade into the background of any well-run establishment. She curtsied at herself and wondered why the silly female with those softly haunted brown eyes stared back at her with a hint of reproach in their depths.

Even if she wanted him to, Mr Ben Shaw would never look at such an antidote with the feral glint silvering his grey eyes she had seen when he looked at Mrs Lavinia Ramsden last night. She shivered at the very idea of feeling his molten gaze linger on her curves, if she ever found the brazen nerve to display them, and on her sinuous, silk-clad limbs. Her hair would probably have to be dressed more simply than Mrs Ramsden's, of course, for no lady as tall as she was would risk adding to her ridiculous inches with such a style, but a few long silky ringlets kissing the side of her long neck and lying teasingly along the curve of her cunningly displayed bosom might fire his imagination to even greater flights of fancy.

'And pigs might fly, Charlotte,' she informed herself in her best Miss Wells voice and swung away from those betraying eyes in the mirror to armour herself with real life and schoolbooks.

'Don't you ever picture yourself as one of them, miss?' Jessie, the second housemaid, asked Charlotte as they strolled along Bond Street on the way home from walking Kate to a friend's house the following afternoon.

'One of whom?' she replied absently, watching a crossing sweeper and doubting her companion had him in mind.

'Those young ladies,' Jessie replied with a nod at a group of girls giggling over a stylish bonnet artfully displayed in a very exclusive milliner's shop window.

'Not really,' she said truthfully enough, having been young and almost as silly herself once upon a time; she had no wish to go through it all again.

'Oh, but I should,' the maid said with a sigh.

'You're nowhere near foolish enough, Jessie,' Charlotte told her with a sympathetic smile.

'But sometimes I should like to be,' the maid replied with a self-deprecating shrug and a faint sigh.

'It would be a luxury, would it not?' Charlotte asked gently and thought the delights of too much leisure and far more money than they had sense would become Jessie rather better than it did the clutch of overgrown schoolgirls making a figure of themselves yonder.

'Oh, yes, miss, even if it was only for a day I should like it above anything,' she admitted as if revealing her deepest and darkest secret.

'Even more than marrying James the undergroom?' Charlotte asked with gentle mockery and Jessie blushed, despite the fact that she'd been engaged to that gentleman for over a year.

'I should like him to see me so, miss,' Jessie admitted with a nod at the showiest of the young ladies.

'Well, I should not,' Charlotte said and considered the little maid for a moment, 'you would suit a much plainer style, more like Miss Kate's new day dress with a pretty blue spencer rather than all those frills, and perhaps a bonnet with a silk rose on it, not a flower garden or half an ostrich,' she concluded, warming to her subject. 'It would be elegant rather than ostentatious and show off your pretty face and figure into the bargain.'

'Ooh, it does sound lovely, miss,' Jessie enthused and her eyes went starry at the thought of her James seeing her decked out thus, while Charlotte wondered if there was any way something like that could be contrived for her wedding dress without wounding her pride.

'And much more appropriate than that overblown marshmallow; the girl looks as if she's about to be launched into the atmosphere like a hot-air balloon,' a deep voice observed in Charlotte's left ear and she turned to meet Mr Shaw's amused grey eyes with a sense of inevitability she really must learn to fight.

'Sir,' she acknowledged with a slight nod and an odd feeling at the pit of her stomach she assured herself was dread of what he might say next, not something far less excusable such as a ridiculous, secret desire for improper attentions he would never dream of showering on a respectable, overgrown and painfully plain governess.

'Madam,' he replied solemnly and Charlotte felt like kicking him as Jessie giggled at his parody of her own stiff manner and distant bow.

'How do you do, Jessie?' he asked with an easy smile for the little maid that had Charlotte fighting a most unworthy attack of jealousy.

She didn't want his smiles, she assured herself crossly and, even if she did, she had no right to begrudge them to a girl who worked relentlessly for her wages and already had a love to take her mind off a smile that would've warmed *her* to the very tips of her toes. But he never offered Charlotte such uncomplicated greetings and never would, and she couldn't afford to be friends with a man who made her feel so very uncomfortable with herself and her lot in life.

'Are you heading for Carnwood House, Mr Shaw?' she asked innocuously enough, and hoped he was heading in the opposite direction.

'Indeed, I hope you'll accompany me there and enliven my way,' he replied politely enough, but she saw mockery and something darker, more primitive, more furious in his grey eyes as he did so and silently squirmed. Just why he always brought out the worst in her she refused to consider, but just at the moment she wished him a hundred miles off and wasn't sure she cared to be a fleeting amusement to enliven the odd second he had to spare for the trivia of life.

Since he looked to Jessie as much as to herself for an answer, Charlotte forced herself to be fair and admit his manners were a great deal better than many of the highest in the land, who seemed to have very little idea servants existed at all, let alone showing any inclination to consult their wishes about even the most important aspects of their lives. Which didn't make him an easier companion as far as she was concerned, she reminded herself, and managed a weak smile of reluctant compliance to echo Jessie's much warmer invitation to join them.

Walking democratically between the two of them, at least he didn't try to take her hand and force her into even closer contact with his ridiculously mighty body. Despite her unease with him, she felt much more comfortable than usual with her unwomanly height in his company as she strolled along, doing her best to enjoy the leisure to look about her just as much as she'd been doing before he came along. Difficult to savour such unaccustomed pleasures, when walking side by side with a man who set her nerves on edge and did such unwelcome things to her composure that it was in danger of shattering completely, she decided crossly.

He obviously had no idea that he affected her so deeply, she reassured herself, and even if he did he would probably be deeply embarrassed that a superannuated governess felt her pulse race and her heartbeat flutter whenever Mr Benedict Shaw hove into view. At least being part of no particular sphere in life, a governess could keep her secrets, and take them to the cold grave with her, a taunting voice whispered as Charlotte stalwartly did her best to ignore it.

'Do you have any further errands to perform today, ladies?' he asked and Charlotte could hardly be properly angry at his drawling tone and provoking look in her direction when Jessie flushed with pleasure at being included in that select grouping for once.

'No,' she said after a pause, in case Jessie should feel the need to fill it by inventing one to keep them out a little longer, 'we're almost at leisure.'

'Only almost?'

'Undoubtedly a flurry of tasks await us at home, Mr Shaw. The Earl and Countess are intent on leaving town as soon as Miss Alstone's new chaperon arrives,' she said stiffly then immediately regretted it when she saw Jessie's pretty face fall at the reminder of all the work awaiting her.

'How mighty my friend has grown that it takes days of fuss and palaver to get him from one house to another, both of which he owns and can stock as he pleases. Time was it only took him time to pack a valise,' he said with what she was quite certain was meant to be a provoking glance in her direction.

'I dare say,' she replied placidly.

'Refusing my fly, Miss Wells? That's not like you—do you think Miss Wells is quite well, Jessie? Perhaps we should take her home immediately and force a powder down her throat.'

'Best not, sir,' Jessie replied with a grin and Charlotte silently fumed, but could say nothing without sounding as if she were rebuking the maid, when it was the man she would very much like to rip up at, if she weren't a lady, of course, which unfortunately she was by profession and birth and thus denied the luxury of telling Mr Shaw exactly what she thought of him.

'You think she'll come about, then?' he added with exaggerated concern as he tried to examine Charlotte's averted features.

'Very likely,' Jessie said with a distinct giggle, the traitor.

'I am here, you know,' she said through gritted teeth and would have sped off ahead of their dawdling pace, if it wouldn't amuse the pair of them all the more.

'And quite impossible to ignore, I assure you,' he told her as if that was something she ought to be proud of.

'I'm quite aware that my height renders me ridiculous without you pointing it out to me, Mr Shaw,' she informed him stiffly, then could have kicked herself for revealing how vulnerable to mockery her extraordinary inches often made her feel, try as she might to pretend otherwise.

Something about him made her feel itchy in her own skin, ill at ease with problems she'd long ago decided she could do nothing about and must endure. In the company of Mr Ben Shaw she felt like the silly débutante she had once been. The one who longed to be prettier, and shorter, so she'd attract admiration instead of mockery. Best not to remember how it had hurt when luckier chaperons condoled with her own over the enormous task of marrying off *her* charge with any credit at all.

'Now that would be the pot calling the kettle black with a vengeance, but I actually meant your decided and disapproving presence, Miss Wells. I could hardly ignore the chill that comes over you whenever I am by; indeed, I wouldn't dare do so,' he finished with a surprisingly boyish smile that made her want to smile back at him like a love-struck girl.

She frowned instead and his smile broadened into a grin. 'I'm so glad you take some note of me, sir, for sometimes it seems to me that you fail to listen to a single word I say,' she said as sweetly as she could in the face of his provocation.

'On the contrary, I take in a great deal, Miss Wells, far more than you could possibly believe,' he returned and it was his turn to frown over that conclusion as if he disliked it nearly as much as she ought to.

'Well, we won't argue about that,' she replied repressively, with a warning glance at the eagerly listening Jessie. He chose to return with a bland smile that set her pulse racing because it seemed to contain a promise of 'later'. As if there would be any later! Not if she had a sliver of sense left in her head at any rate, and luckily, she reassured herself sternly, she had always had plenty of that.

'Have you heard anything about the fighting in France?' she asked instead and trusted the end of this interminable war to divert them all from the unwelcome topic of Mr Shaw and the governess.

'Only that Bonaparte can't hold on much longer, now so many have turned the other way,' he replied with the suggestion of a frown.

'And you find that execrable?' she asked gently.

'I find it opportunistic and disloyal, but so wags the world, Miss Wells, as I'm certain you know, being so well versed in history and all its quirks.'

Jessie nodded sagely as if ranging herself alongside Ben in his necessary absorption in the here and now, not having the benefit of her education and wide reading. Little did either of them know that she'd read so widely to escape too many childhood years totally lacking love and attention from those who were supposedly her carers once her parents were both dead, and that was another subject she refused to dwell on.

'Every event is unique, for all it might look like a copy of the last,' she declared lightly enough, 'and you're better placed than either of us to know the ins and outs of this one, sir.'

'Yes, I can see how the business world rearranges

itself, but, no, I don't have spies at the French court to know just who is sidling out of the room as if he can't imagine how he got there, and who is determined to stay until the last man falls,' he replied and the look on his face made her wonder if he was regretting such disloyalty in defeat. He shrugged as if dismissing the fate of emperors and became facetious again. 'England will be *en fête* whenever the little Emperor decides he can't pull off another miracle and gives in at last, and London will be nigh hysterical with joy. So the question is, Miss Wells, shall you permit your charge a holiday from erudition and grammar, or do you propose to behave as if this is just another spring?'

'Oh, the latter, of course; being a tyrant of the worst sort, I can't countenance such unbridled joy as must surely greet the end of five-and-twenty years of war.'

'Won't it be lovely?' Jessie said, unconscious of, or prepared to ignore, the undercurrent between her companions as she contemplated an end to the strife and anxiety she'd grown up with. 'I can't remember what peace is like.'

'I doubt you were even born last time we had a real one, for that fiasco at Amiens was only meant to give Boney a breathing space, for all we hoped for so much from it,' Ben recalled rather bitterly.

'And were so bitterly disappointed,' Charlotte agreed soberly.

War had cost her a doting father, killed at the Battle of the Nile, but how many other lives had it taken or ruined? She tried to shake off the memory of her shattering grief at her father's death, only a year after her mother's. At least she'd been safe, even if it was in her grandparents' grudging care. Would she have been married to a handsome and hopeful naval officer by now if her parents had lived? she wondered. Recalling impromptu balls at the homes she had shared with them, before being sent to England for a sound education, she thought it highly likely. Still, at least that learning stood her in good stead, even if her loving parents would disapprove the use she'd been compelled to put it to.

'A penny for them, Miss Wells?' Mr Shaw's deep voice brought her back to the present in very short order.

'Oh, I was just wondering what it would be like not to fear invasion and conquest after all these years, Mr Shaw,' she told him.

'Lovely, that's what it'll be,' Jessie said firmly, as if she could sense argument trembling on their tongues and would have none of it.

'Of course it will,' Charlotte agreed lightly, but she knew deep down that nations so geared up for war and resistance would find the world a very different place when their euphoria had died down.

She met Ben's eyes with agreement in her own that, yes, it would be wonderful to escape the grief and grind of war, but then there were all the other problems the war had masked still waiting to be solved. Then she found herself just looking up at him, all the serious business of the fate of Europe quite forgotten. She felt her breath catch, her cheeks flush with heat and her imagination threatened to shock her deeply. If not for the fateful battle that killed him, then maybe, in the company of her sociable father, she might have met an up-and-coming young captain of the merchant marine, her fantasy went, and he would have met her gaze for gaze and stolen her heart away.

And maybe he'd have ignored such a gangling young woman and walked into the arms of some more fortunate, more normal female! Charlotte tore her gaze from Mr Ben Shaw's and shook out her governess persona and donned it like a suit of armour, with good strong chain mail underneath.

'I shall be late for tea with Miss Isabella if we linger for very much longer,' she informed Jessie with a hint of apology for hurrying her indoors when she was enjoying being out of them so much, before she stepped out at a very determined pace all the same.

'And I'll be quite breathless by the time I join you,' Mr Shaw lied as he stepped up his pace with no effort whatsoever, 'but Jessie will be far too exhausted to do anything but seek her bed for the rest of the day,' he pointed out insufferably and Charlotte forced herself to slow down and wait for the little maid to get her breath back.

'I apologise, Jessie, that was most inconsiderate of me,' she said stiffly and squashed a wish to be among the lordly of this world rather than the lorded over, so she could banish her companions and stride off alone. Not even the greatest ladies could ignore proprieties, she told herself with a sigh, and endured it for the sake of her pupil's reputation, if not her own.

'And unusual,' Ben said gently and risked undoing all the good she had just done herself.

She turned to challenge him for interfering and encountered a look of genuine respect for her habitual consideration for the servants. Fool that she was, she felt a misty glow threaten to engulf her at winning his approval without even trying. Another internal yank of sharp temptation whispered, 'if only', and silly tears even threatened as sensible, workaday Miss Wells informed Charlotte she was a fool, and likely to end up whistling everything she'd worked for down the wind for a few moments of passion and a lifetime of regrets.

'I doubt it,' she snapped repressively and set herself to endure the dawdling pace he and Jessie seemed to prefer as she calculated how many streets there were to traverse before she would be rid of him. Then his words put a curb on whatever joy she'd been anticipating in her release. 'You're coming for tea?' she queried and heard a definite squeak in her voice.

'I was invited,' he told her, apology in his words if not his tone or look. 'Apparently Lady Carnwood thinks her little sister is feeling a little lonely now Miss Kate is in such demand for tea drinkings and walking in the Park and all the other interminable activities young ladies seem to enjoy. She thought we could all take tea with Miss Isabella today and make it an occasion for her.'

Normally Charlotte would applaud such sensitivity on Miranda's part, but today she just wanted to be quit of Mr Shaw's annoying company as soon as possible. Some very unladylike words she'd learnt at her father's knee when he wasn't paying attention to his language leapt on to her tongue and she only just managed to swallow them. How shocked the world would be if they realised respectable Miss Wells had such a vocabulary at her disposal!

The idea cheered her up a little as she hugged that secret, other Charlotte to herself and gloried in her for once. As the unruly minx seemed determined to whisper wicked thoughts today, she might as well make herself useful and provide more spirit than the Alstones' governess was usually thought to possess. So Charlotte gave him a look that she hoped told him *she* had not invited him, and he would die of inanition waiting for her to do so, and sniffed with satisfying superiority.

If she did but know it, that sniff came very close to proving her undoing. The sound of it taunted Ben's sense of the ridiculous as well as urging him to seize her in his arms and kiss her very soundly indeed, public square or no. At least *he* took some note of his surroundings, he scolded her silently and bowed ironically when he finally ushered Jessie and Miss Charlotte Wells up the steps to Kit's grand town residence ahead of him. Just to torture himself perhaps, he decided with despairing self-mockery, for he was absolutely certain the prickly governess had no idea how that deplorable pelisse of hers draped to her fine figure and gave him a tantalising view of her neat behind and long, long legs as it clung lovingly to them. Although perhaps she had an inkling, or some protective instinct even years of schoolmarming had failed to completely suffocate, for even as he enjoyed and endured the experience he saw her twitch her skirts irritably and hold them a little away from her body, as if chiding them for failing to douse everything about her that was feminine and all too alluring to masculine senses that were suddenly sharply honed on her every look and gesture.

If he had any sense at all, he'd turn about and head straight back to the City where he belonged. No good would come of consorting with a governess who teased and tantalised his every sense without even taking her bonnet off. It was that old tale of what was concealed immediately became more seductive, he told himself severely, and ordered his eyes to look anywhere but at Miss Wells's delightful figure. Which was all very well, but he also had to endure the elusive scent of her as she put off that deplorable hat at last and stood in front of the mirror in Kit's echoing hallway to make sure not a wisp of Charlotte the woman had escaped from under the engulfing cap of Miss Wells, teacher and stern moral guardian of the privileged young.

Sharp, clean lavender, he decided, setting himself to winnow out the composite mystery that was Miss Wells's peculiar allure. And a hint of the cinnamon and cloves she must use in her moth bags to keep them from the noble work of destroying the dire greyish-beige shawl she often carried to douse any last spark of curiosity the world might show her. Except she habitually overdid it, he decided, and the contrast between the youthful clarity of her skin and the slender rounded vigour of her long limbs and the truly awful clothes intrigued rather than repelled him. He watched with a mix of resignation and wry amusement as she stiffened her shoulders and turned about to meet his gaze. Meanwhile Jessie reluctantly headed for the backstairs and her duties and Ben knew he should get himself and Miss Wells upstairs as soon as possible, so he could leave all the sooner.

'I dare say Isabella will be waiting for us,' she prompted coolly at last.

'I dare say,' he replied blandly.

'And Lord and Lady Carnwood as well, I expect,' she said distantly. The fact that he discovered he would very much like to be scandalously occupied all afternoon with the lady beside him shocked him nearly as much as it would have Miss Charlotte Wells, if she could read his mind. Heaven forbid! He didn't much like what was in there himself at the moment, so the very last thing he wanted was for Miss Propriety to find him out in such a lascivious, and highly unlikely, fantasy.

'When is Lady Rhys due to arrive?' he asked with a preoccupied frown, thinking it as well that it be sooner rather than later, if his stupid obsession with Isabella's governess was ever to evaporate as the mirage it truly was.

'I have no idea, and as Lady Carnwood's letter can hardly have been gone for more than an hour or two, I would have to guess it will not be this week,' Charlotte informed him with something like triumph and immediately told herself not to be such an idiot.

How ridiculous to feel wounded that he was so eager

to be shot of any responsibility he might feel for his adoptive family and by tenuous connection herself, at least until his lordship felt at liberty to leave them to his tender mercies. Ben Shaw was welcome to return to the scandalous embraces of the Mrs Ramsdens of this world, and the sooner the better. An image of his mighty form entwined in some louche fashion with the voluptuous widow, rather than taking tea with a very dull governess and her pupils, made her blink for some reason and every muscle, every resolution tightened as the wicked idea slid into her mind that it should be her locked in his mighty arms and it had to be scouted with such brisk resolution she could pretend it had never been.

'When Kit has gone to Wychwood Manor, I hope you'll do me the favour of taking even more care of yourself and your charges, Miss Wells,' the insufferable Mr Shaw demanded as if he had every right.

Charlotte attempted to stare him down coolly, but she should have known better; he just met her angry glare with steady grey eyes and looked as if he was being logical and rational and she was behaving like a naughty schoolgirl.

'If my behaviour were your concern, sir, which it patently is not, I should have to point out that I've done nothing to deserve censure. I've not been out alone, or offered the least temptation for the gossips to whisper scandal about Isabella's governess.'

'I'm not concerned about Isabella's undeservedly spotless reputation, you damned fool woman, I'm worried about your safety and that of your charges,' he snapped, as if she had been defending herself against his ridiculous assumption of authority merely to annoy him, instead of that just being a satisfying side effect. 'Jessie could hardly do anything to protect you if any of you were set upon whilst you were sauntering about Mayfair.'

'Unless you give me a good reason to change my current mode of life, which I can assure you is quite respectable enough to pass muster in the best of circles, I shall continue just as I am. And if you intend to swear at me, I shall retire to my room until you quit the house, Mr Shaw,' she told him with what she hoped was frigid dignity.

Instead of letting her exit the hall with all flags flying, he simply reached out and caught her wrist, stopping her in her tracks without using any force at all. Desperately trying to ignore the hot shiver that ran through her at the feel of his strong fingers on the sensitive skin of her inner wrist, she held herself rigid and refused to meet his intent gaze.

'You're a danger to yourself and everyone round you,' he eventually ground out furiously and it was fairly obvious he had to exert his iron will not to shake her until her teeth rattled.

'What a ludicrous accusation,' she informed him through clenched teeth, wishing that option were only open to her. One glance at his mighty shoulders scouted that idea as even more ridiculous than meekly giving in to whatever diktat he chose to throw at her.

'Call me that one more time, Miss Prim Propriety, and I'll kiss you until you beg for more.'

Chapter Five

The word trembled on her tongue, but just in time common sense intervened and she settled for, 'You're being preposterous, Mr Shaw!'

'Neat,' he informed her with a decidedly wolfish grin.

They were at risk of being interrupted by someone emerging from the backstairs, but, sensing someone was coming before Charlotte had even heard a whisper of movement, Ben took advantage of his grip on her and towed her into the small room the master of the house used as his office and shut the door so softly she doubted the newcomer had the slightest inkling they had ever been there.

'Very efficient,' she observed flatly and looked at his hand wrapped about her wrist with what she hoped was ironic significance. 'Do you manhandle your conquests in such a scrambling fashion, Mr Shaw?' she couldn't resist asking him.

'No, my conquests, as you call them, are far too

willing to need dragging anywhere, except perhaps out of my front door come morning so I can get some work done,' he informed her outrageously and Charlotte felt herself blush at the very thought of spending the night in his bed, and not wanting to leave it in the slightest come morning either.

Now how on earth had they got from Kate and Isabella's personal safety to the questionable subject of his mistresses and on to Miss Charlotte Wells indulging her baser passions to the full? She drew herself up to her usually impressive full height and gave him a look that had been known to halt hysterical children and furious gentlemen in their tracks.

'I have no wish to hear about your amorous exploits, sir. Instead I'm patiently awaiting an explanation of your ludi…foolish conduct and this laughable delusion you seem to suffer from that you can hustle me about whenever and wherever you have a mind to do so.'

'Well done, my dear, you nearly let the word slip again then, did you not? What admirable self-restraint you do possess,' he said silkily.

'Unlike you, Mr Shaw,' she replied impulsively, then immediately regretted it when a flare of something very hot and decidedly feral lit his silver-grey gaze.

'Considering I'm so far behind you in propriety, if not in good sense, I think we may take my self-control as a given,' he told her and suddenly she mistrusted the reasonableness of his tone, the expression of conscious virtue on his intent face.

'We may?' she asked suspiciously.

'Of course we may. No doubt you would poker up like a dowager and turn into a stone statue if I were to forget myself in your presence and do this?' he rumbled softly before one tug on her wrist landed her smoothly in his arms as if both of them had been made to fit that way.

Struggling with her inner self, she did her best to be predictable and stiffen like a marionette against him. Common sense and a strong instinct for self-preservation urged her to work a hand free and slap his face, so at least he would let her go before he did irrevocable damage. That instinct told her he would release her if she truly protested, say what he might about his origins and that strong masculine urge to conquer. The trouble was that for the life of her she couldn't make herself do or say anything discouraging, so she conspired with her eager senses by saying and doing nothing at all.

'Oh dear, you seem to have failed us both rather badly, Miss Wells,' he said even more softly, before lowering his mouth to hers and gifting her the gentlest, most seductive kiss she had ever dared dream of.

She moaned, for if she had failed him, just what had she done to herself? Hearing it, his pleading kiss turned to one of utter possession and Miss Wells left the room in disgust. Charlotte turned in his arms so she could plaster herself a little closer to his impressive body and raised herself on tiptoe so she could meet his kiss more ardently. His tongue made determined sorties against her lips until she opened them to him, as if her instincts knew exactly what to do when she was with him. She contrasted the only other intimate kisses she had ever received and fought a shudder of revulsion as she banished the memory utterly and they leapfrogged over it, into a new world of utter sensuality.

His tongue dipped between her parted, willing lips and it was as if he drew honey from some well she never knew she possessed. She learnt at first hesitantly and then all too boldly to echo his exploration of her mouth with one of her own. He tasted so right, felt so warm and welcome, that joy threatened to overwhelm her and an odd craving set up in the heart of her that seemed to promise infinite bliss, if only he'd carry on holding her as if she meant the world to him and he to her.

That thought plagued her as she did her best to ignore it and function purely on the physical plain she was so eagerly exploring with him. One large and very gentle hand ran down her supple backbone, exploring and approving her subtle strength, appreciating the contrast to his own powerfully muscled torso that suddenly seemed like a banquet under her own seeking fingers. Maybe he sensed that whisper of unease under her sweet compliance—no, not compliance, utter surrender. Not letting her mouth do aught but breathe under his, he thrust his tongue into the eager, silky depths of it to stir up such unnameable longings deep inside as Charlotte had never dared imagine in her wildest dreams. Meanwhile his hands explored a little lower than before, resting for a moment on the curve of her buttocks and the intimate place where they met her long, long legs, and that heat at the centre of her threatened to melt all traces of will until she was a mass of delight and eager compliance.

Just as he had predicted, her nemesis insisted this was wrong, and Charlotte gave another moan, this time of protest, as her sensible self charged into the breach and informed her it had never been her style to become one of a crowd and this was a poor time to start.

Taking it as an awakening of her usual prim self, mistakenly, Charlotte concluded with bitter self-disgust, Ben raised his head and looked down at the chaos he had wrought. Looking hastily away as if she might have to defend the darkest secrets of her soul from him if she let him see any more, Charlotte met her own eyes in a gilded mirror Miranda had probably placed there to lighten this rather dark and masculine room when she sat in here while her husband worked.

Refusing to consider the difference between this and the undoubted seductions that had taken place in this very room between two real and utterly devoted lovers, Charlotte itemised what the man who still held her as if he had the right to had done to her. The reserved and professionally proper Miss Wells had just been very effectively transformed into a creature of fire and fervour. Her lips were moist and reddened from their mutual enthusiasm for that kiss; her eyes soft and vulnerable as magic lingered in them and an untamed hope for more lay irrepressibly in their velvety depths for all to see, like some voluptuous high summer bloom worshipping the June sun. She could have all that: the heady scent of fulfillment, the heat of everything a woman could dream of in a lover, the warmth of momentarily sated passion and the forbidden promise of something more, some consequence that must never be. Then she recalled how brief the abundance of June was, how so many flowers rushed to perfection and then faded and died in that heady, glorious peak of mid-summer.

No, she had no mind to be just one more heat betrayed bloom, flowering and peaking under his knowing, generous but relentless attentions, until she became nothing but his and then had to watch broken-hearted as he walked away. For walk away he would—something beyond her governesses training and sheer native wit warned her of that. There was a gap, a void in his other-wise generous heart put there by deprivation and hurt at too young an age, so it had set and hardened him against the passions that drove his fellow men and women.

'No more,' she managed to tell him in a soft voice she hardly recognised as her own, so unfamiliar as it felt between lips that still wanted his kiss rather than to form the thorny words she knew she must speak to make sure he didn't offer her any more of this sweet devastation.

'No,' he agreed on a sigh, sounding as little like his usual, decisive, self as she fell short of proper Miss Wells. 'That's more than enough folly for one day,' he informed her tersely and put some distance between them by dint of straightening the arms that had just held her so compellingly, holding her away from his body as if she was dangerous.

A suspicion sprang to life that he was less defended against her than either of them had thought. It sowed a small seed of hope that she dared not examine just now, in case it sprang into full-blown certainty. Maybe his heart wasn't as stony as he thought. He obviously believed he was incapable of giving anything of himself to a woman—or at least any woman who might be more than a brief delight, a mutual passion to be savoured and then concluded with a mild friendship if possible. Even if the besotted creature refused such an offer and left him with bitter reluctance, never to find his equal again, he would still pull away from her, perhaps even more eagerly, because Mr Ben Shaw would not be chained down by anyone. Once upon a time she had agreed with him, but now?

Charlotte forced herself not to linger on her own uncertainty, or that faint flicker of optimism, while she was so vulnerable. One day she might be cool enough to rationally consider the idea there could be something special between a plain governess and a fabulously wealthy man who'd made himself a force to be reckoned with out of sheer will-power and hard work. Now all she could do was patch up as much damage as possible and try to put Miss Wells back in charge of her life, until Charlotte was prepared to be rational and could be reunited with her more sensible self.

'I want you to promise me you'll not go out without one of the footmen or a groom with you, at least until Kester and I have tracked down our enemy and put an end to his game,' he demanded while she was still struggling with her baser self and frantically smoothing down the betraying creases in her cotton gown.

'Why would he bother with me?' She was shocked into saying, 'I'm just the governess, not some valuable hostage who might make him money. I see the logic in protecting Kate and Isabella, for either of his lordship's sisters-in-law would be a fine bargaining tool, but me? I think you have let your imagination run away with you, Mr Shaw.'

'No, it's you who's failing to use yours. Apart from anything else, can you really see Kit and Miranda ignoring your plight if you got captured while you're too busy proving to me that you're invincible to remember your usual common sense?'

Would that be the reason? Charlotte considered it and concluded there was an element of truth in what he said and even felt a little ashamed of herself. Not that she had the slightest intention of letting him see it. It was true that her employers wouldn't sit back and leave her to her fate, in the unlikely event that she ever got kidnapped. They weren't like some of their kind, armoured against the ups and downs of the world outside their immediate family by supreme selfishness, and the assurance they were born to dictate rather than be dictated to. Bitterness threatened to overwhelm her at the thought of her past experience of such privileged beings, so she forced it back into the past where it belonged.

'I confess I can't imagine them being easy if any of their household were taken in such a way,' she finally admitted.

'Good, so we have that much reason to work on at least,' he said, rather unreasonably in her opinion, and then began pacing about the room as if only action would keep him from shaking her, or kissing her witless again just to keep her quiet and eager in his arms.

Hastily dismissing a picture of herself wanton and beyond rational thought, Charlotte decided it was time for a little judicious diplomacy, as she felt quite unable to weather another clash of personalities with him and come out victorious, or at least intact, just at the moment.

'I'll do as you ask for the time being,' she conceded, 'even if I do think you're jumping at shadows, for I doubt anyone outside the family has even noticed I exist.'

'I certainly have,' he snapped, and again a suspicion rose in her mind that he was more impassioned about this whole business than he pretended.

Cautioning herself against hope, she did her best to give him one of her best ironic looks, to remind him that most of what he had noticed he certainly didn't approve of, but he met it with a look almost of despair in his eyes and she let her own drop after all. If things had been different there might have been hope for them, despite him and his silly resolutions not to depend on any other human being for his happiness. And of course there was her own determination to make her way through life alone. Nor was she exactly who he thought her to be, and she knew that complication would jar against his notions of honour and truth, if she were ever so stupid as to let herself grasp the very brief joy of becoming his mistress.

She could see now why his mother had behaved as she had if that was all she could have of a man like this, and she began to wonder about the father Ben never spoke of after all. His silence on the subject was all too eloquent, at least according to Miranda, who seemed to have the idea that Ben owed his determination never to love or be loved to his absent and apparently uncaring father. If he'd been even half the man his son had become, Charlotte thought that was far too simple a summary of the facts. Another idea to put aside and consider when she was cool and logical enough to do it justice, she decided, and braced herself to dismiss him as if he meant nothing much to her at all. After all, that was exactly what he kept attempting to do to her, and she was feminine enough to wonder how he would feel on the other end of the determined distance he was trying to keep from her. A faint, worryingly indulgent smile crooked her mouth, before she controlled it. What a darling he was, in his own gruff and overbearing way, her heart whispered. And what a stubborn mule of a man he was to deal with on any other level but the most superficial one, her everyday self reminded her.

'As you don't want to kidnap me, I hardly think that counts,' she said at last.

'So long as you do as I ask, I suppose it matters little enough why you do so,' he informed her grudgingly and stopped his incessant pacing to peer at her as if he suspected her of something devious.

'While we're in London, I shall do as you ask,' she improvised, for it seemed a shame to disappoint him by being too reasonable when his expectations of her were so low.

'But as soon as you're outside it, you reserve the right to do just as you please? What an ungovernable female you are, Miss Wells.'

'Which even you must admit is rich coming from you, Mr Shaw.'

Instead of sparking his already impressive temper into full life, her comment forced a reluctant chuckle out of him and once more Charlotte's flimsy resistance threatened to melt at the deep, warm sound of it, the sheer intimacy of that richly masculine sound in this relatively small room.

'Aye, we're neither of us given to slavishly following the crowd,' he admitted and for a moment there was a precious accord between them.

Then he recalled how aloof he was determined to stay from the rest of the human race and his expression was as cool and shuttered as any humble governess could hope for in the presence of a man who would never willingly ravish her, let alone marry her afterwards.

'I have already conceded the sense of what you say,' she said and hoped her cool tone would tell him he'd done what he set out to do, so he could safely leave her to sink into her role once more.

'How magnanimous of you, Miss Wells,' he said with an ironic bow and, thinking they had done each other quite enough harm for one day, Charlotte curtsied very slightly and turned to leave him in possession of the field.

'Then I will wish you a good day, Mr Shaw,' she said and, feeling the cool metal of the door handle under her fingers with what she informed herself sternly must be relief, she went to turn it and leave before she betrayed herself any further than she already had.

'Not good day, Charlotte, I will see you in a few minutes, if you recall,' he said with a slight smile, but he looked as if he was saying farewell to rather more than just a plain governess who wasn't quite sure if she disliked, distrusted, or wanted him most.

Forcing her will on those wilfully reluctant fingers of hers, she turned the doorknob at last and opened the door a crack to check for unwanted spectators. Luckily nobody was in the hall. Somehow unable to just turn and walk away as if indifferent as she ought to be, Charlotte gave Ben a faint nod to acknowledge his words, then stiffened her backbone and walked away. Miss Wells intended to develop a slight headache in order to avoid taking tea with Mr Shaw and the other available Alstones, and she hoped he had the good sense to leave her to endure it in peace.

Watching her go, and cursing his ridiculous inability to tear his gaze from her rather spectacular rear view, as the unconscious sway of her hips and those lovely long legs did far too much damage to his resolutions to forget her, Ben did his best not to think about Charlotte Wells's effect on his rebellious body even as it resolutely refused to mind him. Lucky for him that she was innocent in so many ways and had no real idea of the pain his thwarted need of her had left him in. If she had the vaguest notion how easily she could have led him about by a certain susceptible part of his anatomy, what a dangerous woman she might be. His Charlotte was a prickly, demanding, rewarding, unique woman and, if only he had been worthy of her, she might be his downfall.

As it was, he wondered about a visit to his mistress as soon as he could get away from that infernal tea party, and decided he wouldn't insult the woman by slaking his passion of another, more intriguing, more dangerous female on her. Just because he had no intention of falling in love as his mother had done so recklessly, that didn't mean he couldn't like and value any woman he did become involved with, and while the lovely Mrs Ramsden knew very well what was what, she was also showing a worrying tendency to feel a little more for him that he was comfortable with. Maybe taking out his feelings for another woman on her might make her see him for what he was, but still he refused to use any woman as his father had used his mother.

He groaned out loud and fell to pacing Kit's study once more as the very real effect of Miss Charlotte Wells on his disobedient body put him on the rack once more. Curse the woman; anyone would think a man would be safe with a female who set out to extinguish any trace of the true sensual Charlotte under all that propriety and disapproval. But, no, he must look deeper, tread more carelessly and then risk falling headlong into a mire of his own making. Still a part of him rebelled, even as he knew a part of her could not help doing. She was made for better than the half-life she currently allowed herself, as if she was twenty years or more beyond her true age; now he thought about that, he wondered if she were not considerably younger than she would have the world believe.

He pictured the Charlotte of a few, heady, foolish moments ago as she melted in his arms and tried to set her in her true place in the world. Dressed in anything other than that shapeless parody of a gown, her delightful body would show itself for the superb example of the female form it truly was. He could visualise the lovely sway of her hips, the delicate curves of her very feminine breast outlined by the high-waisted, softly draped gowns currently fashionable, and his mind's eye very nearly undid all the good her absence had been doing him. Curse the woman, why hadn't she stayed cold and aloof in her schoolmarm's persona? Now he knew better—there was a tall and lovely Juno under all that protective cover, and what a crime it was against nature to see such a vital creature eclipsed by her occupation and low expectations of the world.

It occurred to him with a flash of shock and temper that someone must have hurt her very deeply in the past to put her so firmly behind those barriers of hers. Teetering on the edge of a powerful fury and a crusading zeal to punish whoever had failed to value her as the rare being she truly was, he just managed to pull himself up from roaring upstairs and demanding the right to avenge her wrongs and slay her dragons. He reminded himself sternly that they had just agreed to be nothing to one another. Well, they hadn't precisely agreed it, but their silent dismissal of the vast possibilities that had sprung into life between them had been agreement enough for him. They were to be as they had been: occasional foes, habitual sparring partners, and reluctant allies in their quest to see the Alstone sisters happy as they deserved to be, after their uncertain start in the world and the dangers their fortunes posed to that happiness.

Even as the very instincts that urged him to protect the females he regarded as the family he had never had stirred, he suffered a reluctant conviction that Miss Charlotte Wells had insinuated herself among their number without the slightest effort on her part. Not an adopted sister as Kit's and now Miranda's siblings had become, never that. Nothing he felt towards her fitted into the sisterly category and the very idea filled him with revulsion. No, she was threatening to be far more dangerous than that, but he could contain her threat if he watched over her from a safe distance. Firmly resolved to keep that distance, while at the same time somehow contriving to see she was kept safe as only he knew how, Ben went upstairs to the young ladies' sitting room, fervently wishing life was as simple as international trade and the more complex methods of financing it had always been to him.

Chapter Six

It took ten days for a large and old-fashioned carriage to turn into the square and come to a halt before the Earl of Carnwood's splendid London residence. Despite its distinctly travel-stained appearance and a very weary-looking team of horses, Lady Rhys sprang down from her carriage to take a quick look around the square, before bustling up the wide steps to Carnwood House and stirring up the quiet elegance of that noble establishment to a bustle of activity and anticipation.

'Good day, Coppice,' she greeted the butler. 'Do me the favour of sorting them all out for me, will you?' she asked with a wave of a plump hand at the equipage, coachman, guard and her rather ineffective companion, who was twittering over the whole to very little effect.

'Very well, my lady,' Coppice agreed with a quiet sigh, but Lady Rhys was already gone.

Shaking his head, Coppice moved forwards to render chaos orderly and decided it was as well he liked a challenge, considering how unconventional a household he presided over nowadays.

'Miranda, my love!' her ladyship called out, and if Ben had been present he might have pointed out it was just as well the noble couple had finally quit their bed-chamber, for no doubt Lady Rhys would have burst in on them anyway and behaved as if their presence there in the middle of the day, as well as her own, was perfectly normal, almost conventional even.

'Godmama!' Miranda gasped and ran out of the schoolroom where she had been hiding from the legion of well-wishers her husband inflicted on her whenever he had to leave her for the City nowadays.

'It's Lady Rhys—oh, but that's famous,' Isabella exclaimed and sent Charlotte a look of piteous appeal. 'Can I have a day's holiday from Italian verbs please, dear, dear Miss Wells?'

'Very well, if you undertake to become a little better acquainted with them before next week's lesson,' Charlotte agreed, finding it hard to be suitably severe, considering she valued the lady very highly herself.

'My dear,' the lady greeted, walking towards her with hands held out in welcome. Lady Rhys gave her a delighted hug before releasing her to examine her admittedly execrable gown with raised eyebrows and a shake of her suspiciously blonde head.

'Will you never get this girl to forsake her interminable beiges and greys, Miranda, my love?' she asked as if the sight pained her.

'Charlotte's determined to remain invisible in mixed

company,' Lady Carnwood observed shrewdly, and Charlotte shot her a reproachful look.

'I certainly don't have the least wish to shine in society,' she said repressively, one eye on her very interested pupil and one on Lady Rhys. Both bore watching, in her opinion, and she could do without her employer complicating her life with misplaced humour at such a time as well.

'Well, there's very little risk of you shining anywhere in that deplorable gown,' Lady Rhys informed her brusquely and Charlotte suppressed an internal groan.

Somehow the lady would drag her off to her dressmaker during her stay and order at least one highly unsuitable gown, and she already had one lying unworn in the otherwise sparsely filled wardrobe in her ridiculously luxurious bedchamber. Ridiculous for a governess, that was, and she reminded herself every time she took the gown out and looked at it wistfully that soon she would have to go back to being one of those in a more conventional household.

'Which is exactly what my position requires of me,' she told her would-be fairy godmother with as much severity as she could muster in the face of her ruthless good will.

'Miss Wells is a very superior governess indeed, isn't she, Miranda?'

'Of course she is,' the countess replied with a rueful smile for Charlotte, as if disclaiming whatever came next as no fault of hers.

'Then she should dress as accords her station, instead of aping the appearance of a coal heaver's wife.'

'Not that many self-respecting coal heavers' wives would go about in such very dull feathers, unless they were helping their husbands heave coal, of course,' Kate observed from the doorway and at least the topic of Charlotte's inadequate wardrobe was forgotten for the time being as the whirl of greeting and kissing and exclamation started up all over again.

'Now tell me where you've been and whom you met and whether your fickle young heart is captured yet,' Lady Rhys demanded as soon as they had sat down to the tea Coppice produced, along with the slightly less harassed-looking companion and a loaded tray of baked treats to tempt them all.

'I've been everywhere that is anywhere, met everyone who's anyone and, so far, my heart is quite my own,' Kate replied succinctly and Charlotte wasn't sure if she should be proud of her, or ashamed not to have turned her into a bread-and-butter miss—a challenge beyond the sternest educator in her opinion, but she supposed she could have tried a little harder.

Lady Rhys chuckled, her sister raised her eyes to the heavens and the companion looked utterly, delightedly scandalised, so Charlotte supposed Kate suited them all very well just as she was. She accepted a cup of tea from the companion, who glared at her as if expecting her to usurp her place in Lady Rhys's life if she wasn't watched, and sipped it gratefully while she enjoyed hesitating between a Bosworth Jumble and a Bath Bun.

'Spoilt for choice, Miss Wells?' a familiar, deep, dangerous voice observed and Charlotte nearly dropped her teacup she jumped so ridiculously high, both at the sound of him and because he had chosen to single her out so noticeably in such company.

'Good afternoon, Mr Shaw,' she greeted him sternly and with an internal moan saw a spark of mischief light in the depths of his changeable grey eyes and wondered what on earth he would say next.

'It certainly is when Cook's best efforts are on offer,' he told her succinctly and Charlotte grabbed a Bath Bun before he could demolish it and everything else on that groaning plate.

Surprised at herself, she eyed her booty with sceptical appreciation. A moment ago it had seemed worth attracting attention for, however benign, but now she had somehow lost her hunger for it. Taking it before he could seemed to betray an intimacy she knew he would reject with what amounted to revulsion and she squirmed at the very idea of such a public humiliation, even if it would serve her purpose. If the family thought her so encroaching as to angle for the attention of one of their closest friends, perhaps they would stop trying to force her out of the mould of respectable governess she knew she had to cling to if she was to pull the role off successfully after all. Then there was Mr Shaw, who had haunted her dreams, both waking and sleeping ever since she had seen him last, so she now had shadows under her eyes and an even gaunter frame. Her role as the upright educator of young ladies represented safety to her, and she told herself that to be safe was all she required from life. She had good company and considerate employers here, but even if her next position was much less salubrious, she would be independent and that, she told herself, was all that mattered.

Coward, a part of her muttered darkly as it looked at what she had become and contrasted it unfavourably against the wild young girl she'd been as a child. That Charlotte had been headstrong and emotional and above all happy, but the woman she had become told herself it was easy to be daring and joyful when you knew yourself to be loved as deeply as her parents had loved her. It was far harder to keep faith with her loving, laughing, unconventional mother and father when they had both been laid in their early graves too many years ago to recall just now.

'And you, my boy?' Lady Rhys saw fit to interrogate Ben, just in time to prevent him seizing the plate and demolishing its contents entirely. 'Are you settled yet, or do I have all that to do as well?'

'No, that I'm not,' he replied with every sign of revulsion at the very idea. 'And you certainly have nothing to do on my behalf to remedy that,' he informed her sternly, for all the good it did him.

With a sceptical sniff, Lady Rhys slyly eyed Charlotte before she examined Ben as if he were an insect on a pin. 'Not a débutante, I think,' she mused aloud. 'Someone more up to your weight, so to speak, a lady of character and principle who'll refuse to be managed for her own good.'

'Miss Dwight?' Miranda asked as if seriously considering the idea, which Charlotte found outrageous and not a little hurtful, her hurt being purely on Mr Shaw's behalf, of course. Particularly as he looked as if there was a cesspit he would rather be cleaning than enduring such unwanted speculation on his personal life.

'No, she has political ambitions and I doubt you have the least desire to enter government, do you, my boy?'

Ben's look of loathing might have amused Charlotte as much as it did Lady Carnwood, if she didn't hate the subject nearly as much as he did.

'How about Lady Rowena Aysell?' Lady Rhys suggested, just as if she was considering form on the race-track, Charlotte decided in disgust.

'Horse-faced,' Miranda parried.

'And that just wouldn't do for a beau like our Mr Shaw. I think perhaps Lavinia Ramsden might suit him,' Lady Rhys considered with such apparent seriousness Charlotte would have liked to shake her, so it was as well she was seated across the room and governesses didn't do that sort of thing. 'She's no shrinking miss and she's certainly a beauty, despite being on the shady side of thirty. I dare say once she's settled again she would behave herself too, since nobody whispered scandal about her while Ramsden was alive. And I doubt she knows the name of our current prime minister, so she certainly wouldn't expect Ben to join his administration.'

'Mrs Ramsden's far too old for Ben,' Isabella protested and took the words right out of Charlotte's mouth, not that she could have spoken them aloud. She shot her pupil an approving look and signally refused to rebuke her for such a personal remark, as the companion seemed to expect her to for speaking her mind quite so forthrightly in adult company. Absurd when she was rising sixteen and very obviously capable of more common sense than her elders. 'Besides which, she's angling for a rich husband and I doubt very much if Ben wants to be married for his money—I know I don't.'

'Thank you, minx, if you're still unwed when *you're* on the wrong side of thirty then I'll marry you myself and save you from such a dire fate,' he quipped, but his grey gaze was warm and his smile open, and Charlotte felt an unworthy twinge of jealousy at the contrast between his easy manner with Isabella and his ambiguous attitude toward her.

Of course she didn't want him to smile at her with such uncomplicated affection; she didn't want him to smile at her at all, in fact, for when he did he was at his most dangerous and she had endured quite enough jeopardy from that quarter to be going on with, thank you very much.

'Thirty?' Isabella said lightly, looking as if such a ripe old age were virtually unimaginable. 'I should hope I could manage to find myself a kind, decent and rich husband before I'm that far into my dotage.'

'Kindly remember we're not all in the first flush of youth ourselves,' her elder sister chided mildly. 'Indeed, you may be in danger of offending the very person you set out to defend, for I happen to know that Ben is *more* than thirty and he still won't put his head in the noose.'

'Then there's Miss—' Isabella began with a pitying glance at Charlotte, who was watching the pallid companion she suddenly suspected Lady Rhys employed solely out of compassion, for she'd never met a woman more capable of amusing herself, but luckily Isabella was stopped before she could commit any far greater, and even more hurtful, *faux pas*.

'Stop right there, Isabella Alstone,' Lady Rhys ordered with unusual sternness. 'You were doing so well before you got carried away.'

'Indeed, and I think that's quite enough excitement for both of us for one day,' Charlotte observed sternly and rose to her feet to bear her charge back to the school-room and give her a lecture on the virtues of considering other people's hurt feelings before she rushed in to any attempt at doing them good.

'Never mind, I think you're wonderful,' Ben murmured to her charge as Charlotte whisked her out of the room.

'I might have to hold you to that promise then, because I don't think anyone else does,' Isabella whispered back and once again Charlotte found herself prey to the most irrational, unworthy emotions as she longed for him to look at her with such rueful understanding as they parted, instead of avoiding her eyes altogether.

If he was afraid he'd roused some stupid hope in her own breast that *she* might call on his chivalry when she was still unwed at thirty, then he could just think again. She'd turned her thoughts from marriage with a hop, skip and a delighted jump the moment she took up her new life, and it would take much more than a reluctant offer from a man who thought her a complete antidote to change her mind now. Not that he had thought her quite so antiquated and undesirable the other day in Lord Carnwood's bookroom, she reminded herself, but that had been propinquity and she'd been a fool to sink into his arms like a trollop, instead of sternly reminding them both who and what they were. Honoured guest and servant; man of spectacular means and a woman of none but the savings she'd managed to make from her generous salary against a rainy day, or a dearth of suitable young ladies to teach.

'Of course Ben will wed long before I get to that age,' Isabella observed sagely and the very notion quite took the sunlight out of Charlotte's day. She fervently hoped he would do so after she left Lord and Lady Carnwood's employ if he was going to abandon his opposition to marriage, for to be forced to stand on the sidelines and watch those particular nuptials celebrated in style might crush her very soul. Not that he'd dream of marrying her, and she stalwartly told herself she'd refuse him even if he did.

'Never mind Mr Shaw,' she said a little gruffly once they were back in the schoolroom. 'It's you we have to worry about just now. How could you put that poor creature in such a position, Isabella?' she demanded.

'What poor creature?' her pupil asked, obviously mystified.

Charlotte struggled to hide her own chagrin as she realised her pupil had her in mind when about to point out that if they were talking of elderly spinsters, her governess qualified as one, and was certainly no biddable débutante to be bossed about and moulded at Ben Shaw's whim.

'Oh, you mean Miss Burrage, don't you?' Isabella asked incredulously. 'But she wouldn't suit Ben at all, beside being so far on the wrong side of thirty I doubt she even remembers what it's like to be young any more.'

'I very much doubt that, and we've already heard quite enough on that particular subject, Isabella. Not all ladies are born to become wives or mothers, and *you* have a duty to show compassion toward those whose circumstances gave them no chance to become either. Although Miss Burrage may be very content as she is, of course.'

'I thought we weren't going to dwell on Miss Burrage, and I promise you that I'd quite forgotten she was in the room when I spoke, Miss Wells,' she ended with a significant glance at Charlotte, whom she very obviously had not forgotten.

'Then you consider *me* to be in my dotage?' Charlotte heard herself ask as if the idea grated on her pride; after all, she was only five and twenty, not at least ten years older as Isabella appeared to think her.

'No, but I do think you might be unhappy with another family when I finally make my come-out and Ben would make you a very pleasant husband, if he could be persuaded to see that marriage to you would suit him very well, of course.'

'He couldn't, even if I were the least bit willing to marry him. Which I'm not, by the way, and he's clearly not a marrying man,' Charlotte managed to say cheerfully enough, as if she was faintly amused by the whole idea.

With the right wife she could see him being the rare sort of husband his best friend had proved to be to Isabella's eldest sister. With the right wife, Ben Shaw would undoubtedly be loving, protective and gloriously vigorous, and perhaps even deeply in love. Part of her longed to be *that* wife to him very badly; the other part was a realist, and knew Miss Charlotte Wells lacked both the fire and the beauty to inspire such passionate devotion.

'I dare say Kit wasn't either, until he met Miranda,' Isabella insisted with a sidelong glance at Charlotte that informed her that Isabella was stubbornly convinced her governess was just the woman to change Ben's mind.

'We're not discussing your sister and her husband; in fact, we aren't discussing that topic at all, but rather your singular inability to guard your tongue in company, miss. You have a deplorable tendency to speak your thoughts as soon as they come into your head, Isabella, and somehow you must learn to keep them to yourself. Inadvertent as it may have been, you just risked causing great hurt to a woman who, as I said before, is perhaps single despite all her youthful expectations and desires.'

'Then I'm sorry for that,' Isabella had the grace to admit, but her intent blue gaze informed Charlotte she wasn't sorry to have pushed her at Ben Shaw as if she were a parcel he might one day want to open, if he ever found the time or the inclination.

Deciding to take what she could realistically get, rather than aiming for the moon just now, Charlotte cast about in her head for a task that might make Isabella think a little harder about interfering in other peoples' lives for their own good. 'I would like you to make a close study of *A Midsummer Night's Dream*, Isabella, and produce a properly considered essay on the consequences of interfering in the lives of others for our own gratification.'

'You think yourself such an ogre, Miss Wells,' her remaining pupil informed her cheerfully and went off to extract the play from her brother-in-law's library without much sign of thinking it a punishment at all.

Wondering too late if his lordship kept Shakespeare's plays in the original or a more polite form in his London library, Charlotte rather thought Isabella was right to be sceptical and flung herself into a less-than-comfortable chair to consider her own folly instead of that of an imaginary fairy king and his queen.

Life at Carnwood House settled back into some sort of routine, occasionally disrupted by Lady Rhys, who had far too restless and lively a mind to fall easily into anything so mundane. Lord and Lady Carnwood departed for Wychwood by very easy stages and Mr Shaw took to haunting the mansion in Berkeley Square far too often for Charlotte's peace of mind, but if that was what it took to keep Kate and Isabella safe then she supposed she must endure it, and even she couldn't deny that his massive presence and acute mind would guard Kate and Isabella even from the most determined kidnapper.

So far as she could see there was nothing unusual to trouble herself over as they all went about their daily lives and she began to wonder if Lord Carnwood and

Mr Shaw hadn't exaggerated their danger just to make everyone extra-vigilant. Once or twice she had glimpsed the same footman strolling along in her and Isabella's wake, as well as the stalwart one Ben insisted they took with them whenever they walked about Mayfair, but she noted his distinctive livery and concluded he was in the Marquis of Pemberley's employ and, as that gentleman lived just across the square, he had every right to be sauntering about it. Satisfied that he was merely an idle servant taking advantage of the fact that his master was in Paris just now, Charlotte decided he represented no threat and relaxed her guard a little once again.

There was certainly enough going on this summer to distract anyone from their worries. There was a general air of heady relief and rejoicing at the longed-for peace. Even the London mob was remarkably good humoured and the only danger they presented to anyone this June was to those who didn't show sufficient lights to prove their delight at Bonaparte's downfall. Half the *ton* had flocked to Paris to see for themselves how much Bonaparte had changed it, and sent excitable letters home telling all the ladies of their acquaintance that their gowns were not in the first stare now Paris had spoken. Their waists must rise even higher, their skirts be even more belled with buckram and primped with frills and rosettes and anything else their dressmakers could think of. Then there were their bonnets—laughably unfashionable, of course, and what had they all been thinking of?

'I need to consult my dressmaker,' Lady Rhys announced as she waved one such letter at them over the breakfast table. 'It would never do for us to appear shabby and behind the times if the Allied Sovereigns are to come to London as the Prince has announced. Coppice, would you tell Miss Kate not to be lying abed all morning today, for we have serious matters to attend to without delay.'

'Certainly, my lady,' the butler replied imperturbably and went to send her maid up to inform Miss Kate that coming home with the dawn was no longer a defence against Lady Rhys's boundless energies. After all, there was no point being the head of the servants' hall if you couldn't allocate the least desirable tasks to your minions.

'Can I come?' Isabella asked. 'It'll be my turn for all the folderol and fussing in a couple of years, so I might just as well accompany you and Kate while you consult with Celestine and find out what I have to look forward to.'

Instead of condemning that idea out of hand as Charlotte expected her to, Lady Rhys looked thoughtful and then eyed Charlotte herself with a most peculiar, speculative glint in her apparently guileless brown eyes. Now what was she up to? She liked Lady Rhys very much indeed, but the lady was always on the lookout for a satisfactory way to settle the affairs of anyone she took an interest in, and Charlotte had an uneasy feeling she saw her as her current project.

'I see no reason why not,' her ladyship said, raising her eyebrows at Charlotte in a question she evidently thought only had one answer.

'Very well, if Isabella will undertake to study a little

harder when she comes home,' she replied with a stern look at Isabella, for she wasn't quite sure she didn't share some of Lady Rhys's more outrageous ideas on the subject of her governess's future.

'Oh, very well,' Isabella said with a theatrical sigh and Charlotte was tempted to tell her she was overdoing it. 'I suppose you'll be contriving some elaborate plan for my betterment while I am away, won't you, dear Miss Wells?' she asked artlessly, making it clear she didn't expect Charlotte to join in the orgy of shopping offered by one of London's most exclusive modistes.

Now not just suspicious, but downright wary, Charlotte began compiling a mental list of errands she must run this morning, many of which might involve that elaborate plan for Isabella's punishment she had just hinted at herself, and this time it would certainly not encompass anything as pleasant as Shakespeare. Some time later she was struggling with an unworthy urge to applaud Kate for keeping the scheming pair waiting for upwards of an hour while she breakfasted, had her fiery locks dressed in the latest fashion and dawdled about the choice of gown and spencer to do justice to such a fine June morning.

'Lord,' Isabella exclaimed when her sister finally came downstairs,' I hope I never take hours to get ready just for a visit to my dressmaker.'

'Don't worry, little sister,' Kate returned rather snippily, 'I doubt there's the least danger of that.'

'And just what does that mean?'

'Children!' a deep voice rumbled from the door of Lord Carnwood's study and suddenly Charlotte knew all too well why Lady Rhys and Isabella had been conspiring all morning to leave her in the house while they all went out and left the field clear for goodness knew what ridiculous encounters they had fabricated in their over-fertile minds.

'Ben!' Isabella exclaimed, giving an artless start. 'I had no idea you were planning to spend the morning here, and now we have all agreed to go out and I can't bear to put it off.'

'Can you not, dear Isabella?' Kate put in sceptically and Charlotte would have liked to kiss her for her unspoken support as Kate's fine eyes darted suspiciously from her sister to Lady Rhys, who came bustling into the hall with her usual whirlwind energy in time to be included in Kate's condemnation. 'How unlike you both to abate your curiosity about everyone's comings and goings before you make arrangements for your day—are you both sickening for something, do you think?'

'No,' Isabella almost yelped and gave her mentor a rather desperate look of appeal, certain that her sister knew both of them too well to believe they had no idea Ben had been planning to work from Berkeley Square this morning. 'I feel perfectly well,' she added rather lamely.

'Excitement,' Lady Rhys announced briskly, 'and I swear the girl will go off like a volcano if we don't get her to Celestine very soon, for you *have* taken a very long time about dressing today, my dear, and it really was most inconsiderate of you.'

Kate was so astounded by her ladyship's brazen assumption of an air of gentle, regretful reproach that she let herself be dragged out of the front door and down the steps before she gathered her senses to protest their duplicity. Charlotte heard her struggle to condemn them both in front of the servants, without giving them any hint of why, and decided that at least one of her pupils seemed likely to do her credit. She might have to strangle the other one with her bare hands, of course, so perhaps she had no need to worry about how her future, and present, conduct might reflect on her teaching.

Ben quirked an ironic eyebrow at her as she stood silently fuming as she watched the Carnwoods' town chariot leave the square with its usual elegant display of wealth and good taste. Nothing about it gave away the fact that two schemers worthy of Machiavelli himself were aboard, Charlotte decided vengefully.

'Lost for words, Miss Wells?' he quizzed.

'No, I could find a good many if I were not a lady,' she told him with her best attempt at regal dignity, 'and probably without pausing for breath,' she added in a furious murmur he surely couldn't hear, and yet there was such an expression of laughing understanding in his eyes she felt compelled to frown at him, just in case she forgot herself and laughed at such transparent manoeuvring, when she would probably be as safe with him this morning as if they had been shipwrecked on a deserted island.

'Doubtless,' he said and she could see that he had recalled how little he wanted to be left to her exclusive company as the laughter faded and he stared at her as if not sure whether to expect hysterics or icy fury.

'I believe you were busy, Mr Shaw,' she reminded him briskly. 'I know I have a great deal to do this morning.'

'Poor Izzie,' he said softly, even as he glanced back into Lord Carnwood's study as if impatient to be safely closeted inside it once more.

'That is debatable,' she replied shortly. 'I wish you good morning, Mr Shaw,' she added as she turned to climb the stairs once more and at least put a few floors of elegant Palladian architecture between them.

'Good morning, Miss Wells,' he replied absently, yet when she could not help herself taking one last look before the stairs turned he was watching her go, just as if he could see inside her silly head and knew what an effort it cost her to stay straight-backed and buttoned up in his company.

Memory of that kiss crackled in the air separating them as her eyes met his and a flush burnt along her cheekbones so fiercely she prayed he couldn't see it from such a distance. Maybe he could and maybe not, but he took a step forwards before good sense obviously overcame the impulse and he swung about and marched briskly back to sanctuary, leaving her looking at the shining mahogany of one of Lord Carnwood's fine doors with wistful bewilderment.

'Can I help you, Miss Wells?' Coppice asked when he stepped out of his pantry and spied her frozen on the stairs like Lot's wife.

'No, I think not, Coppice, I doubt if anybody can,'

she told him with such a note of wistful regret in her voice that he gave her a sympathetic look and she cursed herself for showing yet another member of the household she had feelings for Ben Shaw, even if she wasn't quite sure exactly what they were just at the moment. 'Could George be ready to accompany me outdoors in, say, ten minutes?' she asked with a look at the neat little watch pinned to her bodice so she could be spared the pitying look he was surely sending her.

'Certainly, ma'am,' he told her, but something told her he thought she was running away from the inevitable.

Well, if she was, long may it continue, for it seemed to her that the so-called inevitable was a cruel illusion she wished Lord Carnwood's household would forget, before it did serious damage to the objects of so much misplaced good will.

'There's no need for you to inform Mr Shaw that I intend to run my errands while my pupil is otherwise engaged,' she told him, with a straight look she sincerely hoped would deter him from such a course.

'Of course not, ma'am.'

'I am not the Queen, Coppice,' she informed him with gentle irony and fervently hoped she had put paid to the epidemic of conspiracy she and Ben suddenly seemed to be surrounded by.

'Of course not, Miss Wells,' he replied reproachfully and departed to find George, every line of him proclaiming that he had the last word and if she was foolish enough not to know where her own interests lay there was nothing he could do about it. Charlotte was feminine enough to give her very modest bonnet a rueful look before she put it on and wonder how this morning's shopping expedition would turn out. If Kate managed to get her sister and Lady Rhys out of the modiste's exclusive establishment inside three hours, then doubtless the milliners would prove their next destination and nearly every hat in their shops would have to be tried on before she could get them home. Suddenly she was stricken with a ridiculous yearning to visit one herself, as she eyed the unappetising creation in her hand. Fashion had never entered her thoughts even when she bought it and, who would expect a humble governess to be *à la mode* anyway? They would be disappointed if they did, she decided repressively and determinedly sallied forth in it, despite the chagrin most other ladies would feel at being seen dead in it, let alone walking about Mayfair.

'Where to, miss?' the footman asked cheerfully when she joined him in the hall in her repressive bonnet and equally sober walking dress.

All very well for him, he had a fine day and the prospect of very little to do beside walk deferentially behind the governess while she carried out a series of trivial errands. Strongly tempted to bid him decide and see what novel byways that might take them down, she hit on a trip to Hatchards to begin her enforced leisure; after all, she might as well enjoy her modest holiday as best she could as well as find an improving tome for Isabella to wade through when she got home. Then perhaps afterwards she would take a stroll in Green

Park, safe among the nannies and other governesses where she belonged, and give herself a lecture on how desirable it was to stay one of their decent company while she was about it.

'I won't have to carry nothing, will I, Miss Wells?' George asked her uneasily.

'I very much doubt it,' she replied, rather startled by this question as they made their way towards the famous bookshop in procession.

'Only Mr Shaw said I was to keep my hands free and always be on the lookout for anything unusual,' he replied apologetically.

'Drat Mr Shaw,' she snapped and set such a pace there was a danger of them both becoming overheated before they got anywhere near the shop or the park.

'Hatchards, Mr Shaw,' Ben was told solemnly by his friend's butler at approximately the same time he was being traduced by Miss Charlotte Wells.

'Cursed female, why can't she crave fripperies instead of improving tomes?' he asked and caught Coppice out in a secret smile. 'You're not in on it as well, are you?' he asked suspiciously. For this match-making conspiracy was beginning to feel as onerous to him as it obviously was to Charlotte.

'In on what, sir?' Coppice asked, with that politely blank look they must teach butlers on their first day of training, Ben decided crossly.

'Lady Rhys's campaign to do me good, as opposed to mine not to be done good to, of course,' he replied rather bleakly, for that long look he had exchanged with Charlotte had rendered him nearly as sharply on edge as it had her and he was, therefore, not in the mood for hints or clever evasions.

'Oh, that,' Coppice allowed himself to say dismissively.

'Yes, that—and…?'

'No, sir, I am not part of that campaign, being of the opinion that there's no point trying to do you good when you're so determined to go to the devil your own way, as it were, Mr Shaw.'

'And you think me a damned fool?'

'I think Miss Wells is a very clever and elusive lady who has a mind of her own.'

'So you doubt that I could win her even if I had the least intention of trying to do so?'

'I have not considered the matter with any degree of seriousness, sir, you being so determined to the contrary, as it were.'

'Then you didn't get our names in the sweepstake they are undoubtedly running in the servants' hall now Lady Rhys's machinations are becoming so obvious?' Ben asked shrewdly.

'What sweepstake would that be, sir?'

'You're a rogue, Coppice—how on earth you've contrived to hide it from the world so successfully all these years is beyond me.'

'Maybe it takes one to know one, Mr Shaw?' Coppice observed impassively and had ghosted out of the study before Ben could think of a smart reply.

Not that it mattered, he decided, trying to fight the

ennui and resultant bad temper that seemed to threaten his composure so often these last few days. He was quite right not to even consider wedding the disapproving governess after that shattering kiss they had shared. It was the sensible course of action to avoid her whenever possible, in case he was tempted to repeat that folly or even crown it with a greater one. She didn't even like him, he reassured himself, as he threw himself back in his chair in disgust when the total of a column of figures that would normally have added themselves up in his head without much thought eluded him once more.

His resolution never to father a child hadn't been made lightly, though it might have been made when he was too young to understand exactly what he was denying himself and some nebulous, unlikely female he might one day want to love and not be able to. Yet the reason for it was as valid today as it had been all those years ago when he sat by his mother as she died and heard her cry out for his father with her last living breath. How the hell she could still love that devil after all he had done to her, Ben could not imagine, but at the time it had seemed perfectly reasonable to swear he would never open himself up to such irrational, destructive passion, nor subject any child of his to the threat of such unstable emotions. Better that they were never born than that they should see their father brought low by some fantasy masquerading as love.

The trouble was, he decided disgustedly, his grief-stricken oath to a dead woman had never been properly tested before. He'd managed to go through thirty-four years of life without once wanting to throw himself at a female who seemed to dislike him almost as much as she wanted to kiss him back. Maybe that was why she was so close to changing everything he had thought set in stone though, for nobody in their right mind could accuse Miss Charlotte Wells of casting out lures to unwary gentlemen. Yet he *had* been unwary, her very prickliness had made him complacent; her ugly gowns and extinguishing caps had deluded him into thinking that she presented no danger to him whatsoever. Now here he was, frantic to find out what she was really like under all that starch and bombazine. After that regrettable episode in this very room he knew for a fact that the body it was designed to cunningly conceal was matchless, so what, a demon's voice of temptation whispered, was she like without a stitch of that smothering disguise to her name?

The need to know nagged at his senses whenever he tried to submerge himself in work, it murmured forbidden enticements as he tried to sleep and failed for the heat the stubborn idea of feeling her next to him lit in his disobedient body. Charlotte, the woman she could be, the creature of fiery responses and passionate need under all that caution and distrust, lured him on as no other woman ever had or ever would. Yet why she did so, he had no way of telling. She did nothing to secure his attention, slid away from him as if he might scorch her whenever they were within a mile of touching each other, and now she'd gone out to avoid him and he should be thanking her for it, on his knees if necessary, but instead he was absurdly hurt and longing for any excuse to follow her.

He ought to go anyway, he persuaded himself; George was strong and quick enough to frighten off any casual attacker, but the enemy on his tail was subtle, and infinitely more dangerous than the common run of criminals. He probably owed it to Kit, Miranda and the entire Alstone family to follow Miss Wells and make sure she got home safely, for he was reasonably certain they would pay handsomely for her return if she was ever taken. Yes, it was his duty, so at last he could do as he'd been longing to, when he heard her departure through the carefully cracked open door and forced himself to stay exactly where he was, and sprang to his feet.

'Your hat and cane, sir,' Coppice said, impassively holding them both out for Ben to take impatiently as he exited the room in a great hurry.

'How long have you been standing there?' he asked harshly, but the butler just looked blank and gave him an inquiring look.

'Sir?'

'Oh, never mind,' Ben replied impatiently and ran down the steps of Kit's ludicrous mansion as if Bonaparte's rapidly disbanding army were after him.

Chapter Seven

Ben's relief when he caught sight of Charlotte and her acolyte sauntering ahead of him, towering over the general run of strolling ladies and most of the gentlemen, as well as hurrying tradesmen and the usual idlers, felt almost physical. He'd been struggling with a sense of impending disaster ever since Hugh Kenton informed him that he'd caught the disgruntled captain that Ben and Kit had once turned off for the cruelty with which he treated his crew at last, and that he was in Newgate awaiting trial for piracy, extortion and murder. Although Hugh seemed to think they had found the head of the conspiracy against them, Ben had never been quite so sure. Hugh was too busy gleefully decimating Stitchforth's gang to remember that, while the man was ruthless and as cold-hearted as an Arctic winter, he hadn't the subtlety or the influence to succeed in his foul trade alone.

Ben wished he could go to Wychwood and discuss

the whole rotten conspiracy with Kit, but his friend had a new life and the burdens of running several great estates, as well as a pregnant wife who knew a little too much about the dirty underbelly of Kit's former world to be easy while he still had half his heart there. Well, Ben decided, he was certainly big enough to carry his own burdens and, with no family to hold him back, he could put his nose where the enemy he still sensed lurking and eager to pounce whenever he got the chance certainly wouldn't want it to be. And if only that were true, how much better he would feel! Since he was old enough to walk, Kit and his sisters had become his family, and now he had the Alstone sisters, and their exasperating governess, to add to the mix.

Something about the way that lady's appalling bonnet kept outpacing his attempts to catch her up suddenly struck him as peculiar and Ben's attention sharpened on the buzz of humanity about her and realised she was being shepherded in a certain direction by a crowd he doubted were as random as she thought. Quickening his pace, ready to shove and elbow as ruthlessly as necessary, he felt his heart leap with terror like he'd never felt before as suddenly neither her head nor that of Kit's largest footman towered over the crowd any more.

Torn between fighting to see what had happened to them and the primitive urge to lash out at anyone in his way and force a passage towards her, Ben suddenly knew this was no ordinary knot of innocent strollers on the strut in the West End. The deliberate impetus of a large group of people intent on mischief had already carried them into a court where no respectable person would dare linger even for a look and Ben cursed the nature of his native city, where so much wealth and privilege sat side by side with the deepest and darkest deprivation, as if they were twin entities, each equally disgusted at how the other had turned out.

'Hello, lover,' a remarkably vigorous-looking crone quipped as the ill-disposed crowd jostled him into her arms, then closed up behind them.

As Ben met her hard eyes, his heart sank—not only was there little humanity left in them after years of degradation, but he recognised her as the keeper of one of the most notorious flash houses in notorious St Giles. Not only did she know him, but she hated him like poison for doing his best to close her down and remove as many children from her brutal grasp as he could rescue, even when he couldn't stir the magistrates to action. He thrust himself away from the fetid rags that covered her wasted bosom and resisted all the attempts of the crowd to push him back there. Now he could see Charlotte draped lifelessly over the shoulders of a man nearly as broad as himself, although much less lofty and, with a sinking heart, realised he knew him too. He was one of the enforcers used by gang masters to keep their unruly subjects in line, and in abject terror of ever stepping out of it in the first place.

'You've no chance, my fine buck. Might as well give it up now,' the evil old madam told him complacently.

Then even she jumped back and span out of his way, as Ben furiously milled his way through the mob by sheer force of his superior reach and vigour, blinded to the futility of his efforts by the sheer anger and terror he felt over his Charlotte's plight. The crone's evil, gloating laugh was among the last things he heard, as so many blows from the cudgels and fists of men without pity or conscience finally overpowered even his mighty strength. Losing even his iron grip on his senses under such an onslaught, his last thought was that he'd failed Charlotte and must now endure that terrible burden on his eternal soul, if this was indeed his last breath.

Of course, at the first sign something was amiss, he should have discreetly followed the mob for any clue to where they were going. He was perfectly capable of doing it without them ever knowing he'd been there, even inconveniently dressed as a gentleman as he had been today—if it was still today. If only he'd done that, at least he'd know where she was being held and could plan her rescue, but, no, instead he'd lost his head and got himself caught in the same net. Unfortunate that such a common-sense scheme didn't occur to him until he came to in utter darkness and every reeling sense he possessed informed him the steady breathing next to him belonged to Miss Charlotte Wells, and that it took a gallant fight for her to keep that breath slow and steady. He tried to open his eyes and even that movement cost him dear. Although there was certainly no light to hurt them in the absolute darkness, that didn't currently feel much of a blessing as just the effort of making his eyelids open told how battered he was. He must have moaned as his hurts made their presence felt, as he heard a harsh groan that could never have issued from Charlotte's lips, so at least his ears still worked as well, even if his head felt as if it had been stamped on by giants.

'Keep still,' she admonished in a severe whisper and he felt an insane urge to laugh.

Here was his Charlotte, in as dire a situation as any woman could ever frighten herself even imaging, and still she clung to the ridiculous persona of the severe governess that she tried so hard to impose on the world. Well, it wouldn't work with him any more, not after their scorching kiss had haunted him. He was reckless enough to think exploring her true nature might cure him of his ridiculous infatuation with her. After that shattering kiss, at least he wasn't taken in by her hard-hearted dragon act any more, but he also knew that she meant more to him than any female he had ever thought to meet. Now he also dreaded finding out how bravely she faced adversity, as the hardest of the hard choices she had had to make so far in her life would fade into nothing next to the one she might face now.

'Where are we?' he muttered in a voice that shocked him by sounding all at sea. They must have hit him very hard, he decided sagely, and fought the temptation to defy his fierce nurse and feel the swelling on the back of his head after all.

'Don't bother, you've a lump there the size of a cobblestone, and how on earth it didn't kill you I'll never know. You must have a very thick skull,' she snapped, wondering how she managed it without raising her voice above a breath of sound that occupied a few pain-filled moments as he fought to resist the seductive notion of letting go his flimsy grip on his senses and forgetting their appalling situation in sleep for as long as possible. That would make him a coward, he decided, and leave Charlotte facing it alone, so somehow or another he had to resist the siren pull of just letting his eyelids drop and his mind drift back into oblivion.

'How d'you know I meant to move?' he murmured rather idiotically.

'I felt you tense your arm,' she told him flatly and, at last, he could hear the heartbreaking effort she was making to pretend he was back in the nursery he'd never had and all was well with their world.

'Have you any idea where we are, or how long we've been here?' He finally managed to ask the question that should have leapt into his mind the instant he returned to consciousness.

'No, I was knocked out myself, if you remember?'

'How could I ever forget?' he gritted though sore, stiff lips as the image of her, boneless and heartrendingly unaware as she lay across that brute's shoulder, jarred through him and sobered him as swiftly as a pail of clear icy water might have done, if only this place rejoiced in such a luxury, which he severely doubted from all the evidence so far.

'Then have you heard anything that might tell us where we are?' he asked and felt her tense against the harshness of his tone, something he seemed powerless to soften as he struggled with a dragging sense of utter failure.

All his life he'd tried to protect the innocent from the guilty, but he'd failed to guard Charlotte, the one woman who mattered far more to him than he dared admit just now, from *his* enemies. Given that disaster, was it any wonder he sounded like a hanging judge examining a witness as he asked that question?

'No, and don't think I haven't tried to find out all I can, for I've had nothing else to do since I woke up beside you and found you apparently dead to the world,' Charlotte informed him crossly and did her best not to let him know how terrified she had been that he actually was dead, until she forced herself to calm down and listen for his breath and feel for his pulse. At least that had been reassuringly strong and she concluded now that he had a head like a stone statue and the constitution of an ox, and only the fact that she faintly hoped they might get out of here alive was preventing her from clinging to his mighty body like a limpet at high tide and weeping all over him.

'I'm sorry,' he mouthed and she was sorely tempted to beat her fists against his thick hide, and might even have done so if it wasn't so battered already.

How dare he apologise when he'd obviously fought like a fiend while she had been unconscious? The cuts and lesser scratches, as well as the swellings that indicated deep bruises, told of a merciless beating and her hands fisted at her sides at the very thought of such a cowardly attack. She hadn't the slightest doubt it *had* been cowardly either, given how many of that mob it must have taken to overpower him in the first place and then hold him still while they battered him unconscious. And how could she have been unaware of him enduring such pain and suffering? Logic might tell her she'd gone beyond knowing anything at the time, but somehow that seemed like betrayal, and she stubbornly felt that she should have known, should have stayed home and risked her heart, or maybe even her virtue, anything rather than blithely luring him out of the safety of Carnwood House and into the hands of his enemies.

'You can be sorry for following me if you like, I absolve you from everything else,' she told him and, considering she was torn between railing at him, weeping all over him or kissing him even more witless than he currently sounded, the least she could do was try to stop him blaming himself.

'And if I hadn't done so, you'd now be here alone,' he pointed out.

'With the certainty that you and your friends were moving heaven and earth to find me,' she whispered back fiercely.

'There is that, of course,' he admitted ruefully and Charlotte once more struggled with the complete unreality of it all.

They were trapped in some limitless darkness, by who knew what villains for demonstrably sinister reasons, and still attraction ran like an indestructible thread under all their danger and dread. She suddenly realised she would rather be here with him than back in her comfortable bed at Wychwood and safe as houses and wondered if she had run quite mad from terror.

Although, come to think of it, best of all would be for him to be there with her, in her bed, in her life, for ever at her side to reassure her he would never let himself be overcome by more than a dozen ruthless ruffians ever again.

'I'm glad you're here,' she informed him tersely.

'I can't reciprocate,' he replied gruffly, 'but better that I am than you face this all alone.'

'Humph,' she gritted, deciding he was easily the most infuriating man she'd ever encountered and why she loved him so deeply was beyond her. As the full import of that conclusion hit her, she sat up and put her hand to her forehead in a theatrical gesture that ordinarily would have struck her as ridiculous, but their situation wasn't in the least bit normal, and anyway he couldn't see her.

'Has anyone been in to inspect us?' he asked, clearly oblivious to the seething revolution her mind was struggling with.

'They came in once and tried to see what we were doing, or not doing, from the doorway—I think they're scared of you,' she admitted distractedly.

'Who were they?'

'Men,' she replied tersely.

'What a surprise, now for goodness' sake use the sense you were born with and think, woman,' he demanded, and if he hadn't already taken a battering, she might have slapped him. How could she have fallen for the high-handed, unreasonable, rude creature?

'I forgot to ask them for their calling cards, but one of them had a high-pitched voice and a country accent,' she informed him after a dignified pause that seemed utterly wasted on him.

There was silence for a long moment and Charlotte sensed Ben searching some internal gallery of rogues for a clue to his identity. She tried to think of anything that might help him, although she didn't see how knowing who held them could possibly help them escape.

'They gloated about the safety of their hiding place from any interference and informed me how grateful I should be that they had smuggled a bed into it while his nib's back was turned. It's my opinion they did that for their own benefit, by the way, for they didn't strike me as overflowing with kindness at the best of times. I dare say they've been using it themselves while hiding from whatever justice they go in fear of. And although they shackled one of your ankles to the bed when they brought you in, they were too cowardly to risk getting any closer once there was the slightest risk you might wake up and overpower them,' she told him disgustedly.

Something told her Ben was startled by that information and she heard the faint clink of the shackle they had used to pin him in place like a lion in some foul cage, feeling his prodigious strength tense against it for a long, futile moment. Desperately worried that he could be so unaware of the ills and restrictions of his suffering body, she fought the urge to weep. She wouldn't be any good to him if she succumbed to the hysterics that had seemed such a good idea when she woke to find herself being imprisoned next to Ben's giant form and the terror that he might die was much greater than any for herself.

'The bed's bolted to the floor. I ascertained that fact while you were unconscious, so you can save yourself the effort of finding it out for yourself. Oh, and the other one said something about the upright man singing like a lark and them needing to stay close hid for a while, and he insisted that they had to keep you alive until the big nob from nob house got here,' she told him as coolly as she could.

'Oh, God, Charlotte, what have I got you into?' he said with a groan and she could feel him run his poor battered hands over his swollen eyes, as if to try to shut out a reality even he could no longer cope with.

Pity wrung her heart; what had she reduced this mighty man to by allowing herself to be bundled into a trap without so much as a scream or a protest, while they had been out in the open street and within a hairsbreadth of rescue? Now they were in this seemingly limitless darkness with little hope of rescue, and she had to bite back a groan of her own.

'Never mind how we got here, how do we get out?' she snapped, fighting hard not to simply sink into Ben's arms and hide from reality.

'They'll make very sure we can't,' he replied, grimly determined not to give her false hope.

'And we're going to lie here and accept whatever they have in mind for us?' she asked incredulously.

'Since I'm shackled and they're some of the most hardened rogues who ever came out of the stews, I can't currently think of an alternative.'

'So we just wait, like rats in a trap?'

'Damn it, woman, what would you have me do? I'm not a shape-changer or some other supernatural being, so how the devil do you expect me to get us out of this infernal pit of darkness when I can't fly or walk through walls, or even get myself free of this confounded chain?'

'I don't know, but we can't just give up and wait for whatever evils they have in store for us.'

There was a brooding silence in the room as she felt him trying to fight darkness and despair. Maybe she should be sorry for taunting him, trying to goad him out of this uncharacteristic acceptance of a fate outside their hands. On the other hand, they might not have time for him to recover his indomitable will along with his full senses, so how could she sit by and commiserate while he brooded on past mistakes and a blank future?

'We need to find out everything we can about this place and the confounded rogues who brought us here,' he finally informed her, sounding more like himself than he had since he woke up.

'You must have seen something before they knocked you unconscious,' she prompted. 'You're far more likely to know them than I am, sir, as I'm not at all used to the company you seem to keep.'

'Shrew,' he accused her briskly and she could have cried at the sound, for it seemed to say that Mr Benedict Shaw was once more willing to take on the world and win.

She chuckled at an epithet that only hours ago would probably have made her bristle with hostility, but pretence seemed useless in their current situation and there was no point in putting Miss Wells's chilly armour on again. 'What did they mean by "nob house", Ben?' she asked, more for the sake of curiosity than because she thought anything useful might come of knowing.

'Parliament,' he replied grimly.

'Then they're expecting a Member of Parliament? Good Lord, how high does this damnable business go?'

'Or a representative of the Lords,' he returned brusquely, almost as if the admission hurt and she suddenly felt irredeemably stupid as she realised exactly what he was thinking.

'Oh, no, Ben, it can't be your father,' she gasped impulsively, 'that would be wickedness beyond belief. No father could do such a thing to his own child.'

'You have no idea what a man will do *in extremis*,' he said and she was sure his mind had gone back to his childhood, and he was quite right—she knew nothing of how a man might meet, or fail to meet, the challenges of extreme poverty, but, being a lord, she doubted Ben's father had ever had to contemplate them either. 'I never wanted to believe it, whatever else I might think of him, but I have to consider it again now. Kit won't have it that he's involved, but too many things are adding together for me to go on deluding myself. My lord Pemberley is a law unto himself,' he added grimly, 'and you've no idea what he's capable of, thank God.'

'Nor have you from the sound of things, for I know him to be an honourable man,' Charlotte replied sincerely, startled that his lordship was Ben's father and searching her memory for clues that would connect them. Only their silver-grey eyes and perhaps their lanky inches, so far as she could remember, she decided—oh, and their good hearts and urge to protect the vulnerable. She heard Ben take a deep breath as if to calm his temper and then let it out on a long sigh as if hurt by the thought, even if he was prepared to think a good man a black rogue, and she instantly forgave him.

'Do you? I must admit that I never actually had a chance to become acquainted with his noble lordship, considering he dismissed my mother to perdition before I was born,' he said.

'Tell me,' she whispered, intrigued and more than half-afraid of what his tale might reveal.

She felt him hesitate, wondered if she had asked too much of him in her need to know everything she could about him. Now they were faced with such a dark future, in more ways than one, she refused to hide the truth from herself any more. Ben Shaw fascinated her; his every movement, the complex thoughts in his extraordinary, bull-headed mind, every nerve and impulse that made up the one man on earth who could have persuaded her out of her stony isolation was uniquely interesting to her.

And even that impressive list left off the effect of the whole, physical promise of the man on her senses of course. *They* were singing a descant of delighted anticipation over all her terror and the shock of uneasy darkness, just because he was lying so close to her and she was struggling to condemn that part of herself for taking their plight far too lightly. Somehow the blackness only served to sharpen the effect he had on her other four senses, as her eyes became useless in it and her imagination provided the gaps. No! He was injured and they were both in appalling danger.

Controlling a misplaced need to reach out and discover if his senses might be experiencing a similar heightening, she still couldn't make herself put cold space between them in a vain attempt to snuff it out. Impossible, an inner voice scoffed, and she acknowledged a tightening of the sensual tension she'd been trying to ignore from the moment she first laid eyes on his giant form. At the time using the prim repressed governess persona of common belief had seemed a much better idea than staring at him open-mouthed and hungry-eyed. She'd been too wrapped up in controlling her reaction to his size, his powerful presence and the sheer vitality of him to realise how deep the damage he could do to her precious self-reliance. That wholly feminine reaction should have warned her how dangerous he was, but she'd been too busy putting up the barricades against him to take the common-sense course and refuse to leave her post in Bath in the first place.

If she could go back and do just that, would she? No, of course not. The answer leapt into her thoughts so instantly there was no denying the truth of it. She was a fool and, even to save herself the prospect of an early death at the cruel hands of Ben's mysterious enemy, she wouldn't give up the potent challenge of meeting him, sparking arguments off each other, enjoying the heady secret of her wildly feminine reaction to him, and being so deliciously intimately close to him for that long unforgettable kiss. A lifetime of crushing propriety spent serenely teaching good behaviour to the daughters of the nobility and gentry could only pale by the side of their odd, instinctive compulsion to bring out the worst, or perhaps the best, in each other. No, she wouldn't forgo Mr Benedict Shaw for Miss Thibett's entire academy.

Yet now, while she was struggling with her wanton need to stop their mouths and thoughts with one another, he was facing his own demons and she very much doubted they were the same ones. She unwarily shook her head at her own folly and felt her senses swim. The blow their captors had dealt her didn't appear to have knocked any sense in, she decided ruefully, and ordered herself to concentrate.

'I'm no tattle-monger,' she told him softly and felt a chuckle rumble through his powerful torso.

How intimate, how seductive to feel rather than just hear the rich depth of it, rather than just stand apart and try to pretend amusing him beat dining with the gods. No, she wasn't supposed to be doing that, was she? Miss Wells made a temporary return to duty and ordered Charlotte to behave, or stand in a corner until she could do so.

'That you're not,' he agreed.

'And I assure you that anything you tell me will never be repeated without your permission,' she added earnestly.

'Small enough chance of that,' he said bleakly, then seemed to remember they were being hopeful after all. 'Anyway, it's not a secret, or at least not so far as I'm concerned. Just a topic I don't care to linger over.'

'Since it seems to play no small part in our current dilemma, then perhaps you should.'

'Maybe you're right.'

'Well, of course I am, it's my job.'

Again she made him laugh softly and didn't know whether to be glad or sorry as she also felt him flinch as the vibration of it played havoc with his cuts and bruises and he muttered a few soft and rather potent curses.

'I'm cold,' she said pettishly and wondered if a governess might be permitted to slap herself for being annoying.

'Come closer, then,' he urged and she felt herself drawn into his powerful arms, then shifted gently until she lay against his chest and sighed with absolute content. She hadn't even had to humiliate herself by crawling over him as if she was trying to climb inside his skin, either.

'Said the spider to the fly?' she managed to ask caustically and felt him smile with an absurd shiver of happiness that only made him hold her closer.

'Your waspish tongue is a constant source of delight to me, Miss Charlotte Wells,' he informed her and she told herself she was a fool for hearing the smile in his voice and wanting to melt.

'I doubt it,' she told him snippily, but the urge to kiss him into silence only fell away when she remembered the feel of his poor battered lips when she felt gently for his hurts while he lay unconscious beside her.

'Pray still your nagging tongue for a few moments, woman, while I get my tale over, since you're the one who wanted to hear it,' he chided gently.

'Very well,' she conceded with a sigh that fought hard not to be openly contented with a very poor lot indeed.

'Once upon a time…' he began.

'That's not very original.'

'Never mind, you can deduct marks for that at the end. Once upon a time there was a beautiful young maiden who lived near to a castle and her father was tenant of one of the farms belonging to the lord of that castle.'

'Was he a wicked baron?'

'I'll let you judge for yourself, but later perhaps, after I have got this sad tale over with. If you can spare me a few minutes uninterrupted, that is?'

'Hurry up, then.'

'Why, are you going somewhere?' he asked, and reality almost crashed in, until he ran his broad hand down her back and dispelled it.

'No,' she admitted on a stutter of pure sensation, 'I think I'll stay right here for the time being.'

'Good—now, where was I?'

'Her father being a tenant,' she said, glad she was about to hear the true story of Ben's origins at long last and, if he thought she'd flinch from it because he was born a bastard, he'd best prepare for disappointment.

'Ah, yes, well, the maiden grew ever more beautiful, until the day came when the lord's son was completely dazzled by her as soon as he came home from completing his education at court. Being a sensible maiden, she told him to go away, but he wooed her with every conceit and device open to him, damn his black heart. He plagued her with promises of his eternal devotion and a lifetime without care or hardship. He offered her jewels and velvet gowns and every temptation women are supposed to dream of, but she turned them all down. Seeing at last that she wouldn't yield to any man without giving him her heart and soul first, he set himself to convince her she meant the world to him and he'd never know another happy day without her. Being far too kind to let anyone suffer such misery, and because she'd come to love him far too much herself, she yielded at last, convinced he loved her as deeply and enduringly as she did him.'

Charlotte heard the depth of contempt for his father in Ben's voice and dug her fingernails into her palms as she fought the urge to reach up and silence him with a gentle touch, then kiss away the pain. To finally understand something of his past, she must hear his tale to the end.

'Afterwards she always insisted they were blissfully happy, until they grew careless and the old lord found out how deeply they loved, and how little his son wanted the noble lady he should have wed. Myself, I think she believed her lover to be the noble being she wanted him to be. Then he proved her wrong by upping and marrying the lady he'd been destined for before he met her the very next time he went to London. Afterwards he stood by and let his father and new wife banish his supposed love for ever. She was to leave her home and not come back, or her family would be thrown on to the streets with nothing. The lord's son must never see her again, or write, or send her money, and in return the old lord would make sure she lived in comfort for the rest of her days.

'Which sounds fair, doesn't it, Miss Wells, since the lords of this land usually run their lives with little thought for the less fortunate? It might have been so as well, except that comfortable life never materialised, even when she wrote and told the old lord she was big with his grandchild and would soon be thrown out of what work she had found as a seamstress and embroiderer. Nothing stood between her and ruination but the fact that she had the sheer luck to land at Mirabelle Alstone's lodging house when she first went to London. It might have been in danger of tottering into the very slums it backed on to, but not even her brute of a husband could beat the darling into throwing my mother out.'

No wonder she loved him, she decided with a smile she hid against his waistcoat, although he couldn't possibly see it. How could she not when he was so gruff and defensive, yet so loving and furious on his mother's behalf?

'Not a very edifying story, is it?' he asked curtly.

'It certainly does this lord and his son little credit, but I can't see how it reflects on you, Ben, not when you were the most innocent party of all.'

'I doubt my father would agree,' he replied cynically and yet she wondered how on earth Lord Pemberley had been fooled into letting go of him, when all she knew of the man argued he would hold to such a son with the last breath in his body.

Even the most loving and scrupulous mother might exaggerate her enemies' misdeeds to a beloved son and how much more understandable that she'd want this wonderful man to think the best of her. Charlotte longed for the same weakness as far as he was concerned, and yet why not? It wasn't as if they had room to hide anything from each other here, and what would it matter if she finally let him know the truth about Charlotte Wells?

'How could he be anything but proud of you?' she protested hotly and felt his strong arms bind her gently even closer to his giant frame.

'I could be Lord Mayor of London and king of every walk in town and he'd cross the street to avoid me,' he told her with an attempt at lightness that nearly broke her heart. 'Once he even sent his legitimate son and heir to gloat over our lowly situation, living as we had to in one room of a shabby lodging house and taking whatever work we could get to keep even that. The preening little idiot didn't look quite so pleased with life when Kit and I ran him out of the house by the scruff of his neck and threw him in the gutter.' The smile that accompanied that sweet memory was there in his deep voice as he recalled their youthful triumph. 'I dare say it took his doting mama a week to get the stink out of her nostrils.'

'She knew?'

'She came with him, although I never saw a so-called great lady move so fast as she managed to once we dealt with her whelp and came back to see why she was still defiling the air my mother had to breathe. I hope I never again feel such deep-in-the-gut hatred for two people I hardly know, Charlotte. It cut into me for years and, even if it spurred me to prove we were worth twice what they were, I would gladly give it back to them to have never set eyes on them or my cursed father.'

'He mightn't have known what they did,' she defended half-heartedly, for something told her that if the young man Lord Pemberley had been were half the person his son would become, he'd have marched away from his heritage with the woman he claimed to love and made his own way in the world in defiance of anything his family had to say about it.

'He came to find me when my mother died and offered to bring me up with that little runt of his. Apparently his wife told him we'd spent all the largesse the old lord had poured into our pockets and were living in squalor because of my mother's foolish extravagance and my precocious vices. Kit had to nigh knock me senseless to prevent me strangling the—' He broke off, gallantly stifling his true opinion of his sire for her sake.

'I suppose it might have caused problems if you'd killed your own father,' she said sagely.

'Just a little,' he agreed with a laugh in his voice to lighten her heart, and she was sure she felt him kiss the top of her head as if he couldn't help himself. 'Anyway, at least throwing his so-called charity in his face spurred me into proving him wrong and making a man of myself.'

'And what an excellent job you did make of that task, Mr Shaw,' she murmured appreciatively as she nuzzled even closer to his powerful chest and gloried in what nature and Ben Shaw had made of his lordship's by-blow.

'Such praise from you, Miss Wells? I might yet grow swollen-headed, if you promise to stop that fearsome trick you have of looking at me as if I might eat with my knife at any moment.'

At such an unlikely suggestion she gave a little splutter of laughter against his chest and wriggled with silent enjoyment of being free not to feel the least disapproving at long last.

'Keep doing that, my dear, and you'll very soon discover the limits of my self-control,' he admonished and she thought about a delicious little shiver against his taut muscles just to test it to its limits, or beyond perhaps? Nobly restraining herself, she lifted her head a little to stare futilely up at him in the dark, hoping somehow to gauge his response to the question she had to ask, useless though that might seem in this seemingly limitless darkness.

'You truly think your father's your enemy, don't you?' she made herself say and felt him stiffen, then armour himself against such an unnatural notion to reply carelessly.

'Aye, I dare say he's convinced himself he's reclaiming the investment his father never made in my upbringing.'

'Which, if you think about it, makes little sense, since it argues he has no idea your mother was turned out with nothing, don't you think?'

'Or he pretends not to.'

'But it could mean another hand lies behind the whole repellent business, don't you think?'

'Why, because he was innocent of one crime, he must therefore be blameless for the rest? You're overgenerous, my dear.'

'I wish you'd stop calling me so in that superior, sarcastic tone,' she complained absently as she considered his opinion of his father, because thinking about his probable view of her hurt too much. 'And I think you're wrong. How could he not regret what he threw away, wed to such a woman, and father to a son who'd smirk so snidely at anyone just for being poor?'

'Serve him right,' Ben declared unsympathetically.

'Maybe, for he was undoubtedly at fault for abandoning you in the first place, but couldn't his wife or son be behind your later woes, or even your grandfather, perhaps?'

'He's been dead for twenty years, so I sincerely doubt it.'

'Well, he began it, and perhaps he passed his hatred of you and your mother on to his other grandson.' Her words seemed to give him pause, but then she felt him shake his head.

'You haven't met my father or his son, and my little brother lacks the simple courage to swat a wasp on a summer day, let alone deal in piracy and fraud on the scale my enemy's up to his evil neck in.'

'It doesn't take much strength to intimidate and manipulate when you possess both power and a great position,' Charlotte argued with a reminiscent shudder, realising the particular man who'd used them against her, before she escaped his repellent clutches with Lord Pemberley's help, was in fact Ben's brother. Best perhaps if she kept that horrifying conclusion to herself while they were locked in such a prison and helpless in the hands of Ben's enemies.

'Luckily you don't know anything about the sort of toughened rogue my enemy must deal with if he sups with those particular devils,' he countered.

She probably didn't, Charlotte reflected wryly, but evil was still evil, whether dressed in fine lawn and best superfine, or roughest rags and hobnails.

'Having seen you and Lord Carnwood in action occasionally, I do know it's not merely bodily strength that gives you power over your own destiny. Since I'm not a fool, I can also tell from the toughness you both had to develop to rise as you have something of what you had to fight to do so.'

'Then you think we're also capable of such extreme violence and intimidation?' he asked, sounding contrarily hurt.

'No, but neither of you would have risen from such beginnings if you'd been less…well, just less, I suppose.'

'Less impressive, less handsome and dashingly appealing to even the most discerning lady—even one not given to handing out admiration unless it's wrung from her like blood from a stone, perhaps? Although I sincerely hope you don't admire my dashing friend the Earl half as much as you do me—for if you do, the lovely Miranda might scratch your eyes out and I might be forced to challenge my best friend to a duel.'

'Who said I admired you at all, Mr Shaw?'

'You did, my dear, most ungovernessly Miss Wells,' he mocked gently, as he lifted her hand away from its exploration of his heavily muscled chest and neck, one she hadn't consciously known she'd embarked on. Even under the occasional stiffness that told her his shirt was bloodied from his wounds and the torn broadcloth of his coat, her touch definitely appreciated the man underneath, and he'd be a fool to think otherwise.

'I have very good taste,' she informed him half-seriously.

'Indeed you have, and, oh, for the time and place to explore it further.'

'You're thinking of going somewhere, then?'

'Very likely to hell, if my detractors have their way,' he said tersely and if he thought she only admired him when she squirmed closer to him, as if she might somehow become part of him at the very thought of their being divided so brutally, then he was welcome to that delusion.

'They're fools, and it's not like you to give up,' she chided in a rather muffled voice, hoping he would put the hint of tears in it down to fear for her own skin.

'If you think they're stupid enough to risk letting either of us go, then you lack imagination, Charlotte,' he informed her sternly, obviously trying to steel her against the true horror of their situation and, if he did but know it, making her love him more.

'I've a perfectly adequate supply of that, thank you very much,' she countered and, as he didn't seem to intend taking their current intimacy further, she shut her eyes and luxuriated in the moment.

After all she was in his arms, locked against his strong, battered body and her fantasies beat reality hollow. Revelling in them, she felt her heavy eyelids drift down and fought to keep them futilely open in the heavy darkness. It proved a useless endeavour as the shock and horror of what they'd endured finally caught up with her and she went to sleep in his arms, even as arguments against his ridiculous refusal to make love to her formed on her wanton tongue. Maybe later, when she didn't feel quite so content, quite so warm and sleepy in his arms, where she so much wanted to lie…

Lying in the dark, bound like a brute beast and ridiculously helpless, Ben held Miss Charlotte Wells in his arms while she slept and wondered at fate to divert his disobedient body from what it really longed for. What might he have been if not born to penury and a bastard's lot in life? he wondered. Then he might have loved such a true lady, if not for that reckless promise he had once made himself, and if he were a completely different man, what then? No good wishing for the moon and she had no idea what a dark soul he possessed, how hard the fight was to stay out of the very world they'd now been dragged back into. He and Kit had never stooped to murder, but they'd stopped short of very little else, so how could he ask a unique woman like Miss Charlotte Wells to love *him*? Even if either of them had a future, he couldn't let her throw hers away so criminally.

Anyway, he didn't believe in love, so how could he ask her to commit herself to such an unequal match? Look where love had got his mother, after all, aye, and Kit's for that matter. Admittedly Bevis Alstone had married her, but, considering what he put her through, she must have bitterly regretted ever setting eyes on him. Growing up with two women determined to love a pair of unworthy, ungrateful and even downright wicked men, was it any wonder he'd set his face against love? Yet he considered one or two cases he'd witnessed since and wondered if he could be wrong to dismiss it.

Kit loved his Miranda as surely as the sun rose and set every day and the moon waxed and waned. And Sir Hugh Kenton, once the despair of anyone foolish enough to care a snap of their fingers for the contrary, restless rogue, adored the very ground Kit's youngest sister Louise walked on. And her deepest-blue Alstone eyes sparkled with delight and mutual laughter every time she so much as set them on her lawfully wedded lord, or at least they did when he wasn't infuriating her into sparking back at him like the virago he'd so often named her in the old days. Yes, he decided with a reminiscent smile for his true brother and sister's undoubted happiness, love definitely existed, but could it for him? If it couldn't, then why did it feel like a homecoming he'd waited for all his life to hold this particular, argumentative, challenging, and utterly desirable woman in his arms? Even though his enemies would very likely make sure neither of them survived, he could almost be happy here with her in this infernal darkness, if only he didn't know he'd brought her to this in the first place, just by knowing her.

Whatever he felt for her, he couldn't let himself explore it here. He knew they were only alive now because someone had given orders they were to be kept so, until he had the twisted pleasure of dispatching them himself. At last his own eyes grew heavier and he let them drift shut. He wouldn't be much use to Charlotte if he stayed awake in some futile vow to guard her sleep, especially when he'd signally failed to do so while she was awake. Better to allow himself the luxury of sleeping next to her. And his Miss Wells wasn't in the least bit stiff or stern as a bedfellow, nor could he feel that neat little dragon tail he'd once fantasised she might possess wrapped about them. Not that he'd mind it, he decided sleepily, not if it twined them even closer, as if neither of them ever intended letting go of the other...

Fathomless hours later the door of their prison opened and Ben squinted against the faint gleam of light as a loaf of bread was thrown on to the floor, followed by a cask of something and a bucket.

'He alive?' a rough voice mumbled behind the thin man he could just see and he surmised the other was holding the dim lamp at arm's length.

'How'd I know?' the other grumbled.

'By goin' over yon and looking.'

'After you, then, Cubby,' he told the bruiser scornfully.

'Not I, he's dangerous as a maddened bear at the best o' times and I ain't a fool.'

'What about the wench, then? She'd warm this ice house up a bit for both of us, gentry mort or no.'

'She'll keep,' the thin one muttered.

Maybe the furious tension in Ben's long body was wound tight enough for even them to sense it as they hovered by the door. As Charlotte felt him flex his stiff muscles and gather himself for action, however desperate, she too doubted even two of them could wrench her away from him, pinned down and injured as he was.

'Aye, for 'is nibs,' the other grumbled, but he moved back for the other one to scurry out again behind him and snicked the door shut with a particularly unpleasant snigger. 'They'll both wish they was dead when 'e gets 'ere,' he risked saying loudly, once there was a stout door between him and Ben's bunched fists.

'Did you know them, Ben?' Charlotte asked into the brooding silence they left behind them, once she was fairly certain she could keep her voice from shaking and giving away her terror at the very thought of being torn from him and into the hands of those repellent brutes.

'Aye, you described them perfectly.'

'So who are they?'

'Scum,' he gritted furiously.

'I took that as a given.'

'And I'll kill you rather than let them lay a finger on you,' he said grimly and she shuddered.

'I prefer hope to death,' she told him painfully.

'Hugh Kenton and whichever of my men have the most cause to hate the man behind all this will do all they can to find us, Charlotte, but I have to warn you the odds are against them and us,' he warned her.

'The odds have always been against you,' she whispered, determined nobody outside this cold prison would hear a word. 'I can't see how it ever stopped you before.'

'No, but I still won't let them get at you,' he insisted savagely.

'And I still don't want to die,' she said painfully.

'I don't want you to either,' he finally admitted on a huge sigh and laid his head against her brow in an intimate gesture that brought hot tears to her eyes.

'Then let's believe in Sir Hugh and your men, at least for now, please, Ben?' she murmured and felt his lips gently kiss her brow.

'It's devilish hard to be pent up here and dependent on someone else,' he whispered as if to explain his difficulty, which she supposed it did.

'And how bitterly you hate to lean on anyone,' she chided.

'True,' he admitted as if it almost hurt him to say it.

'Let's sleep again, Ben,' she whispered, knowing it wasn't an admission he would care to linger over and dreading to hear an invitation to rely on her love leave her lips and be fumbled aside as an embarrassment. 'You need to recover your strength.'

'We'll eat first,' he said calmly, now they'd got that painful admission out of the way, 'if you can feel your way to the loaf we've been thrown, that is? I hate to ask it of you, or to take a thing from those two flashmen, but neither of us will be in good shape to resist whatever they have in mind for us if we're starving, and I certainly won't be going anywhere for the time being.'

'Wish me luck, then,' she said with an unsteady laugh, feeling as if she was ripping herself away from every security she had ever had in life as she stepped out of his arms and into the dark.

'Ever and always, Charlotte,' he said and sounded as reluctant to feel her leave his arms as she was to quit them.

Setting out on legs that seemed to have forgotten how to hold her at first, she shivered uncontrollably once she was away from his warmth and the reassurance of his sheer physical presence. Recovering herself as best she could, she held her arms out in front of her to ward off any obstacles and felt horribly vulnerable. What if they came back and caught her so far away from Ben that they could wrest her from him without any danger to their hides but what little resistance she could offer? What if it was all a trap designed for that very purpose?

'Get on with it, then,' he muttered brusquely and infuriated her so much she forgot all her fears and strode out as confidently as it was possible to do in the pitch darkness.

'Found it,' she muttered with satisfaction, then, emboldened by her success and cross with him for prompting her like an adult ordering about a foolish child, decided it was high time she explored their prison a little more.

'You're going the wrong way,' he told her brusquely.

'How do you know?'

'I just do,' he told her, sounding so puzzled by his affinity with her that she almost forgave him for being bewildered by it.

'Well, I want to know where we are, even if you don't,' she told him rather unfairly and went on.

'Don't fall over.'

'I thought I was supposed to be the stern teacher here, not you,' she mumbled, then marvelled at his acute hearing as she caught a faint laugh at her flash of temper.

'You do it so much more gracefully than I,' he informed her, 'but I am ravenous, Miss Wells, so could you return with our lunch before I pass out, if you please?'

'Very well,' she whispered and grabbed even more booty before creeping back toward his so-welcome warmth as quickly as possible.

'What took you so long?' he asked softly as she scrambled back on to the rough bedstead and snuggled her freezing toes against his legs.

'We're in a wine cellar,' she informed him triumphantly, 'and let's hope it's a good one,' she added as she handed him a rather dusty bottle.

'For once, Miss Wells, I find myself in complete accord with you.'

'Ungrateful wretch!'

'Well, what's the use of a bottle without a corkscrew to open it with?' he grumbled facetiously.

'Some people are singularly ungrateful,' she told him sternly. 'And I did find a glass, so if you can't smash the top off cleanly enough, then you shame your upbringing, Captain.'

'Do you really think we merchant-venturers spend all our time in Hispaniola, seducing pirates' molls and smashing open bottles of rum, my lovely?'

'Well, you might have done for all I know,' she told him and offered him the bottle to open as best he could.

'I never did, which is an oversight I must see to if we ever get out of here.'

'Take me with you?' she heard herself say wistfully and wondered if the fumes of good red wine that were released as soon as he had neatly smashed the neck against the side of their bed might have already gone to her head.

'Where to, the West Indies?'

'Anywhere,' she admitted, unable to disguise her longing for adventure in his heady company.

'You have no idea what life is like for a lady aboard ship,' he countered roughly, as if it were a serious possibility he might take her with him, which she knew in her heart of hearts was impossible, even if she longed for it to be otherwise.

'And that's where you're so wrong,' she muttered mutinously.

'How could you have any notion? It's not at all like they describe it in books, Miss Wells—my world is full of danger and discomfort.'

'Considering your height, I should imagine every step would be a danger to you, but I spent my early childhood aboard a man of war, so pray don't try to tell me I know nothing of the life.'

'You're a navy brat, then?' he asked with perhaps a little more respect in his voice.

'I was born on my father's frigate and in the midst of battle apparently, the shock and noise of it all often bringing about such a consequence, you see? I probably escaped being called after it only by virtue of my sex, at least according to my mother.'

'What a very unexpected female you are, Miss Wells,' he told her as he handed her the glass half-full of what smelt like a rare vintage even to her inexperienced nose.

'I suppose you're cautious of getting me unexpectedly and uproariously drunk?' she asked him unsteadily, suddenly back to wanting him immoderately with the yearning idea in her head of drinking this in a lover's toast, from his hand entwined with hers, as they sipped from the same spot and pledged more than just a necessary drink to lighten their captivity.

'I expect a female of your exemplary background to hold her drink.'

'How comforting, but I left the sea at the age of ten, which was a little too young to become hard-headed, and much to my disgust I was deemed too old to wander the world any more.'

'Just at the age I embarked for the first time.'

'Did you, so young?'

'You know that's considered almost grown up at sea, and I was big for my age.'

'I can imagine, but your mother must've hated seeing you go all the same.'

'She died,' he informed her brusquely as if that explained everything.

'While you were gone?'

'No, just before I was due to leave.'

'I'm so sorry.'

'It was a long time ago now, and she'd been ill for months.'

'Which didn't make it any easier, I dare say.'

'I thought if she no longer had me to provide for as well she might look after herself well enough to recover, but that was a boy's wishful thinking. Still, I suppose I must thank my father for speeding me on my way so effectively, if for little else.'

'I don't believe he's behind this, Ben,' she was bold enough to tell him with the warm glow of half a glass of excellent burgundy inside her.

'Why not, since he's done plenty of harm to me and mine already?'

'How could you be as you are, if he were truly as you think he is?' she went on bravely in the face of his obvious impatience.

'I think there's a huge compliment in there somewhere, but I suggest you soak that wine up with some bread before we both say or do something we'll regret,' he cautioned gruffly and passed her a heel of the rough loaf he'd torn off it for her.

Impossible man! Charlotte bit a mouthful off her crust and lingered over it as if it was the finest she ever tasted. Day old as it was and the adulterated rations of the poor rather than the more wholesome fare she was used to, with the salt of a sharp appetite and inside this odd bubble of intimacy with Ben Shaw, it tasted better than anything she'd ever eaten.

'No point saving it,' Ben said as he handed her another chunk, 'I doubt we'll be able to break it by tomorrow, let alone chew it.'

'We'll be free by then,' she insisted doggedly.

'Maybe,' he replied and risked pouring her another half-glass from the jagged bottle and passing it to her as if determined to change the subject.

'You're a stubborn man, Ben Shaw,' she told him as she handed him the empty glass with a sigh.

'I am that, which makes us very well matched by my reckoning,' he told her and sank back on the bed with her in his arms, and she melted into them more thankfully than into the finest down pillow and feather bed.

'True,' she agreed hazily and tumbled into sleep just as he intended.

Chapter Eight

How many hours later he awoke Ben had no way of knowing, since there was nothing to indicate day or night in this prison. His sharp ears caught the sound of movement outside the door, even as he felt Charlotte tense in his arms and knew she was awake and her senses were straining to gauge just what, or rather who, was coming. If the head of this gang had any sense he'd make sure only one or two of them knew him or his true purpose, for too many of the gutter sweepings he'd seen today knew enough about Ben Shaw and his brothers-in-arms to fear the consequences if he was killed. He doubted they'd a twinge of conscience left in them, but fear for their own skins would make them very wary of harming him. He imagined the full force of Kit's fury if anything happened to him and a woman Kit considered under his protection, and even shuddered himself as a faint glow at last blurred his sight after so long in the pitch dark.

'Well, isn't this delightful?' a thin tenor voice enquired as its owner swept a commanding hand at the man holding the lamp to illuminate his captives better. 'My, and what a long time it has been too,' he drawled with oily satisfaction oozing from every pore.

Shocked to see his half-brother and not his sire and fighting not to show it, Ben was puzzled to feel Charlotte suddenly go stiff as a statue in his arms at the first sound of that objectionable voice. What did she know of the most ignoble Lord Beldastowe? A little too much, from the feel of her resistant body and the tremor of revulsion that shot through her. He felt ungovernable fury threaten to rip through him at the very idea of Beldastowe so much as laying a finger on his Charlotte. Would his father pollute everything in his life that was good, and had he once more sent his legitimate son to mock his bastard? Charlotte's story suddenly seemed far more of a mystery than his and he marvelled at himself for not seeing that sooner.

'So you caught two fish in your net, Statton?' vacant-looking Lord Beldastowe mused, but if Ben had underestimated his enemy, he didn't now.

It wasn't vacancy that ruled those flat grey eyes, but a pitiless inhumanity. Any hope of trading himself for Charlotte's freedom leached away; he'd rather kill her himself than let her fall into such hands.

'Come now, my dear, don't be shy,' the obnoxious light voice encouraged, from a safe distance.

Charlotte refused to raise her head from its pillow against Ben's shoulder and nothing on earth could prevent him raising his large hand to cover as many of her fiery locks from Beldastowe's soulless scrutiny as possible. He caught the coppery glow of one stray curl in the dim light and fought surprise himself at what she'd been hiding so determinedly. Beldastowe gave his henchman a significant nod, as if he would have them pulled apart by force, but the bully at his shoulder shook his head.

'Ain't goin' within ten feet of 'im on me own, guvnor,' he informed his employer and folded his arms across his chest to signify his determination not to feel the full benefit of Ben's fists.

'You're not on your own, you fool,' Beldastowe insisted, but from the veiled contempt in the man's eyes, he might just as well have been. Ben doubted even the terror of his lordship's cold temper would overcome the man's more immediate one of a good beating.

Unfortunate that the bully knew him too well, he mused, for he could deal with such spindle-shanked ruffians with one hand tied behind his back, or his leg shackled to a sturdy bedstead, and at least capturing him would even the odds a little. Pushing Charlotte further behind him as the lamp swung back toward Beldastowe, Ben hid her as best he could from his half-brother's reptilian gaze and hoped the resty female would stay where she was put for once.

'I doubt if the filly will prove so shy when I finally decide how to kill you, brother,' Beldastowe said with a smile that made Ben want to shudder over her fate at his slimy hands.

Refusing to consider what Charlotte might suffer if he allowed it to happen, he merely stared at the wall beyond Beldastowe's shoulder and waited wearily for him to take himself off. Behind him, Charlotte amazed him further by squirming as far beyond the range of that one candlepower of light as possible and he could feel the physical effort it was costing her not to give way to the revulsion Beldastowe seemed to invoke in her.

'You won't dismiss me so lightly when I have Gurley strip the skin off you bit by bit, Shaw, or perhaps I'll prefer another of the other delightful methods of torture he has at his disposal. Most creative I find him, but I doubt you'll like him half as well as I do.'

'I never did share your peculiar tastes, *little* brother,' he mocked back and surprised a spark of hatred in those cold eyes after all.

It was an emotion, if a Cain-like one, and once Beldastowe let that into his dealings he might make a slip. Perhaps he'd give himself away to Ben's friends before it was too late if he found it so impossible to hide. Refusing to let hope show in his eyes, he met Beldastowe's with a stony gaze and saw the thug his brother had brought with him glance from one to the other as if confirming their kinship by the only legacy his father had passed to them both—those grey eyes he had cursed himself for inheriting from Lord Pemberley as a child, instead of his mother's far more guileless blue ones.

'Who'd'ave thought it?' the man finally concluded and shot a speculative glance from one to the other.

'Who indeed?' Beldastowe replied sourly.

Had he been born on the right side of the blanket, Ben would have beaten him to title and fortune, but as he was the senior by age and not status, he had no idea why Beldastowe hated him so bitterly. It was another potential weapon, however, and he stored it away in the slender hope of finding a way to use it somehow. Yet he saw the hatred die out of that flat gaze as quickly as it appeared and had to admire the little rat's ability to stamp on any emotion that might put his foul enterprise at risk.

'You won't stop the hunt for your black soul by killing me, Beldastowe. In fact, you'll just make all the others on your tail the more determined to chase you into hell,' Ben informed him as cheerfully as he could.

'Oh, I think not, both your confederates have wives. I doubt they'll risk them meeting a similar fate to your charming companion. Sorry, dear lady, but an example must be set and you can blame the company you keep for that.'

His mistake, Ben felt, for suddenly instead of a shrinking kitten cowering at his back, he felt as if he was masking a spitting tigress. Attuned to Charlotte's responses as he now was, Ben knew some word, some taunt had sparked his fiery, defiant lady's temper. It was a relief to know she was herself once more, although that conclusion baffled him—for hadn't he often wanted to shake her for being the contrary, stubborn conundrum she was? He faced his repellent brother with a bland social look he knew would drive him to the edge of reason—how humiliating would Beldastowe find it if the bastard aped the gentleman better than the lord?

'You really are the most tedious of fellows, Beldastowe,' he murmured as if about to return to comfort and company infinitely preferable to what was presently on offer. 'I do wish you'd take yourself off.'

He caught the henchman hiding a grin and wondered if he might be worth cultivating after all. Beldastowe had no concept of how the gangs and victims of the underworld thought and acted, however many of them he had running about doing his bidding. Loyalty was rare as hen's teeth there, and probity even rarer, and Ben doubted the fool had done anything to deserve either. If he could convince their jailers that Kit and Hugh would see them hang if anything happened to himself or Charlotte, and reward their safe return liberally, maybe there was some hope.

'I might deny Gurley the pleasure of flaying you and do it myself,' Beldastowe spat at him and gestured imperiously for his acolyte to light him out of the room.

'Denying us food and water as well as light now?' Ben quizzed cheerfully as even the faint light of the lamp began to fade. 'Lord Carnwood and Sir Hugh Kenton will be deeply disappointed when they find out how poorly we've been housed,' he added as the sound of their footsteps retreated and all he could hear was a receding complaint from Beldastowe that the man who lit his way would suffer if he so much as threw them a crust.

'Do you think it might work?' Charlotte whispered at last from behind him and, by dint of a great deal of wriggling and unladylike muttering over his size and general lack of mobility, came out from her hiding place and stood upright on the floor beside the bed.

'What might work?' he answered grumpily, furious with his body for finding the process of a terrified female extricating herself from hiding so ridiculously erotic he was painfully aroused, and having to hope she'd stay away from him long enough not to know it. To wish otherwise would lower him to Beldastowe's level and he'd rather be dead than share anything with him but the unfortunate hue of his eyes.

'Frightening his cohorts into telling his lordship and Sir Hugh where we are, of course—do you think I'm a fool not to have known what you were at?'

'Was it so obvious?'

'Only to a rational being,' she replied calmly and he could tell by the fluctuations in sound that she was moving about their cell as they talked.

'Oh, that's all right then,' he said flatly and wondered how she'd transformed herself from terrified maiden to superior goddess in so short a time.

'Your brother is clearly not rational, so it might work,' she continued as if she'd never seen Beldastowe before today, which had to be a thundering lie considering she had seemed to know him all too well only a short time ago.

'Half-brother,' he said testily.

'I'm sorry, but I really don't think much of your relation,' she observed as she went about her explorations as if she actually believed she'd find something crucial.

'Somehow I can't bring myself to like him much myself.'

'Yet nothing about his actions proves your father is behind it all.'

Were they back to that painful subject again? 'Nor did I hear a single word that exonerated him,' he snapped.

He could almost see her put her head on one side to consider that statement as he suddenly realised he'd seen her do many times before while she weighed up some problem. When had he begun to watch her with such slavish attention he knew her gestures and responses, even in the dark?

'I really think you're mistaken in him,' she announced, her voice fading further into the darkness.

'You don't know what you're talking about.'

'I do,' she argued, her voice now telling him she was facing him again and embarking on her return journey at last.

'How?' he asked, more because she expected him to ask than out of any great curiosity.

'Because once upon a time I was engaged to his son,' she replied coolly and perhaps darkness could be good, if it masked the fact that he was sitting here like a tethered ass and watching her with his mouth open.

'You were what?' he managed to ask in a rusty voice he hardly recognised as his own.

'My grandfather and your father arranged a marriage between their unsatisfactory granddaughter and unpleasant son, in the laughable hope that we'd breed little aristocrats in their image instead of our own.'

'Idiots!' he snapped, revolted by the very idea of Beldastowe so much as standing by her side, let alone marrying her.

'I quite agree, but at least Lord Pemberley supported

me when I finally found the courage to tell them I wouldn't do it. If Grandfather had had his way, I'd have been marched down the aisle and wed whether I liked it or not, but fortunately Lord Pemberley wouldn't countenance the idea.'

'Then I have to thank him for that much at least,' Ben breathed as he reluctantly considered just what his father had saved her from.

'I thanked him myself at the time,' she informed him coldly and he realised he'd taken another misstep with her pride and haughty temper.

'Still,' he muttered to himself, 'at least now I know why it's so fiery.'

'What did you say?'

'Nothing, dear.' He parodied a doting husband and grinned in the darkness as she finally reached his side again and fell over the bedstead and tumbled into his arms. 'What a pleasant surprise,' he murmured into her ear as he explored his squirming companion in the darkness and found her infinitely desirable, despite their privations and her apparent haughtiness.

'We're in a wine cellar,' she announced with a catch in her voice that encouraged him to hope he was rendering her nearly as breathless and heated as he was himself.

'Really? Still? And did you find that corkscrew?'

'Oh, you infuriating man, don't you see what that means?'

'That we'll be drunk or frozen before morning, maybe even both.'

'No, it means we're in Berkeley Square, under your father's house.'

'Why?'

'I was supposed to marry your brother and got to know him too well, so I can see how his twisted mind would work on such possibilities.'

'I'm struggling with the idea you were ever that close to him,' he admitted and immediately regretted it as she began to fight against his hold. 'Not because of any stupid idea about you being defiled, you idiotic woman, but because you came so close to the filthy little brute and survived it, and I'd like to kill your grandfather slowly.'

'You'd have to stand in line, but thank you for seeing how abhorrent I would find the notion. At the time everyone else seemed to think it such a very good one I almost wondered at myself for resisting it.'

It was the overtone of bewilderment that told him how horrified she must have been, trapped in a nightmare and unable to persuade those who should have protected to release her from it. His fists tightened at the very idea of her, young and alone, facing that devil in all his vacant malevolence.

'Tell me about it?' he urged gently.

'Some time—first we have to see if there's a chance of escape.'

'Why Berkeley Square?' he asked the question she seemed to want him to, and avoided the one she was shying away from—that they were trapped and unlikely to be rescued in time to stop Beldastowe wreaking his warped vengeance on them both.

'Because he'd never use his own house and risk it coming home to him if you were found, and just imagine the scandal if your body was discovered beaten and tortured inside your father's house. Beldastowe would revel in causing such a scandal, I think, and he hated his father far more than you ever could, Ben.'

'Then he should have disowned him years ago.'

'I agree, but don't you think it's a fine jest that we ended up imprisoned here together and Beldastowe has no idea who I am?'

'No, I don't,' he replied bleakly, refusing to look on the bright side or hope for a miracle, because to do so would be to fail her once she realised how trapped and hopeless they were. 'Have you any idea how many cellars a town mansion like Pemberley's possesses? And does this one show the slightest signs of being visited by anyone but our jolly jailers and their unwilling guests any time in the last twelvemonth? Who are you really, by the way—I feel a fool calling you by a name I doubt you were born with?'

'Never mind, I prefer this one, but why so pessimistic, Ben?'

'Because I'm shackled like a performing bear; you're cold, hungry and frightened half to death of my foul little brother and we're shut in a cellar beneath a mansion owned by my enemy. Isn't that enough?'

'Yes, Ben, of course it is,' Charlotte soothed him and let her slender hands smooth over his tangled mane of hair, infinitely gentle over his many hurts, almost tender as she tried to smooth away the frown from between his brows. 'I know it's almost hopeless, but I refuse to sit and just admit defeat. That would be to let him take everything from us and I refuse to allow that.'

'Just for now, let's sit and admit nothing,' he said huskily and closed her brave lips with a kiss so gentle, so steadfast that she sighed and seemed to let go of a whole tangle of tension and pent-up energy and simply melt into his compelling embrace.

'If I have to die,' she declared as she lifted her head at long last and he sensed the long steady look she gave him, 'better that it should be with you,' she assured him.

'Oh, my darling girl, better that it should be with almost any man but me, but unfortunately I'm the one you're lumbered with.'

'Just as well you think there's little hope, perhaps, for I doubt we'll get on any better than we usually do if we ever get out of here,' she joked and he felt his heart physically ache at the brave humour in her words as she took what he said as a rejection rather than the protest to heaven it really was.

'We get on very well, Miss Wells, very well indeed, and that's not what I meant at all. What I was trying to say in my clumsy manner was that if you must marry any man to save your reputation, it shouldn't be one whose father lacks the manners to acknowledge him. You deserve better than having to wed a bastard.'

'First that bastard would have to ask me and I'd have to say yes.'

'You know we must wed if we ever get out of here alive.'

'No wonder you've given up, then,' she said face-tiously, but there was hurt underneath it and he longed to pour out his confused feelings to her, if only he understood them himself.

'Charlotte, you're a vixen of the foxiest variety,' he chided instead and rested his forehead against hers.

'And now you've seen my hair, no doubt you find it as foxy and unfortunate as everyone else does; the ones who know about it, at any rate.'

'Idiot,' he told her tenderly and reached up to capture one of her tumbling tresses and smoothed it over his fingers like finest silk.

'Idiot yourself, you don't have to live with it.'

'Would that I could.'

'Was that a declaration, Mr Shaw?'

'If it could be, it would be, Miss Wells.'

'Then I don't mind you knowing that there's no man on earth I'd rather be locked in a midnight-dark prison with, with no food, or water, or privy,' she whispered generously and he didn't know whether to laugh or cry.

'And there's no other woman on earth I'd sooner share my deathbed with,' he quipped rather unfortunately and felt the shudder of denial that shot through her.

'They really are they going to kill us, then?' Charlotte whispered into the darkness that suddenly felt very menacing indeed. Irrationally she hoped she was close enough for only Ben to hear her and nobody who might be listening outside that infernal door would have the satisfaction of hearing how frightened she really was.

'I suspect they intend to try,' he muttered shortly and

she could read impatience and extreme wariness in his soft voice, but no fear.

Perhaps his soul was in a better state than her own, then, because she was having the greatest difficulty controlling her hysterics.

'Suddenly I feel very young,' she admitted, 'for I certainly had a great deal more living to do.'

'Ah, Charlotte, you humble me,' he said softly and his voice had a catch in it, as if he too was holding back emotions that threatened to overflow, 'such courage,' he said softly and kissed her full on her surprised, willing mouth, 'such gallantry,' he followed up with and kissed her again, more passionately this time, so deeply in fact that she felt that threatened soul of hers warm and at the same time weaken.

'I want you to make love to me. Fully and in every sense of the word,' she finally admitted. In the face of what could be imminent death, she couldn't lie to him and she wanted him desperately. More than she wanted food or even good clean water, her own bed and the safety of Wychwood's, or even Carnwood House's, strong walls around her. 'I need you to,' she corrected herself as she squirmed on the hard palliasse and somehow got closer to him than he seemed to altogether like from his startled reaction.

Although perhaps he did like it after all, for his mighty arms came round her like a vice and he held her there as if she was his only hope. 'You really have no idea what you're asking, Miss Grammatical,' he grated even as he smoothed a large hand over the long and

lovely line of her hip and down on to her thigh with possession in every bone and sinew of him.

She smiled in the darkness, letting her mouth curve
against his stubbly cheek so he could feel it even as the
blackness all about them forbade sight. 'Oh, but I do,
Mr Mathematical,' she teased so softly only someone as
close to her as he was could hear her. 'I know very well
what I ask of you,' she taunted, 'and it's such a sacrifice I wonder that I dare.'

Although her need of him was the bare truth, she
wanted all the truth in the open. 'I want you to be my
lover, Ben, and I'd ask that of you now, even if I didn't
know Beldastowe will force me the instant he realises
who I am. I couldn't bear him to be the first, you see?'

'Such an honour…it will be my infinite pleasure,' he
told her with a stumble in his gruff whisper that jagged
at her heart.

Enthralled anew by the novelty of lying half across
him and breathing as he did while they warmed each
other as only intimate contact could in such a place,
feeling him in every sense and pore of her, she luxuriated in the reality of Ben Shaw. Somewhere deep within
she finally admitted the written-in-stone fact that she
loved him. And at last the rest of her surrendered and
meshed with the young impulsive Charlotte she thought
she'd buried with her parents and the carefree life she'd
lived with them.

'The honour would be mine, if only I could finally
attain it, even in the face of death itself,' she breathed
boldly.

'What, in some God-forsaken pit and without benefit of clergy?' he asked gruffly, as if holding back only on a hairsbreadth of his self-control.

'With you, anywhere,' she told him brazenly, surprised to find herself the confident one for once, and so deeply certain in the face of his doubts.

Even so, she held her breath as she waited for his annoyingly chivalrous mind to catch up with the roar and demand she could sense in his voraciously male body, as he reacted to her proximity so fiercely even she could hardly miss the rampant craving he had for her.

'We might yet get out of here,' he protested rather lamely as she sought to fan the flames with a provocative little stretch that took the length of her, the promise of her, even closer to his straining, heated length.

She shrugged and plastered herself even closer to him. 'You have a magic wand about you after all then?' she asked facetiously, knowing she should take their situation more seriously, but finding her present needs far more pressing than grim reality.

'No, you tart-tongued little torment, I haven't and well you know it, since you must be intimately acquainted with every inch of me by now,' he replied, and with a soft moan seemed to give up fighting them both at last.

'Not quite,' she muttered wickedly and leaned down to stop his mouth with her own, resting it luxuriously against his, sipping and then licking at him until he gave in to the inevitable and took over their mutual seduction.

At last his mouth firmed on hers and a sigh left him as if he knew they had both met their fate, and what point fighting such a mutually satisfying one? He teased her beestung lips into opening and goaded her neat white teeth apart with a wooing, pleading, commanding touch she couldn't refuse, and she let him in with a glad gasp.

'Shush!' he softly muttered, taking time to reluctantly leave the enthusiastic welcome of her mouth to whisper into her dazed ear, and wasn't it a surprise to feel the shiver of arousal even his warm breath on her soft lobe could send through her? What useful things senses were, Charlotte decided with dazed approval as, deprived of sight, the others sprang into acute, sensitised action and touch took over the lead. 'We might be making love in the darkest place I ever beheld, but I'm damned if I'll let our jailers hear us do it,' he murmured, nuzzling at her earlobe as if he was almost as surprised at the possibilities it offered for seducing every inch of her as she was.

'Yes,' she replied, and maybe neither of them was quite sure if she were agreeing with him, or urging him on to ever more passionate efforts.

'Oh, yes, my darling,' he encouraged again in that heady murmur that was almost breath audible and the most significant, potent sound she'd ever heard.

She promptly forgot all about their potential audience again and had to smother a moan of approval against him as he took that seemingly innocent lobe into his mouth and nuzzled on it. Breathing in the scent of him, the heat and spicy fact of him under her exploring mouth, made her realise she'd never taken in the full possibilities presented by a man's firmly muscled neck, any more than she'd delved into the unlikely sensuality of having a man whisper open-mouthed kisses along the cord of her stretched and eager throat, until he reached the hollow at the base and lingered there to evaluate it with his exploring tongue and find it very satisfactory indeed. Luckily, she had his abundant hair to mask her approval of what he did there and something tempted her into reaching round and loosing the leather thong that as usual kept it in check.

She didn't want any part of him held in check since they must give in to silence and that seemed restraint enough, and she felt the springy, silky strands fan about her fingers with a contented sigh. It was so thick and vigorous and manly she had no idea how anyone could think his maverick style anything but a joy, to the lucky woman who felt his mane loose to spring under her hand and curl about her questing fingers. So much a part of the man he was that she smiled against him and knew he felt it when he did the same against her throat.

Her breath stuttered and she wondered how she'd find the patience to get through whatever layers of seduction he'd demand of himself to ready her for him without screaming with need. Somehow, she promised herself, if only because for him it would be unendurable to take her when she was less than absolutely, pleasurably desperate for his taking. Feeling she could hardly be more so than she already was, she ran slender fingers over his hair and on to his shoulders; over his impressively muscled, rigidly controlled back she felt the smooth silk of his waistcoat take on some of him, become almost as heated and supple as he was under it. Not for them the luxury of nudity—she knew it even as she regretted it and went on to make the very best of what they did have. She wouldn't ask him to render himself more vulnerable to their enemies than he already felt; she loved him far too much to risk that.

'I like your tailor, Mr Shaw, he has talent,' she whispered in his ear as he rested his head on her very willing bosom and savoured her instinctive exploration of the man under that gentlemanly attire.

'Just as well, I don't think he'd like you, then,' he growled back possessively.

Charlotte almost giggled at the notion of some exquisitely turned-out gentleman's outfitter looking down his long nose at her handiwork as she mussed as much of his as she could. Who would have thought loving in the fullest sense of the word would bring with it such a leaven of humour? A breath of joyousness, while at the same time being serious and sensual and so deeply important even the darkness they were trapped in served to heighten it all instead of blight it.

'I like *you*, Mr Shaw, oh, I like you very well indeed,' she muttered encouragingly, as she felt his hands making very interesting forays at the laces that held her gown in place.

Cool air caressed hot skin as she felt the fabric first resist, then part inch by tantalising inch. She quivered under the slide of workaday cambric against the silk of her chemise and gloried in the wet velvet of his tongue as he opened her gown ever wider with his white, even teeth and his fingers lingered over every inch of her torso. Almost she forgot to taunt him with her own exploration of every inch of him she could currently get hold of, almost.

'Ben, not Mr Shaw to you,' he chided in a voice so roughened with need she might have had a job to recognise it as his, even if everything about him seemed as sure and familiar to her as her own voice in her sensitised, straining ears.

'Ben,' she murmured slowly, 'Ben, oh, Ben, oh, Ben…' She exhaled on a long, wondering sigh as finally he pushed the shucked halves of her gown aside and set his fingers to exploring her suddenly so-full, so-eager breasts, and she had to fight not to gasp her satisfaction to the world as he cupped them in gentle, eager palms and softly gave a satisfied grunt at the bounty they had uncovered between them. Nothing he did felt like an intrusion as any other man's touch would have done—more a very delightful reality, a lovely sharing she could never have dreamt of until actually experiencing it. He ran his thumbs up the sides of her breasts and then smothered her moan of delight with his open mouth on hers as he rubbed his thumbs over her pebbled, ravenous nipples under the thinnest veil of much-washed silk her chemise now provided with more seduction than the most expensive of lady's attire.

'Lovely Charlotte,' he exhaled against her, 'delicious, wondrous, beautiful Charlotte.'

'Lucky Charlotte,' she added with irrepressible enthusiasm.

'Some might argue,' he cautioned soberly, as if offering her one last chance to come to her drowning senses.

'Idiots,' she proclaimed as boldly as she could under the circumstances and nuzzled against his mouth until he opened it and gave her the open-mouthed, passionate kiss she longed for and returned to her seduction with single-minded determination.

'Now be quiet for once,' he cautioned and slipped aside from her ravaged mouth to trail kisses down her throat once more, this time tracing fire much further down and finally taking one of her tight nipples in his mouth and teasing and suckling until she felt fire and delight roar through her, leaving her wanton and ready to gasp her delight to both of them, if only it would be for them alone. Since it could not be, she bit the lapel of his coat between her teeth and held her pleasure in, refusing to allow the intrusion of those who held them into her thoughts to blight them, but concentrating every fibre of her being on the sensations he was provoking in her instead. Fire shot through her and she felt his echo of her pleasure in the way he cupped her other breast and bent his head to feast on it, even as he abandoned the first one and it tightened even more under the seductive chill of wet silk. How could she doubt he took satisfaction in driving her witless with desire when he made it into such an art?

Even so, she wished she had experience enough to pleasure him a quarter as much as he was pleasing her and ran exploring hands between their heated bodies to see how his flat, manly nipples might respond to an echo of the chaos he was causing with hers. She had her answer as they tautened under her touch through his fine lawn shirt, and he hummed a soft paean of praise in her listening ear as he held himself as tense as a bow in her arms.

'Much more of that and you'll be unceremoniously seduced and sadly unsatisfied, my siren,' he cautioned, taking her hands and raising them to once more clasp his shoulders, as he held himself above her and taught himself constraint again. And devilment, she decided, and felt her hands tighten on the splendour of those broad, muscled shoulders as he slid his hand from the hem of her gown up one long leg, to rest just above her garter and pause to feel the unexpectedness of that lace-edged band and taunt her eager skin with the tip of one long finger.

'Now that's not in the least bit governessly, Miss Wells,' he whispered tauntingly.

'Even I have my secrets, Mr Shaw,' she replied pertly and felt his fingers stop their probing and his strong hand settle and brace on her as if in rebuke.

'Ben,' he corrected her as sharply as their present circumstances allowed and somehow it felt important, although it was outwardly so trivial.

'Ben,' she corrected herself softly and felt the tension leave his grip as he softened it once more and trailed a wicked touch along her thigh, until she quivered with nerves and need and anticipation, and longed to order him to get on with it considering she was growing so hot and impatient for him.

Charlotte discovered herself to be a very vocal lover, given the opportunity. Such a shame they would probably never have the chance to explore that demanding, expressive Charlotte along with the silenced, eager, wanting one she was now. No, thoughts of the future were not allowed, this was their exclusive now and it was wondrous, and that was all she needed. Then that knowing, seeking hand reached its destination and she couldn't have thought about anything but Ben if Bonaparte's Imperial Guard had been pacing about the cellar with them, fully armed and bent on revenging their beloved Emperor's defeat.

A last maidenly sliver of her past self hesitated as he gently lifted her shift and rested his hand very close to the knot of springy curls at the very heart of her. She was humming with need of something just there—him, she intuited—and this was the final yielding to him, to them as lovers in the deepest sense. Then she felt the lure of it, the love of it and parted her thighs in welcome, as generous and eager as the rest of her was for him.

'Charlotte,' he murmured against her lips, as he once again took them in a kiss that branded her his as surely as he was hers in that moment.

'Oh, decidedly I am she,' she agreed, Miss Wells quite forgotten and shamefully unmourned in the ecstasy of his loving and the promise of yet more heady delight.

Then she felt his long finger part her and settle on her secret centre with possessive certainty and, now she had accepted his touch, she revelled in it and writhed in blissful welcome. Breathless with anticipation, she wondered if she might break apart with sheer sensual anticipation as he moved it within her and she felt the gnawing, driving hunger bite even deeper; then blossom into something more delightful than she'd ever dared dream.

'You're certain?' His question was tense and painful and it sounded as if she had his heart in her hands, as they tightened involuntarily on his shoulders and she felt his potent muscles tense in response.

'Yes,' she whispered in his ear, 'yes, yes, a shameful number of ayes to that, lover.'

For once she'd rendered him speechless; he just gave a tight nod against her forehead to tell her it was a very mutual agreement and gently probed that finger higher, brighter and his thumb rubbed somewhere she hadn't even known she had until fire gathered and flamed, then seemed to tighten in coil upon coil there, ready to shatter her with sensation. 'Not enough,' she managed to gasp against his heated kiss.

'Enough for now,' he insisted, 'there's more.'

Then his knowing, caressing touch shot her into that molten mass of sensation and she felt herself tighten, then loosen into the most joyful, wide and wondrous world she'd ever even dreamt of. Her body spasmed with seemingly endless delight, but all the time a part of her was protesting that he wasn't with her, that he was a bystander in her pleasure, not a partner.

'Now you,' she murmured when she finally gave up that quivering wonder and drifted back into being merely half of them again. 'It's lonely without you,' she protested and felt his mighty body jerk, as if he'd let it off the leash for an unwary moment.

'Now us,' he corrected and she smiled a besotted, glorious agreement she somehow knew he'd sense, even though he couldn't physically see it.

'Oh, I *love* us,' she encouraged wantonly, felt his deft hand leave her for the buttons of his breeches and smiled even more wantonly at the notion of feeling the whole of him close, but not close enough.

Suddenly not quite as brave as she thought, she licked her lips and opened her mouth to question him a little further on whatever came next, then he caught her tongue with his own instead and lured it into his mouth to dance it into a new rhythm, advance and retreat, thrust and parry. It sent hot shivers of anticipation down her back and earthed them in the throbbing centre of her she'd so recently thought beyond further pleasure. If he'd been struggling to hold back such a gnawing, fathomless need all this time, he was more of a hero than even she thought him. Suddenly everything she guessed at and all she knew of the mating between man and woman became infinitely desirable and, instead of retreating, she advanced, boldly luring him to take everything she had to give and add to it with his own need and their joint pleasuring.

'Ben,' she finally confirmed, 'Ben and Charlotte.'

'Indeed, we are,' he confirmed and she felt him tense for that final act that would make them exactly that, but somehow more than that as well. 'Together,' he bit out as he gently, oh, so gently entered her, stretching the unstretched secret place no other man could, or should, ever find.

Feeling as if she was banqueting on endless delights, she let herself accommodate the potent breadth of him and surprised herself by feeling only pride that they could do this for each other, pleasing each other as they undoubtedly were. He let them rest on that laurel for a brief, precious moment, then slid a little deeper into her silken depths and she sensed the full, potent length of him as a promise of wonders yet to come, and she knew he was holding himself back even now rather than plunging them both into something she'd yet to fully comprehend or consent to.

'Come right into me, lover,' she whispered and felt as if she'd finally abandoned all the inhibitions that might have held them back.

'It'll hurt,' he warned in a driven murmur and she sensed the bunching of any remaining muscles that weren't yet intimate against her, his hard masculine plains and strengths against her supple feminine frame as he butted against her maidenhead.

'Much?' she managed with the last shreds of her maidenly self falling away as he shook his head and she felt the fan of his loosened mane against her cheek and nuzzled deeper than ever into his kiss to encourage him on, even as he held himself back with a truly noble effort.

'Just a short, sharp sting, I hope.' He tore his mouth from hers with an impressive effort to reply with such passionate honesty she almost giggled, but only almost—the iron tension as he held himself so near and so far from his ultimate goal was too much to be treasured for that.

'Then please could you hurry up?' she urged, sensing something wonderful beyond that pain and eager to get it over with so they could get there and both feel it.

'Your wish is my pleasure, lady,' he gasped into her mouth and thrust home as if it truly was.

It did hurt, a stretching snap that almost broke her attempts at silence, until he took it into him with a passionate kiss that seemed to take the sting out of her protesting body with it. Then she flexed experimentally and heard him gasp as if in torment and did it again. The novel sense of fullness, of utter, mutual possession, enthralled her and she opened eagerly, wonderingly to him when he began to gently thrust and withdraw in a sweet rhythm she caught eagerly and then echoed as smoothly as she could with the bow and curve of her own body as he rode her gently. Then even that wasn't enough. Urgency tightened her breathing and she moaned a faint, inarticulate protest as his tongue thrusting into her mouth took on a deeper beat and his body failed to echo it.

'I'm not made of porcelain,' she protested as she snatched her mouth from his for long enough to breathe her words into his ear.

'No, you're made of fire and satin and sheer contrariness, my darling,' he argued and plunged so deep and long into her welcoming softness at last that she felt as if he now knew every inch of her and she him, and didn't she just love the stretch and thrust of his impressive manhood within her? Again he gathered all that velvet sheathed force and strength and thrust into her, until she could have sworn she felt the stars melt as she whooshed up to meet them.

Clenching about him as eagerly as he thrust into her and claimed the very heart of her, she felt her eyes roll back in her head in a moment of sheer bliss and let the most extraordinary golden delight claim her in wave after wave of satisfaction, as he took her gasps into his mouth and silenced them, then gave them back to her new-minted. At last he thrust one final mighty spasm of ecstasy and she thought she saw the sun as well as the stars, even as she finally melted into Ben Shaw's slackened arms, her lover and her love, as they collapsed into each other's arms sated, softened and blessed with something she knew without a doubt went way beyond mere passion.

Too satisfied, too loved to try to put anything into words when there didn't seem words made to tell him how she felt, she sighed contentedly and nuzzled into his arms, feeling him draw his coat over them both to cover them as best he could. He pulled her as close as he could get without repeating a seduction she was too sated and possibly too sore to repeat just yet.

'Sleep, love,' he murmured into the wildly curling mass that was her glorious hair, now they'd both finished reducing it to total disorder.

Miss Wells would have been furious, he decided whimsically, but Charlotte seemed to care not one whit. Lovely Charlotte, he decided, and pulled her a little closer so she'd sleep across his still-heaving chest, and bless him with her lovely, boundless confidence and her glorious hair spread over them both for just a little longer.

Eyelids heavy as she smiled into his sweat-dampened torso and luxuriated in the warmth and the feel of his living, infinitely precious silk-and-satin skin, tight over bone and muscle and deliciously roughened with the light pelt of hair she discovered felt just right against her flushed cheek, she decided they deserved the sweet aftermath of their loving without lingering on the terrifying probabilities to come. 'You too,' she whispered.

'In time,' he muttered, 'all in good time, my darling,' and she felt consciousness slide away from her even as she wanted so badly to hold on to it and for their glorious, never-to-be-forgotten completion to stretch on for ever.

'Love you,' she muttered and exhaustion claimed her as peacefully as if they were wrapped in silk sheets and cosseted among finest feathers.

Ben enfolded her in his mighty arms, holding her as carefully, as tenderly, as if she were made of spun glass, instead of womanly contradictions, stubbornness and pure temptation. Part of him reeled at the very thought of what they'd just done, lady and by-blow as they were; another was longing to snap her up into some hidden lair and keep her exclusively his, in defiance of the world for the rest of time.

Not that he had the choice, he reminded himself grimly and wondered how he'd bring himself to kill her as he surely must if he was right and there was no hope of him staying alive to protect her from the brute lust of Beldastowe, or their guards, and being sold into slavery in one of the seedier brothels in the stews once they were done with her. Only if he loved her beyond his own soul could he put his hands round that long, lovely neck of hers and squeeze the life out of her and, once that was done, his own death couldn't come soon enough. Not that it would matter, for he'd be dead inside the instant the last breath crossed her lips. He sighed in the darkness, careful not to wake her, but now fully awake and aware himself as he brooded on their dire situation.

If only there was the slightest hint of hope, he silently raged, and glared into the darkness as if he could somehow fight it for her. If there was some way, he would exchange his life for hers. It would be agony to part from her even if he could. Yet even knowing there would be no second conflagration of the senses for them, he wanted to bargain for some long-in-the-future death for her, when she might lie in her grave next to another man who would have the endless privilege of calling her wife. The only thing that could hurt more than letting her go to that theoretical, already hateful, husband, was the knowledge she must die too. Not with him, but before him, and by his hand. Ben held out one of those offending hands in the darkness and cursed it; he might as well kill his own soul as kill her, he decided. But if he didn't make himself do it, he deserved to lose whatever remained of his better self for not saving her from his repellent half-brother and his unsavoury cronies.

The terrible dilemma of when he must decide to do what he had to do, and the strain of wondering how he could judge the moment when his brother had done with playing with him like a cat torturing a mouse, kept him awake even as Charlotte slept so peacefully, so trustingly in his arms.

Chapter Nine

Somehow Carnwood House seemed echoing and empty
without either its master's or Ben Shaw's vital presence,
despite that of the usually lively Misses Alstone and Lady
Rhys. Sir Hugh Kenton decided he'd rather deal with half
the London underworld on his own than face three
females wallowing in self-reproach for leaving Miss
Wells without their eagle eyes on her, as well as taking
most of the blame for not being available to fight off the
gang of abductors required to kidnap Ben Shaw as well.

'If not today, then another; if not this week, then
whenever they did get a chance to grab either of them,
ma'am, none of that being your fault so far as I can see,'
he reassured as patiently as he could manage.

'There's a person below insisting on seeing you, Sir
Hugh,' Coppice interrupted Lady Rhys's bitter self-
reproaches and earned Hugh's everlasting gratitude.

'It could be a ransom demand,' Isabella speculated
dramatically.

'And you could take a blue pill,' her sister informed her sharply, glancing at Lady Rhys as if warning her sibling to keep her wilder speculation over their friends' fate to herself rather than upset her duenna even more.

Hugh decided that if he wasn't already married to the most wondrous female who ever stepped, he might propose to Kate Alstone on the spot, and cravenly left her sister and their tearful chaperon in her capable hands.

The younger Miss Alstone might be bitterly disappointed if she could see the burly 'person', dressed in the Marquis of Pemberley's livery and looking distinctly unfootman-like, for he quite evidently wasn't a kidnapper.

'What do you want with me?' Hugh asked, after eyeing the man for long enough to make him look more uneasy than ever in his borrowed plumage.

'To tell you what I know of Mr Shaw and his lady,' the man replied.

'At a price?'

'My employer pays me well enough, I need no more.'

'How remarkable.'

'Well, I ain't always been a footman,' the man said, after several minutes trying to meet Hugh's darkly cynical gaze as if he had nothing but good deeds on his conscience.

'You do surprise me—Bow Street?'

'Before I took to private work, yes, but I've always run best alone.'

'Doubtless, and your name?'

Once again the stranger shifted as if even admitting

that much might do him some physical damage. 'Charlie Hodge,' he finally said.

'I've heard of you.'

'You ain't heard aught wrong, because there's naught to know.'

'That could be because you haven't been found out yet.'

'They said you was a hard man, but I can tell they didn't know the half of it,' Mr Hodge told him bitterly.

'I've seen enough of this fair world of ours to make me so, but I take it you didn't come here to exchange cynicisms with me?'

'Better things to do, I came here because I didn't see where else there was to go.'

'Good, then if we might get on?'

'You sure you want to hear it?'

'I shouldn't be here unless I did, and as you admit that you wouldn't be here unless there was nowhere else to go, can we please get down to business?'

'Aye. Your friend Shaw…now, he's got enemies enough to fill Newgate, seems to me, but there's one as hates him more'n all the others put together.'

'So I'd already surmised—his name?'

'Not sure you'll believe me. Nobody did at Bow Street, laughed at me and threw me out with a flea in me ear, they did,' Charlie Hodge told Hugh indignantly and he didn't doubt his story so far.

'I, however, have a more flexible mind,' he encouraged.

'You'll need it,' the man muttered and took a deep breath. 'It's Lord Beldastowe as ordered your friend caught, and he'll kill him sure as we're standing here before too long. I heard him tell the gallows bird he employs as his groom and, as his lordship hates your Mr Shaw like poison, I don't doubt but what he means it.'

Several pertinent facts clicked into place in Hugh's mind and he used the trick he'd learnt in his unregenerate days to retreat into himself and assimilate, then process them to the best advantage he could.

'Why should I believe you? And, as he's your master's son, why would you betray him in the first place?' he finally asked.

'Because my master ain't his son,' the man said succinctly and, if his contempt for Beldastowe was assumed, he was a better actor than any on the London stage.

'And what a man he is, who could reject his eldest son for such a runt,' Hugh challenged.

'And bitterly regrets it,' the man told him.

'How touching,' he said carelessly, and continued to watch his visitor with cool, wary eyes.

'I delved into this whole business as deep as I can on the Marquis's orders, Sir Hugh, both of us thinking the past was the key to what's been happening to Mr Shaw and his friend now. His lordship was young and maybe he was a fool to believe his father's promise the girl would be taken care of, but I wonder if he's paid an even harder price than they did for being fooled.'

'Oh, I think my friend would disagree with that summation,' Hugh said stonily and the man's eyes fell before his ironic look.

'Aye, well, can't say as I blame him. His lordship once saved my life, so I always feel I must look for the best in him. All the same, he set me on his heir half a year ago, so at least that proves he's nobody's fool now.'

'Pity you failed to come up with the goods until Ben Shaw and a perfectly innocent lady under his guardianship went missing, then.'

'The little cur's a damn sight cleverer than I thought possible, Sir Hugh. Every time I got near to catching him someone would be silenced and he'd shut down one operation, then start up again somewhere else. Too many have made too much out of his wickedness for them to let on who was behind it all. Until you caught Stitchforth, I was beginning to think his nibs would beat me every time I thought I finally had him dangling on the end of a rope.'

'Why would Beldastowe take Ben Shaw and not just kill him?'

'Because he hates him more than he fears hell. He'll want him to suffer good and proper before he dies,' Charlie Hodge told him grimly.

Hardened though he was to the darker faces of the city, Hugh gave a superstitious shiver. 'And where's your employer been while all this is going on?' he asked cynically.

'In Paris, trying to looking through Bonaparte's records.'

'Why?'

'So he can wipe out Lord Beldastowe's mucky footprints, before anyone thinks to look for them where they shouldn't be.'

'He's been spying for the French as well as everything else, then? If he were mine, I'd denounce him and leave him to be damned.'

'Would you, Sir Hugh?'

Hugh thought of his own infant sons and paused— would he? But would he leave his younger son at liberty to kill his older one while he cleaned up a mere scandal? He certainly hoped he wasn't going to be that hopeless a parent, for Louise would undoubtedly leave him even if the boys didn't.

'No matter what I'd do, all that matters now is getting my friends out of that gallows bait's clutches alive.'

'True enough, Sir Hugh, and I think I know where he's holding them, only I can't see my way to getting them out safe on my own.'

'Let me worry about that, then,' Sir Hugh Kenton told his new ally and they retreated to Lord Carnwood's much-used study to plan a rescue.

'Ben?' Charlotte woke from a wonderful dream to warmth and a lovely certainty that at least some of it were true. 'What's wrong?' she asked sleepily as she felt the tension in the formidable muscles under her cheek.

'Hush, I'm trying to listen,' he muttered as if she was prattling away like some idiotic female at a tea party.

About to hush him furiously back, she remembered just how perilous their situation was at last and raised her head so she could use her ears for something more than listening to the reassurance of his steady heartbeat.

'I didn't hear anything,' she whispered at long last.

'That's because you were asleep, woman,' he chided

and she could feel him straining away from her, as if her very presence was an unwelcome distraction. So much for her gallant lover, she thought in disgust, and sat up to oblige him by setting as much distance between them as she could manage, without relinquishing his warm proximity altogether of course.

'Excuse me for being human,' she mumbled crossly.

'Gladly, now kindly shut up.'

'Ooh! Why did I ever think I loved you?'

'I have no idea. Now remember where we are, Charlotte, and the danger we stand in.'

Doing so, despite the warm glow that their lovemaking had lit in her, and that she seemed incapable of disowning in the face of Ben's angry silence and Beldastowe's virulent enmity, Charlotte made herself concentrate on what was happening outside their prison instead of inside it. If they were really hidden beneath Lord Pemberley's town mansion, then he kept an unruly house, she decided. Even down here, so far from the normal everyday life of the place, she could hear the occasional muffled thud.

'If he's got rats, then they're extraordinarily active,' she joked and Ben didn't bother to reply.

Of a sudden he seemed horribly remote from her and she wondered if she would ever understand, or even truly know him. If their enemy had his way they wouldn't have the chance to know more of each other's character than they already did and suddenly Charlotte was sad she'd been so reticent. She should have told him of her idyllic sea-gypsy childhood and loving, lively parents. Too late for that now, perhaps, and all she wanted to do was learn more about how loving and generous *he* was with the woman he could be about to die next to.

'How can I know?' she heard him mutter distractedly.

'Know what?' she asked with one ear on the furore in the distance.

'Whether this is rescue or Beldastowe come back to gloat,' he replied.

'You can't, although I suppose if Lord Beldastowe really is using his father's house as a gaol, it's in his interests to be considerably quieter than whoever is making so much noise,' she pointed out logically enough, still wondering at the extreme tension in his mighty body. Yes, they were in mortal danger. He was pinned down, imprisoned and held in total darkness, but he was almost shaking with suppressed strain and that didn't seem like Ben Shaw at all.

'Did he strike you as a man worried about being challenged?'

'No, I suppose he must come and go here pretty much as he pleases, and his father probably took most of his staff to Paris with him,' she acknowledged and once more felt his every sinew harden as if resisting a huge pressure.

'He took everyone but the night-watchman,' Ben told her, revealing how close an eye he kept on his father as she wondered if he hated his sire quite as much as he claimed.

'Not everyone,' she argued absently.

'Who did he forget, then?'

'I saw one of his footmen strolling about the Square the last time I was out walking with Isabella.'

'You're sure?'

'Yes, I even noticed him out and about on several occasions when we went to Green Park. I assumed he had a sweetheart among the nursemaids, so you see Lord Pemberley's household is not quite deserted, and if that's Beldastowe he'd do well to keep a little quieter.'

'That he would,' Ben returned and a little of the tension left his straining muscles and he took a deep breath.

'What's worrying you so much?' she asked as the thumping at last stopped and the usual black silenced reigned.

'I'm a coward, Charlotte,' he whispered as if the words were torn out of him.

'You're the least cowardly person I ever came across,' she informed him in her best governessly tone, for the very idea seemed absurd to her.

'Then you don't know me as well as you think,' he said, a faint unamused laugh in his voice.

'Enlighten me, then,' she demanded.

'I can't do it,' he admitted rather incoherently.

'Can't do what?' she asked, listening more intently to the silence than she had to the previous noise. Suddenly it seemed to have an air of expectation to it and at least soon they'd know if their future was to be good or bad, or indeed if they had one at all.

'Kill you,' he admitted dully at last.

'I should hope not!' she said indignantly, now firmly focused on the tensions inside their prison. 'Why on earth should you want to? Unless you're more like your brother than you like to think, of course.'

'Be damned to that,' she thought she heard him murmur absently. 'I should do it to save you,' he finally admitted as if the words had been wrung out of him under torture.

'Save me?' Charlotte echoed hollowly. 'You intended to save me by killing me yourself?'

'I don't see how else I can protect you,' he replied defensively.

'I don't want you to, I'd rather you give me a chance,' she informed him stiffly, 'or even ask me what I actually want for once.'

'I didn't want to distress you by discussing such desperate measures.'

'Well, you have anyway,' she snapped, 'and I hate men who assume they know best for any female who happens to be vaguely connected with them. Do you think any woman who knows of Lady Rhys and the Countess of Carnwood's charitable work can be ignorant of what happens to women who fall into the hands of villains? For that matter, do you think any one of my sex with her own way to make in the world hasn't considered the possibility of such a fate?'

'Well…'

'Well, what? Every woman you meet isn't going to be convinced death is better than dishonour, Mr Shaw, and you'll not be required to kill me today, or any other day either, thank you very much.'

'Well…'

'And if you expect me to throw myself off Westminster Bridge if we ever get out of this mess alive, just because, in your obviously skewed view of the world, I'm now dishonoured, then you'll be disappointed.'

'I wouldn't dare,' he finally managed to say when she wound down like a spent automaton.

'Good!'

'Will you marry me instead?'

'I'll think about it,' she answered, very much on her dignity.

'Lord above, woman! I can't believe I'm saying it, but for once I think I'm seeing my father's point of view rather than my mother's,' he murmured and she could almost see him shake his head and turn to watch her uselessly in the gloom, as if she was an unexploded bomb of some sort.

'Are you, my boy? Well, that's an excellent start then,' a deep voice very like Ben's own observed conversationally from the doorway and both of them started as if they'd been stung.

'Lord Pemberley!' Charlotte gasped and blinked in the sudden light of a lantern wielded by the reassuring figure of Sir Hugh Kenton, just visible behind the Marquis's large one.

'Hugh!' Ben exclaimed and there was a world of relief and trust in his voice at the sight of his friend. The look he directed at his father was more complex, but Charlotte thought she detected a faint lessening of his usual hostility toward him.

'Is it safe?' she demanded, hardly daring to hope this really was rescue from so desperate a dilemma.

'Of course, but thank you for the reminder that we need to get you both out of here as soon as possible and back to some sort of comfort, my dear,' Lord Pemberley told her and nodded to someone hovering outside the room and murmured something about fetching the magistrates now his son and his companion were safe.

She felt herself relax and believed it at last. That sense of security she had always felt in Lord Pemberley's stalwart presence reminded her so poignantly of Ben that she almost turned to him and told him so, until she recalled she was at outs with him and smiled sweetly at his father instead.

'It's a pleasure to see you, as always, my lord,' she greeted him sunnily and felt unworthily triumphant when she heard Ben grind his teeth.

'Forgive me if I don't rise to greet you, or feel ready to join in the eulogies on your stalwart character just yet,' he remarked sarcastically, with a gesture at his chained ankle to remind them he was incapable of going anywhere at the moment.

'Oh, for Heaven's sake,' she exclaimed impatiently and eyed the offending shackle as if he was making excuses for being too uncivil to rise and make his father a bow. 'The keys must be around here somewhere; I refuse to believe they brought a blacksmith in to make that leg shackle and failed to wake us as well as half the neighbourhood.'

'Logical,' Sir Hugh remarked succinctly and stepped outside to investigate possibilities in the outer cellar, which the two villains Beldastowe set to guard them must have used to store their things once their rough bed was occupied by their prisoners.

'I hope you didn't drink the '88 Le Fleurrey?' Lord Pemberley remarked facetiously and surprised a deep chuckle out of his son.

'We hadn't quite got round to it, although Charlotte did discover an excellent burgundy—it tasted younger than that,' he replied just as flippantly and Charlotte wondered if she'd ever understand men.

'Never mind that,' she ordered impatiently, 'pray tell me what's been going on in the outside world while we were locked away in here?'

'Later!' both men informed her as if they knew best and it was Charlotte's turn to grind her teeth in frustration.

'Here we are, Prometheus,' Sir Hugh remarked from the doorway, glancing from one to the other as if highly amused by all three of them. 'Let's try these for size,' he added, rattling a bundle of keys before kneeling at Ben's poor feet and patiently going through the lot.

'It had to be the last one, didn't it?' Ben observed ruefully as he slid gingerly off the bed and wobbled perilously on to his bare, bruised feet. 'No,' he ordered, backing away when Sir Hugh would have supported him, 'I refuse to leave this place while being supported like an invalid.'

'Good, because I doubt I could carry you very far, even if I wanted to,' Sir Hugh told him cheerfully.

'Stubborn, ridiculous, inconsiderate, top-lofty man,'

Charlotte muttered bitterly as she watched Ben stagger, then right himself by sheer force of will.

'Can't imagine why we put up with him, can you?' Lord Pemberley asked her gently and offered her his arm like the gallant gentleman she'd always found him to be.

'No, and with any luck I'll be rid of him before any of us are much older,' she grumbled with fingers crossed, because deep down she knew very well she'd only feel half-alive if she were forced to live without Ben now.

'Liar,' the older man chided softly and she nodded her admission, only to sense from Ben's stiffly held shoulders that he believed her.

'True,' she admitted on a huge sigh, 'I'd miss him being stubborn and unreasonable after the first week or two, I dare say.'

'He does unreasonable so much better than anyone else, don't you find?' Ben's father teased and she knew he'd seen that braced look about his son's poor battered body as well and sought to banish it. Who could blame him after so many years of standing by while Ben proved he could do without him? Not her, she decided, with a rueful smile at that stubborn back.

'Yes, it's one of two things he excels at,' she said.

'The other being?'

'Private, my lord,' she replied pertly and was amused despite herself when the hint of a swagger suddenly infused Ben's weary stride.

Their route through another two cellars, each better used and closer to the outside world, reinforced the formidable nature of their prison and Ben's face was grim as he eyed the mighty outer door, now broken and listing perilously on its hinges. Glad their gaolers had decided to rely mainly on the lock on the outer door to secure them, and keep the keys to Ben's shackles inside it, Charlotte decided she would never voluntarily visit a cellar again. She supposed some of the thumps they heard were accounted for, but how had they known where to look? And perhaps, more importantly, where were their enemies now?

She climbed the stone steps in silence, preoccupied with Ben's weakened state as he reeled and hesitated, then corrected his wavering balance and doggedly trudged upwards. Yes, he was stubborn, unreasonable and arrogant, but so much a part of her now that every pained breath, every jarring bruise and cut gnawed into her. Then at last they were in the sculleries and what looked like early morning and under the scrutiny of every person who had any right at all to be in Pemberley House, and a few who certainly didn't.

'Mornin', Cap'n,' one particularly unprepossessing rogue greeted Ben as if nothing in particular had happened, but the genuine joy in his gap-toothed smile told Charlotte a great deal about how Ben was warmly regarded by his men, both ashore and on land, for behind him a precise-looking clerk peered anxiously, as if he needed to lay eyes on his employer for himself to actually believe he was alive and likely to remain so.

'Good morning, *everyone*,' Ben replied, but Charlotte thought he was secretly as pleased to see his cohorts as they were to see him.

'Later, I think,' Lady Rhys said gently, with a significant look at Ben's swaying form as she set out for the back door.

'Much later,' he agreed, forging an unsteady path through the knot of spectators in her wake, determinedly tugging Charlotte after him.

'Like a flotilla,' she muttered as she sensed Sir Hugh and the Marquis lining up behind them and won a quick, boyish grin from Ben as he followed Lady Rhys along the mews, hopefully without attracting the notice of more than the score or so of watchers already there.

'Can't be helped,' Lady Rhys informed nobody in particular as she led them through the bustle of the Carnwood House kitchens and finally brought them safely into the breakfast room. 'Hot water and towels, Coppice,' she ordered, as if it was perfectly normal to be demanding such things before the most energetic lady or gentleman would usually dream of being out of bed. 'Then breakfast, if you please.'

'Certainly, my lady,' he replied as if nothing untoward had occurred and Charlotte marvelled at the speed at which all three arrived, even if nobody else seemed to expect less of such a superior butler.

'Just wash as best you can to eat for now; you can have a bath when we've taken care of more immediate needs,' Lady Rhys urged and Charlotte blessed her good sense.

'We haven't been to bed at all,' Isabella informed them impulsively, as if to disarm anyone who demanded to know what she was doing up at such an hour, and

Charlotte admired her tactics, even as she wished she didn't believe her.

'See what happens when I'm not about to see that you behave?' she said in a creditable effort at sternness that was quite ruined as Isabella rushed into her arms and hugged her as if she never intended to let go. 'There, now,' Charlotte said soothingly, refusing to cry in case Isabella caught the affliction and they couldn't stop. 'I'm appallingly dirty and I *really* want my breakfast,' she said prosaically and her pupil gave a watery chuckle before pushing out of her arms and taking a good look at her governess.

'You are as well,' she confirmed with a grin, 'and you certainly won't want to sit down to eat looking like that once you've taken a look at yourself in the mirror.'

'No, I sent for Jessie as soon as I saw you all tiptoeing across the square,' Kate told them from the doorway and Charlotte could only cast Lady Rhys a resigned glance as she was spirited away to be set to rights after all.

Finally clean enough to feel almost normal, as well as dressed in a fresh gown, her hair very carefully brushed and loosely tied back to take the pressure off the large bruise on the back of her head, she rejoined the company feeling considerably better. Seeing that Ben had been similarly tended, even if his hurts were obviously much more comprehensive than her own, she consumed an enormous breakfast under what felt like far too many interested eyes.

'Now what?' she finally asked as she sat back to sip

her coffee and revelled in the feel of a full belly for the first time in what felt like a week.

'Wouldn't you rather go to bed first?' Lady Rhys asked hopefully.

Charlotte refused to look at Ben in case he was struggling with the same scandalous picture as she was. 'Not yet, there's far too much mystery afoot for me to get a wink of sleep,' she said carefully instead.

'Far too much,' he agreed with a significant glance at his father, who sighed and seemed to give up on the idea of putting off this uncomfortable discussion for later.

'Where to start?' Lord Pemberley mused.

'At the beginning,' Charlotte said with an encouraging smile.

'That's a tale you probably know already.'

'Only part of it, and I'm not planning on going anywhere just yet.'

'Very well then, long ago when I was young and about as foolish as a man can be, I fell deeply in love. I lacked the courage to marry her—lovely, spirited and loyal as she was—knowing I would be disinherited and she'd be forced to starve along with me if I did. So I kept her as royally as she would allow me to instead, and thought that would be enough for both of us. Young idiot that I was, I even felt noble at my refusal to marry anyone else if I couldn't wed her. My father had other plans, however, and when I next went to London he had me kidnapped, then drugged and starved until I was confused enough to do anything he told me to. Unfortunately what he told me to do was to marry the woman he'd picked out as the most suitable one to be my wife all along. I still recall nothing, but apparently marry her I did, and in front of witnesses…' Lord Pemberley paused and shook his head, as if he had woken up and found himself wed to a stranger just yesterday.

'Pitiful, isn't it, a grown man being coerced into marriage like the heroine in a melodrama?' he asked Charlotte, seemingly unable to meet his son's eyes with that crucial question on his lips.

'If not for you, that would have been my fate seven years ago, so at least you saved me, even though you couldn't save yourself, my lord,' she told him gently.

'When a marriage between you and Beldastowe was suggested by your grandfather, I agreed because I thought you'd lend him the courage and principles he so obviously lacked, that somehow your character would bolster his lack of it,' his lordship admitted starkly, 'but I couldn't permit a forced marriage even to try to correct his freely demonstrated faults.'

'Try as my grandparents did to persuade you to do so?'

'Indeed,' he agreed ruefully.

'Thank you,' she said and felt Ben's hand grip hers under the table and exchanged a long gaze with him as they both thought of what might have been, if not for Lord Pemberley.

'I suppose that explains why I couldn't discover anything about Miss Charlotte Wells's life before she became a schoolmarm?' Ben asked his father.

'It wasn't an existence I would have chosen for her, but as she insisted on being independent when the old fool cut her off, the least I could do was to make sure no further damage was done to her character by that unfortunate episode.'

'Who are you really then, Miss Wells?' Kate asked, gazing at her former governess with a fascination Charlotte could have done without just at the moment.

'Angela Charlotte Venetia Louisa Standish Kirkwell,' she replied, eyes steady on Ben as she listed the fanciful string of names her delighted parents had burdened her with.

'Standish?' he asked, latching on to her mother's maiden name, added with a defiant flourish by her mother and directed toward the parents who had rejected their only child for marrying a mere sea-captain.

'Yes,' she admitted, braced to watch him turn away.

'As in the Duke of Devingham Standishes?'

'Yes.'

'I seem to gather aristocrats about me like bees to honey,' he told her blandly and held her hand as if he'd no intention of letting her go, much to her relief as she had almost expected him to repudiate her for those aristocratic connections she could hardly be expected to do anything about.

'We can't help being born that way,' she excused herself feebly.

'I dare say not,' he replied consolingly and smiled as if he found her almost-aristocratic birth amusing.

'And I'm only half-aristocratic after all, as my other grandfather was a shipbuilder. Anyway, if it comes to that, you're one yourself.'

'Only a backstairs one,' he argued with a challenging look at his father, who seemed content that his eldest son was even speaking to him, never mind the whys and wherefores of it all.

'Never mind all that,' Isabella said impatiently. 'What about the dastardly villain behind all this? Don't tell me you let him get away, just because he's a lord?'

'Sorry,' Lord Pemberley said humbly, 'a trial would have been such a, well…a trial, I suppose.'

Ben's mouth was grim and his eyes cold again. Charlotte felt him release her hand and a chill cut right through her.

'So you let him loose to kill again?' he accused his father bleakly.

'I gave him two hours to flee before I set the Runners on him,' Lord Pemberley excused himself sheepishly.

'You let him escape,' Ben replied implacably.

'I wanted him gone, out of my life and yours and beyond hurting either of us any further. He's my son as well, you know? And all his life I've felt at fault for his warped nature and his infernal jealousy of you, because I never could love him, try as I might.'

'Jealousy?' Ben asked incredulously. 'What the devil had he got to be jealous about?'

'I realise now that his mother must have instilled it in him from the cradle. Seeing that I could never love her if we both lived to be a hundred, she made sure there was nothing but strife between us. I wonder if she could possibly have known just how bitter and base a man he would turn out to be under her malign influence? It's probably just as well she's been dead for a decade now, seeing what Beldastowe has become.'

'Even if he hated you, why target me? It's not as if you doted on me.'

'Ah, but I did. Fool that I was, I found it no hardship to love you from the moment I knew of your existence, and I never found out about that until your mother died. I made a complete mare's nest of the whole business at the time, but I promise you that I never knew you existed until that very day.'

'You didn't know?' Ben asked, looking as if his world had just rocked on its foundations.

Charlotte felt cut off as he withdrew into himself. He was coping with every shock and setback in his life alone, as he'd done since he was ten years old, and she was back to being an outsider again. How that could hurt her so acutely, when he'd never made her any promises of undying love, or even just trust and friendship, she had no idea, but, oh, how it cut into her. She sat a little straighter in her chair, reminding herself she'd survived devastation before and would do so again. Miss Charlotte Wells, governess, possessed impeccable references and had a place in the world. Somehow she'd continue with Isabella's education, even if it nigh killed her, and then she'd go on to teach in another family because that was what she did now.

'I think it's high time we retired to the schoolroom, Isabella,' she observed coolly, consulting the watch pinned to her bodice as if it was an oracle for far more than simply the time.

'Today, Miss Wells? I really don't think you're up to it,' Kate observed with a worried frown, but Lady Rhys nodded sagely.

'Routine works wonders for the nerves at difficult times in our lives, my dear,' she told her charge, with a sympathetic glance at Charlotte that told her the lady suspected much of her feelings for the stubborn idiot next to her, and thought a few hours' refuge from them might prove beneficial.

'But how can Miss Wells still be my governess when she's also the granddaughter of a duke?' Isabella asked rather desperately, having seen an early end to her studies heave into sight and now having to watch it drift away.

'I was born this way the last time I taught your lessons, and it didn't stop me then,' Charlotte pointed out.

'Don't you need a rest?' Isabella asked a little desperately.

'Italian verbs again?' she asked sympathetically, wondering at the odd nature of her life. One moment she had been contemplating death or dishonour, maybe both, the next she had to consider conjugating verbs with her reluctant pupil.

'Well, yesterday was the oddest of days. It didn't seem like the proper time for such things,' her pupil admitted.

'Then today you may have a rest from them until you have rested. We'll consider the upcoming settlement of Europe instead.'

'Oh, Miss Wells, must we?'

'Indeed we must, you might marry a diplomat after all,' Charlotte said with a faint smile.

'Lord, I hope not!' Kate exclaimed irrepressibly and Isabella smiled as the notion seemed to amuse even Ben, who came out of his chilly reverie for Isabella, even if he couldn't manage to do so for her governess.

'I think you'd make a fine ambassador's wife, brat,' he told her consolingly.

'So long as our country wanted to go to war with whoever he was ambassador to,' Isabella said mournfully.

'Nonsense, anyone can learn tact given long enough, but you've a warm and loving heart and even Miss Wells can't teach that. You'll be a credit to us all one day, minx; in fact, I'm already practising boasting that I knew you when you were a scrubby schoolgirl,' he reassured her and Charlotte wished he was as good with antiquated ladies like her as he was with young ones such as Isabella.

'Indeed,' she confirmed with a nod, 'but as you've already missed two days' worth of lessons, it would be remiss of us to risk further backsliding from such a worthwhile cause.'

With a show of reluctance, Isabella finally submitted to banishment to the schoolroom and Charlotte thought she looked secretly relieved at such a return to normality when they got there, even if she'd never willingly admit it. Indeed, it all felt so ridiculously normal that Charlotte might have thought her time in Lord Pemberley's cellar a figment of her imagination, except for the fact that her hair was ridiculously dressed and her eyes felt heavy and tired. Then there was the slight ache at the very centre of her being to remind her one part of it had felt magical, unforgettable and unique at the time. Now they were safe and about their daily lives once more, she suspected she and Mr Benedict Shaw might go back to behaving like the strangers they'd striven so hard to be since they first met.

It was perhaps the oddest day she'd ever experienced, Charlotte decided, when it finally seemed done with. At dinner, which Lady Rhys had insisted on making a festive occasion, although Charlotte's heart felt heavy and Ben looked as if he might go to sleep at any moment, the others had laughed and joked and seemed almost drunk with relief, while the two most involved in their misadventures tried to pretend all was well with them. Ben hadn't looked at her properly once, she reminded herself painfully, as Sir Hugh and Ben disclaimed the least desire to be left to their port and ordered a decanter to be brought into the drawing room.

'For we'll both undertake to behave ourselves, I believe, and this is no day for such stiff formality,' Sir Hugh observed, with a severe look for Ben and Charlotte, who were once again pretending they were nothing to each other.

'Beldastowe got away,' Ben informed them bleakly, as if that explained his refusal to celebrate. Perhaps it did too, Charlotte mused dully.

'To what, though?' his friend asked him impatiently. 'To a life of relative poverty, for ever on the run from the law and uncertain who might betray him to the nearest magistrate for the sake of the reward put on his head by those he defrauded. An existence without the status or the assets he's accustomed to and the luxuries he considers his by right. Inadvertently, perhaps, your father has damned Beldastowe to a life he'll hate more than he would the condemned cell at Newgate and a criminal's death.'

'Maybe, but he still killed too many good men in pursuit of his dirty trade for me to think it punishment enough.'

'Death would have been too quick,' Sir Hugh told him, with a significant look at Isabella, who sat round eyed and hanging on their every word.

'You're right, I suppose, and this is a day for rejoicing, not chewing over the unsavoury parts of my past,' Ben said, with what seemed to Charlotte a mighty effort at cheerful lightness. 'So let's be wicked and call for some champagne to toast our freedom instead of quaffing port, and we can raise a glass to the most courageous lady I ever had the good fortune to lay eyes on while we're at it,' he said, ringing the bell and fixing his gaze on her as if it had never been away, the wretch. 'And one or two of my senses more, well, immediate, shall we say,' he whispered in her blushing ear as he came close enough not to be heard by anyone else.

'Don't!' she protested as firmly as she dared, dreading he was about to betray more than she had a mind for the world to know, benign though this circle of friends might be.

Too late, Coppice led in two footmen with champagne, suspiciously ready for the occasion, and she was sure Ben winked at him as the dignified butler smiled faintly in acknowledgement. Charlotte sipped warily at her champagne and had to admit it revived her. Or at least it did until she heard Ben's toast and hoped she'd slipped into a dream without noticing.

'To Miss Charlotte Wells, the most extraordinary governess I ever laid eyes on, and my future wife!' he proclaimed as if infinitely proud to announce a marriage they'd never properly discussed, let alone agreed to.

'No!' she exclaimed, protesting his high-handed arrogance and hurt that he hadn't bothered to ask her in private.

Anyway, he didn't want to marry her and hadn't he always insisted he would never marry? She'd heard it said so many times that Ben Shaw wasn't a marrying man it hadn't occurred to her to doubt it once they were free of their prison and about to live after all. Or had it? Weak, wanting Charlotte was in danger of taking charge as she saw at last how long she must have loved Ben Shaw, to have been so ridiculously wounded by his revulsion towards matrimony from the first. Luckily, stern Miss Wells rushed into the breach and ordered her weaker self not to be such an idiot.

'Yes,' he countered, taking her hand and unfairly undermining Miss Wells with the undeniable warmth of their contact, and the endless promise of more of it than she'd ever dared imagine. 'Yes to all of it, and no arguments if you please,' he chided, outwardly as loving as any fiancée could wish. Then in an undertone meant only for her he challenged her, 'You promised yourself to me not twenty-four hours ago, lovely Charlotte.'

She would have spoken, protested that it had been

less than a promise, but he got in first, as if he could sense the protests flying through her busy mind.

'Don't try to deny it,' he whispered, 'or you'll categorise us as two rutting beasts. Do that to yourself if you must, but don't make me less than a lover along with yourself, my sternest, most correct Miss Wells,' he chided softly, and the hint of hurt under his words silenced her when she knew she should speak up and deny it.

'Very well,' she conceded out loud, wondering that the earth didn't shift under their feet in protest at such a travesty of an engagement. Still, it was only an engagement, and could therefore be broken when his pride had cooled down and he was prepared to see sense again.

'Three days' time, St Martin in the Fields,' he informed them all brusquely, puncturing her faith in time coming to her rescue no sooner than it was made.

'That's far too soon,' she protested weakly, feeling again that the world was spinning out of her control and she might do something irredeemably missish like fainting to escape it all, if she didn't keep a very tight hold on her self-control and her senses.

'Not soon enough for me, lady,' he insisted and she felt the heat of his gaze on her, the teasing touch of his fingers caressing her palm in an extraordinary display of secret sensuality that took her breath away.

'We'd best begin our shopping in the morning, then,' Lady Rhys said, as if that was the very foundation of a good wedding, but her dark eyes were alive with happiness as she contemplated the two of them, hand-fasted and seemingly unable to take their eyes off one another.

'I told Miranda you two would finally come about if we left you to it,' she informed them smugly and Charlotte began to wonder just how deep the conspiracy to push her and Ben up the aisle ran.

'Did you now?' he said austerely, but Charlotte thought she heard the hint of a smile in his voice all the same. Did she know him at last, or was she just suffering from the delusion of hope?

'Well, I think it's wonderful,' Kate told them with a sigh and Charlotte briefly wondered if her former pupil wasn't more of a romantic than she would ever admit.

'There you are, Miss Wells, now everyone is happy,' Ben teased her and Charlotte took refuge in her champagne glass and decided to save up her arguments until she knew what they were herself.

Chapter Ten

W here had it all gone so horribly wrong? Charlotte asked herself as she paced impatiently up and down her room, all hint of tiredness temporarily forgotten. One moment she'd been ravished by the most sensational lover any woman could hope for. Then they were freed and he'd looked at her as if he'd never seen her before while he fretted over his brother's escape. Now Ben insisted he intended to marry her in three days' time, with all the attendant illusion it was a love match and he could wait no longer.

He'd been so loving toward her for those golden hours that their time in a lightless dungeon seemed a stolen paradise in retrospect. Still, at least she knew what it felt like to be everything to another creature, even if it had lasted for a mere day. Now they were free and about to live as long, or as little, as any other being in this uncertain world and earlier today he'd looked as if his temper might shatter irreversibly if she whispered,

'Make love to me', in his outraged ear. Now he was intent on making her forget her common sense and agree to marry him.

The trouble was, she missed her bold lover so much she felt torn between shame and longing at the very thought of those magical hours in his arms. Her body ached for him, softened at the very thought of him aroused so rampantly by her proximity and the profound intimacies they'd shared. Silly body, she told it severely and resumed her pacing. If nothing else, it might exhaust her at last and drown her memories of the night when she lay in her lover's arms as if she'd been born for the role.

'And he says he wants to marry me?' she muttered darkly as she completed another circuit and for once wished the room ten times larger so she could really work up some momentum. 'Ridiculous, feeble-minded, want-wit of a man—how can he expect a marriage of convenience after that?'

'Because he's a fool,' the rich rumble of Ben's beloved voice remarked ruefully from the doorway and she was too startled by his presence and his implied apology to say a word when he closed the door behind him and took one of those ground-eating paces of his toward her, as if he was some sleek-skinned predator about to pounce.

'Not only that, he's in my room at God knows what hour of the night compromising what little bit of good name I have left to me,' she informed him implacably, determined not to give in to the internal voice that urged her to take whatever she could get from him and think about it later.

'True, but although I'm a fool, I sometimes realise it in time and try to learn a little wisdom.'

'And it's wise for you to come here and prattle about your precious honour again?' She forced herself to sound incredulous and shot him a blistering look she hoped would disguise the fast beat of her heart and the glittering excitement already building within her, just from his very presence in the same room, let alone the wolfish glint in his tired eyes.

Despair ran side by side with elation as she realised this heady mix of passion and anticipation would tow her under again if she let it, and somehow she must leave London after all, once she finally persuaded him that a marriage between them would be pure folly, for she'd never learn not to love him when he was almost within hailing distance all the time.

'Once a suitable replacement has been found, I intend to leave Lady Carnwood's employ and move to Ireland,' she informed him, surprising both of them with that hasty decision and distracting herself from the scent of him, once more clean and carefully groomed and almost his old self again. 'My mother had relatives there and they are independent enough from my grandfather to make me welcome.'

'So they might, if I had the slightest intention of letting you out of my sight, let alone allowing you to put two kingdoms and a sea between us.'

'You have no say in the matter,' she informed him

haughtily, once more wishing this spacious room very much larger, so she could avoid his piercing gaze more easily.

'I have, you know,' he purred dangerously and strode a little closer.

It took all her pride and resolution not to take a step back and give him the satisfaction of seeing how much he disturbed her.

'That you haven't. We're nothing to each other, less than nothing,' she spat the words as if the wound he'd inflicted this morning might be excised if she got rid of enough poison, although she knew in her heart it could never stop hurting while she loved him and he didn't love her.

'No, my dear, you're wrong. We couldn't be nothing to each other if we both lived for ever and were condemned to exist on separate continents. What we have is rare and I intend to treasure it, even if you're currently too angry with me to tell a hawk from a handsaw.'

'Be damned to that, and to you.' She rounded on him furiously. 'You're the one who believes I must marry you whether I like it or not, since you compromised me by being careless enough to get locked inside an impregnable dungeon with me. I won't wed a man who looks as if he's hearing his own death sentence pronounced when the parson speaks the marriage vows. Nothing on earth will make me marry a man who doesn't want to wed me, let all the proprieties in the world be screaming with outrage.'

'Finished?' he asked infuriatingly and leant against

the post of her elegant tester bed, just as if he was the reasonable one.

'Not even begun,' she informed him huffily and drew breath to denounce him even more comprehensively.

'I'm sorry,' he said with almost painful sincerity, and let his eyes meet hers for the first time since he came into her room and she saw the truth of it raw in the complicated silver-grey depths of them.

Standing there with her mouth open, words of bitter condemnation dying on her tongue, she felt all her carefully crafted arguments fly away without so much as a by your leave.

'So am I,' she murmured and stopped her pacing to stand beside him, awkward, uncertain and suddenly more than a little weary now he'd deflated her fury so unfairly. 'What now?' she asked and met his eyes with so much uncertainty in her own, she wondered he didn't flinch away.

Instead he took her hand as if she were a princess of the blood at the very least and walked her over to her rather tempting bed. 'Sit,' he said and unfortunately she could see no signs of rampant lust on his handsome face and did so with a thump, as if the bones had suddenly been taken out of her legs and they would no longer hold her up.

Making no effort to hide a quick grin at her rather inelegant descent, he startled her by sinking on to one knee in front of her and giving her a quizzical half-smile as he asked, 'Marry me, my lovely Charlotte?' as if he really meant it. 'I promise there's no other woman on earth I'd ever contemplate making my wife, let alone do so joyfully. If you'll only say yes for once in your life, of course.' He shifted a little on that knee and looked acutely uncomfortable as he awaited her verdict.

No promise of undying love, no romantic lie that she was the loveliest and most desirable of women. The romantic girl she'd once been sighed and left the room, but the real Charlotte who'd lived the last seven years in a determined spirit of realism put her head on one side and considered after all. He'd be a thoughtful and interesting husband and there was certainly no danger of them being less than passionate lovers. If she wed him, he'd honour her and see everyone else did so as well, and there might even be children. She hugged that possibility to her like a precious and barely believable blessing and made her mind up.

'Yes,' she agreed at last in a voice that sounded so small and feeble she had difficulty recognising it as her own.

'Thank God,' he breathed and got to his feet as if the weight of tension wound into them over the last days had finally dropped from him and left him hardly able to walk.

He looked so weary. More than weary—exhausted, even, as if that one last effort of getting her to agree to the inevitable had taken the strength to be his usual omnipotent, impatient self from him.

'Come to bed,' she urged gently and held out her hand for his.

'I should go,' he argued almost as if he had to, just for the sake of exerting his own will on the world about him.

'I think we're both done with canting propriety, Mr

Shaw,' she told him with a fine irony he was probably too tired to combat, for once.

'Lead on then, Mrs Shaw,' he replied with a grin she saw had a little more energy in it than she'd thought.

'Not yet, but a very managing Mrs Shaw you'll soon find me to be, sir,' she warned as she claimed the privilege of undoing his cravat and waistcoat without having to fumble in darkness.

It was so very different to just feel than it was to see *and* feel, she discovered, and couldn't stop her greedy fingers lingering on the wonder of hard muscle, satin-smooth skin and fine dark-gold hair as she exposed his chest to her marvelling eyes. Curbing her wanton urges for once, she reminded herself they were here to sleep and not to tumble each other in a careless welter of petticoats and fine linen. Forcing herself to act the valet and not the seductress in the face of their mutual exhaustion, she unbuttoned his coat and waistcoat, then moved to the head of the bed and folded back the covers invitingly.

'I'm not ready to strip in front of you just yet,' she informed him with some of Miss Wells's remembered stiffness, 'so you will kindly turn your back, Mr Shaw, and you may like to remove your boots while you're at it, for I draw the line at sharing my bed with a gentleman who can't be bothered to take them off.'

'Spoilsport,' he muttered, and she wasn't fool enough to think he meant it to go unheard and chuckled as he obediently turned from her to attend to whatever she'd left undone.

Marriage, so unexpected and so unsought by both of

them, promised to be leavened by a good deal of humour as well as passion and Charlotte couldn't bring herself to hate the idea of a marriage of convenience quite as virulently as she ought to for the moment. Whisking out of the gown she'd put on such a short time ago, she laid it aside before removing the snowy lawn cap she'd resumed for dinner, despite Lady Rhys's protests, and throwing it across the room. She was done with the wretched thing and, if the world didn't like her unfortunate hair, then it could do the other thing and dislike it. With a severe nod at some imaginary spectator, she took the pins out of her heavy mass of it and let it down, running her fingers through the weight of it with a sigh of relief.

'I never saw anything so beautiful in my life,' Ben informed her in an awed voice and she eyed him dubiously. Suddenly he looked to have far more energy than either of them would have thought possible a few minutes ago, but alongside a more carnal wonder, there was also such genuine admiration on his face that she couldn't disbelieve his words.

'It causes trouble,' she cautioned him, breathless at the idea that something she'd for so long thought a handicap might prove one of her greatest assets in her lover's eyes.

'I can quite see how it would,' he told her silkily and she felt as if he'd just run an exploring finger down her backbone.

She shivered and turned to face him fully, determined to make him realise what a bane it had been to her, up until now. 'I hid it to avoid unwanted attention, and because governesses should never stand out in any way they can avoid. I could hardly go about on my knees for the rest of my life so there was naught I could do about my height, but this I could hide from the eyes of the world,' she explained uncomfortably.

'And me,' he informed her flatly, a flame in his gaze that warned her when he was not quite so weary, not quite so careful of her own exhausted state, he'd exact a price for that. 'Yet somehow you've held my attention for far too long now without any help from your sharpest weapon, Miss Wells,' he told her and closed the gap between them with panther-like grace and she suddenly knew she'd been a fool to think him too tired to be dangerous.

'It's not a weapon, unless you count it as one to be used against me, of course,' she told him on a rather panicked tide of words. 'I've been teased and tormented about it since babyhood and have hated it with a passion for years. Then I decided that what couldn't be cured must be endured and did my best to pretend it was nothing out of the ordinary, nothing worth the world staring at and plaguing me about, and more recently it seemed simpler just to hide it.'

'Don't ever cut it,' he warned and there was that predator's demand, the possessive assurance of her mate in his voice and his eyes as he finally let his hand reach out and explore its silken softness.

'Not even when it reaches my knees and tangles in the furniture?' she quipped, and did her best to hide a shiver of delight, as his touch on the heavy waves felt as if he was stroking her skin through finest satin.

'Perhaps then, my logic-chopping siren,' he replied and suddenly everything was right between them again after all, and she laughed and sank into his arms as eagerly as if she hadn't left them for the fuss and fears that perhaps they'd both suffered since their release.

'That'll do for now,' she informed him softly as he carried her to the bed and laid her down as if she were far more fragile than she knew she'd ever be. 'You may not need any rest, my fine buck, but I know I do.'

'Do you think we can just rest then, my far finer belle?' he asked as if he was in severe doubt of being able to resist her, whatever his state.

'I think we have to; there's the morning to be faced, after all, and I dare say her ladyship has lived long enough to let me sleep until I decide I've had enough of it for the time being, shopping or no shopping.'

'You may have, but I don't know if I ever will, with you sharing my bed from now on,' he admitted and Charlotte was so tempted to turn in to his arms and explore that statement as he lay beside her and pulled the covers over them both. 'Let's see just how steely my will can be, then,' he muttered as he tugged her into his arms and let one hand play with her hair, then settle to a gentle, mesmerising stroke.

She smiled sleepily up at him, then snuggled her head against his broad chest, sighing with infinite contentment. 'Good night, Ben,' she whispered with an absurd sense of shyness and promptly fell fathoms deep into exhausted sleep.

He lay there, one hand still gently smoothing her

vibrant, silken hair and the other arm holding her as if he had no intention of letting her go, even in his sleep, then he too let himself succumb to the heavy fatigue dragging at his every muscle. 'Good night, sweet Charlotte,' he muttered as he too slipped into oblivion and, for once, dreamt of nothing but the woman in his arms.

Some time during the night they woke and made love because exhaustion could only damp their senses for so long and there was a world of glorious exploration in front of them, so, as Ben said, what reason was there not get started on it right away?

'I do so agree,' Charlotte murmured and embarked on her second voyage of discovery with a delighted heart.

'And afterwards we'll do it all again, only slowly,' he promised as he began a languorous journey from one ear to the other, sweeping kisses down the tender curve of her jaw, then back up the other side.

'I'll probably lose my mind trying not to cry out,' she warned and lay back to facilitate his wicked attentions even further.

'One day soon we'll have all night in our own bed to make love and you can make as much noise as you like,' he offered generously.

'While you remain silent? I think not, sir,' she sparked back and set about making him realise how impossible that would be, when they had the luxury of respectability, and the whole of their lives to enjoy it in.

Every moment, every touch, word and gesture were

precious, lingering and slow as he brought her to unimagined peaks of ecstasy and then did it all over again, as promised.

Morning came all too swiftly, of course, and Charlotte fought her way up from what felt like fathoms depth of sleep to find herself alone in her comfortable bed. After so many years of waking alone, surely that should have been a relief to Miss Wells's governessly soul? But, no, it seemed that Charlotte the woman was well and truly awake now and *she* felt the lack of her powerful lover as acutely as if she was to be deprived of the pleasure of waking up next to him for the rest of her life. Even if he didn't love her, she would wed him just for that pleasure alone...well, almost. There were so many pressing reasons for them to wed that at least she needn't look too deeply into their future, even if she had fallen desperately, irrevocably in love with her husband-to-be.

Of course he'd go before he could be caught out compounding their errors by the servants as they went about their business; she should have known that even before she reluctantly gave up her dreams and tried to snuggle into Ben's warmth and iron strength and found him gone. Despite his ordeal, Mr Benedict Shaw would never let circumstances dictate his life when he could do it himself. She sighed and put a protesting arm over her eyes to fend off the daylight, but after a few seconds of self-delusion she gave up. Wondering if she should go back to being Miss Wells, or give up that particular lie for ever, she was hesitating in front of the clothes press when a quick knock on the door heralded Jessie with the determined look of someone who knew exactly what was owed to her new mistress even if she didn't.

There was obviously no point asking if she would like the post, Jessie had already annexed it and that was that. Anyway, she had no wish to employ a snooty dresser who would look down her nose at such an un-promising mistress as Mrs Charlotte Shaw seemed likely to prove. Nothing could minimise her height, or disguise the brightness of her hair, so a fashionable dresser would probably take one look at her and flounce off in disgust.

'You can't come in, Henry,' Jessie informed the second footman regally, 'but pray pass me the hot water and then go and fetch Miss Wells's tray as soon as I ring the bell.'

Amused by the turnabout in Jessie's position, as well as her own new status as a lady in need of waiting on, Charlotte let herself be ordered about just for the sheer novelty of it all.

'Lord, Miss Wells, you've got the most beautiful hair I ever did see!' Jessie informed her as she ran Charlotte's plain hairbrush and comb through the tangled mass it had become during an eventful night in Ben's arms.

'Oh, that,' she replied with a rueful look at herself in the mirror. 'You don't have to live with it, Jessie, some-thing you should thank your stars for.'

'I'd thank them if I did,' Jessie informed her severely and for once Charlotte felt as if she was the one being instructed to count her blessings, rather than being the governess handing out sage advice to her pupils.

Eyeing the shining mass Jessie's gentle ministrations were making of her despised hair, Charlotte wondered for once if the little maid could be right. Maybe she had agonised too much about what made her stand out in a crowd instead of embracing it. A teacher who drew attention to herself would not have lasted long in respectable employment, of course, but if she was about to become Mrs Ben Shaw maybe it was time to rethink a good many aspects of her life. She wanted Ben to be proud of her, for this marriage to lie lightly on his broad shoulders, and the fierce sense of protectiveness she felt towards him amazed her, for never had she met a man more capable of fighting his own battles. Of course that was only one of the emotions she felt toward him, but the less she considered them while Jessie was trying her best to kit her out as became a newly engaged woman, the better.

'That's much more like it,' Jessie exclaimed with satisfaction as she finished the loose knot with a final hairpin, gently aimed away from the bruise that still reminded Charlotte of her ordeal, and turned to contemplate her work like an artist wondering if one more stroke of the brush might produce perfection. 'Although there's naught to be done about your gowns,' she added in a tone that spoke volumes about her opinion of their inadequacies.

'No doubt Lady Rhys will take me in hand,' Charlotte offered meekly and took a second to wonder at how docile she had suddenly become, now she actively wanted to please her new fiancé rather than infuriate him. Protective cover, she decided wryly, and took a few moments to consider how vulnerable she might be making herself by going without it.

'Aye, well, her ladyship said she'd be along to see you as soon as you'd broken your fast, miss, and it's about time I found out what that idle Henry has done with your breakfast before he eats it himself.'

'Ah, now, that's very much better,' Lady Rhys informed her latest protégée as she bustled into her room a few minutes later, surveying Charlotte's elegantly dressed hair, 'quite magnificent, in fact—you'll astonish the *ton* before we're finally done with you, my dear.'

'I would far rather be ignored by them as usual,' Charlotte told her with a rueful smile that admitted such cowardice was no longer possible.

'Rubbish, you'll enjoy every minute, once we've shaken a few of the odd kicks out of your gait,' her ladyship told her with a steely glint in her eyes that dared Charlotte to argue. 'Now let this poor girl find your most presentable gown and finish dressing you as best she can for now, then we can get the serious business of the day underway at long last.'

Submitting to their inspection in a most un-Miss Wells-like fashion, Charlotte let herself be arrayed in what until now had been her finest. Realising under the eyes of two stern critics that a neat gown of plain lavender cambric, cut high to the neck and designed to minimise her assets rather than emphasise them, was not very fine at all, she was rather glad she was about to acquire something altogether more fashionable, until she got to the dressmaker's and heard the vast order being placed on her behalf.

'And if you can't cut to flatter Miss Wells's magnificent height and proportions as well as choose colours and textures to enhance her colouring, then I despair of you and shall send the whole lot back and refuse to pay a penny,' Lady Rhys informed the middle-aged proprietor of the very elegant Bond Street establishment she'd just marched into and virtually taken over.

'If you thought that I couldn't, you'd never have brought her here, my lady,' the modiste informed her eccentric patroness patiently and Charlotte could almost see her calculating the final bill and deciding it would be well worth putting up with a little plain speaking for such a magnificent order.

Impressed with the woman's pragmatism, and her lack of a *faux* French accent to add glamour to her establishment, Charlotte decided she trusted her not to deck her out in a mass of frills and furbelows that would make her look more like a walking trifle than a sophisticated lady of fashion and style. She wasn't feeling quite so philosophical several hours later, however, after being minutely measured, then having countless lengths of fabric draped over her as if she was a clothes prop.

'No, I like it,' she argued as a lovely, heavy ivory silk, shot through with subtle hints of gold and copper, was rejected by her tormentors. If she was going to be forced into the open by her new circumstances, then she was also done with hiding in corners.

The dressmaker put her head on one side and considered the effect again and slowly nodded. 'Yes, I suppose it has possibilities,' she finally pronounced.

'Good, it'll do to make up my wedding dress, then,' Charlotte said decisively and felt her old self meld with this bewildering new one at last and felt a little better for asserting herself.

Of course it wasn't that easy, so unconventional a choice was never going to go unchallenged, but Charlotte was five and twenty and finally it was decreed that she could get away with such a daring fabric, and from the way it clung to her she rather thought Ben would like it as well, possibly rather a lot. Of course she'd be wearing it for her own satisfaction, she told herself severely, not for that of a husband who really didn't want a wife at all, least of all one like her.

'We'll never find a velvet to match it to make up the spencer, though,' the dressmaker informed her with a sad shake of her head.

'Then it should be made up in this,' Charlotte said, now with the bit fairly between her teeth as she picked out a coppery-gold satin more suitable for summer wear in her opinion and couldn't resist rubbing it against her cheek to enjoy the sheer luxury of it.

From somewhere Ben had released sensual depths in her character even she had never known were there, but now they were loose her appreciation of the world about her seemed oddly heightened and she had difficulty hiding a rather wicked and too-revealing smile at the thought of Ben's hands running impatiently over the lovely soft stuff, searching hastily for the frogging that would close it so he could get to the rest of her. Yes, this was the one, and he'd appreciate her choice even if the rest of the world raised its eyebrows at her ensemble. 'It's really not very bridal, my dear,' Lady Rhys protested mildly.

'Then it's about time brides had a little more choice, especially ones of my advancing years,' Charlotte replied in a voice Miss Wells might have been proud of.

'Very well, then, but I draw the line at ordering a bonnet made up with plumes to match for a wedding. At least allow me one sop to the conventions.'

'Oh, I think I might do that,' Charlotte said with a grin and met Lady Rhys's eyes to see mischief and a little too much understanding in them.

'Cream straw with a ribbon to match and a few rosebuds made up in the colours that run through your gown, and I know just the person to do it,' the clever modiste said with a knowing nod, as if the whole idea had been hers from the outset.

No doubt it would cost a fortune, but for once Charlotte put such practical notions out of her head and thought of her first impression on her groom as she glided down the aisle. He would remember her thus for the rest of their lives, or at least she hoped he would, and that was more important than penny-pinching when he was rich as Croesus, and would definitely not appreciate being presented with a beggar maid for a bride. It would be worth it, she decided, and Lady Rhys evidently agreed. So at last they were able to leave the elegant establishment, but only for the bootmaker and then to search for silk stockings and gossamer underclothes that would do justice to the finery Charlotte was to assume like a very tardy butterfly, finally emerging from her chrysalis at the advance age of five and twenty.

It would probably have consequences, she reminded herself with a shudder, but she would deal with them when they descended on her. For now she was safe and about to wed the only man she'd ever met who could be the other half of herself, and not even the past would be permitted to spoil it.

Chapter Eleven

Nothing did, news of the marriage not being inserted into the papers until well after the deed was done. The gossips had a nine-day wonder to exclaim over and Charlotte and Ben had precious memories to gloat over as the church was filled with those they really wanted at their wedding, although there were notable absences of course. Kit and Miranda couldn't get to London in time, even if his lordship had permitted it in his wife's present condition. Charlotte sincerely mourned their absence, but wondered how they would all get on now the governess had become the wife of his lordship's best friend. Receiving a warm letter of congratulations as she did her best to settle into her new home a few days later, Charlotte knew she'd been a fool to doubt their genuine delight. Even Lord Carnwood had added a brief line to Miranda's letter to thank her for wedding 'the most pig-headed idiot he'd ever had the misfortune to meet', because he doubted any other lady of sufficient character would prove brave enough to take him on.

'Much room he's got to talk,' Ben muttered darkly when she passed it to him to read over the breakfast table.

'So, if you aren't to prove him right, are you going to let Lady Rhys ask your father to our ball after all?' she asked while he was in a mellow enough mood not to get up and walk away from the question as usual.

'Why? He never asked me to any of his.'

'Having little taste for having one of his gilt-edged invitations thrust down his throat, I suspect,' she said with considerable exasperation.

'Sensible man,' he observed blandly and went back to his breakfast with determined dedication.

Charlotte had been astonished by the quantity of food needed to sustain her very large new husband, until he finally permitted her to take a tour of his dock and warehouses and she saw him working as hard as any of the stevedores and sailors. Unable to take her eyes off his giant form as he tossed bails of silk from China and chests of tea bound for ladies' tables around as if they were a child's bricks, she had thought wicked thoughts about being hefted about by him like a flyweight herself. She yawned and was reminded how much he seemed to like the idea he'd obviously seen in her eyes when he came home that night and seized her and threw her over his shoulder and bore her off to their bedroom before either of them even thought of dinner. Having always considered herself ridiculously overgrown and about as fragile as a carthorse, she had loved being made to feel small and fragile far more than she might have done if she actually was so. He was a wonderful, inventive and vigorous lover, but sometimes she wondered if he had an abacus instead of a heart, for she quite despaired of ever hearing him say he loved her.

'I want him to be there, Ben,' she urged, despite heady memories of just how many compensations there were for the lack of a mere word.

'Why? He would have married you off to Beldastowe when you were no older than Kate, who seems to me little more than a babe in arms for all her common sense, so what can you possibly owe him?'

'Is that why you won't let him come?' she asked incredulously.

'Perhaps,' he said as if not sure a full admission might not come back and bite him.

'Then that's no excuse at all, for he saved me from being sold off to the most noble bidder to come along, even if I had managed to refuse your brother. My grand-parents considered me in the light of a mongrel. They would cheerfully have married me off to Bluebeard if he called himself a duke or marquis. I owe your father so much I can never repay the half of it.'

'Why? You earned your own living, made your own way in the world. I can't see that he did so very much for you,' Ben told her brusquely and half of her was delighted that he thought he was championing her. The other half was not quite so happy with his conclusions.

'Then you clearly didn't grow up with two stiff-necked marionettes who thought my only purpose in life was to do as I was bid,' she told him impatiently. 'Nobody ever told you what to do, how to think, who to mix with and who you could never even consider speaking to, for all you think you had such an appalling upbringing. Well, you should try being of so-called noble and legitimate birth and you'd soon find out it's nowhere near as wonderful as you appear to think.'

'I'll think about it,' he said cautiously and took himself off to the City to do it in the efficiently elegant offices Stone and Shaw kept there.

'Mr Benedict Shaw and Mrs Shaw,' Coppice intoned majestically as they stepped into the blaze of light that was Carnwood House's ballroom the night of the ball Lady Rhys insisted on throwing for them, and Ben squirmed as the ringing tones echoed about the suddenly silent room.

The whispers began even before Charlotte paused at the top of the stairs to whip up the curiosity of Lady Rhys's guests to a fever pitch. He could tell his wife was determined to enjoy her sudden notoriety after years of being overlooked, or regarded as an insignificant dependent by the Alstones' less-enlightened acquaintances. Their mistake, he decided with satisfaction; nothing about his wife was insignificant and it was high time the *ton* learnt to see her for who she truly was.

Lady Rhys stepped forwards to welcome them, and a brief smile flickered over Ben's rather forbidding countenance as he contemplated another lady who always went her own way.

'My Lord Pemberley,' busy Coppice pronounced behind them and Ben had the pleasure of seeing his wife's radiant smile for the first time since he had returned home to be told Mrs Shaw was busy dressing and could not join him.

Of course the effect had been worth all the fuss, he conceded, as his gaze lingered on her artfully cut azure gown and the way it showed off her superb figure to full advantage.

His lordship, in the act of stepping forwards to greet his hostess, hesitated as he met his son's steady scrutiny. 'My boy?' he asked softly and rather diffidently for such a famously composed nobleman.

'Father,' he acknowledged with a careful nod and put out his hand in greeting, for the first time in his life able to say that word without feeling a burning sense of betrayal.

His lordship was seen to grip his son's hand with both hands as if he was loath to let him go and those whispers started up again. Rumours had been busy with his lordship's family, both legitimate and illegitimate, for days, and this one was likely to spread even faster than usual. Suddenly Ben didn't care, and he doubted his father did either as he acknowledged all they had in common for the first time in his life as well.

'What a crush,' he informed Miss Kate Alstone mischievously as she meekly stood in line waiting to receive her chaperon's guests of honour.

Obviously remembering the last time they attended a ball together too, she laughed and agreed heartily. 'But at least this time Miss Wells will have no excuse not to dance with you, Ben,' she consoled with a wicked glance at her one-time mentor that made Charlotte itch for a moment for the schoolroom.

'Mrs Shaw knows it's her duty to dance with her husband, however arduous,' she replied repressively.

'And he returns the compliment, knowing just as well as she does that most of the other gentlemen here tonight will give her the neck ache if she attempts to adapt to their lack of inches,' Ben countered, his eyes all the time on her as their true feelings ran like a secret language under their sparring and Charlotte felt her breath quicken, daring to see a message in them she had hardly brought herself to even look for until tonight.

'Except me, of course,' his lordship put in mildly, showing that it wasn't just his inches Ben had inherited from that side of the family.

They stepped into the crowd together just as Ben and his father were vying for her dance card and Charlotte was overcome by a ridiculous urge to succumb to the giggles.

'Last time I ventured on to a dance floor, I seem to remember most of the young gentlemen present running for cover,' she observed happily enough.

'Idiots,' her husband condemned those timorous *beaux*.

'And I always knew you'd grow into those long limbs of yours one day,' his father told her with an encouraging smile, then turned to greet guests Charlotte certainly hadn't been expecting.

'Your graces,' he said blandly as they turned to face the Duke and Duchess of Devingham. 'I don't think you've met my son and daughter-in-law yet, have you?'

Charlotte's grandparents shifted under his lordship's steady grey gaze as if they had suddenly found their expensive evening clothes didn't fit them after all.

'Not quite the match we were aiming for,' her grandfather informed Lord Pemberley stiffly, without looking at either Charlotte or her new husband.

'No, that one would have been a disaster,' he agreed genially and moved that cool gaze of his on to the Duchess, who flushed and looked more uncomfortable than ever.

Charlotte had to fight a smug grin as she recognised the tactics of a master, for the first time since she was ten years old feeling nothing for her grandparents but pity that they'd let pride take the place of love in every aspect of their unbearably narrowed lives.

'We are at home every Wednesday at the usual time, if your daughter-in-law wishes to call,' the Duchess told Lord Pemberley's left ear as if the words pained her.

Suppressing the urge to inform him as their proxy that she was always engaged on a Wednesday herself, Charlotte nodded regally and laid her hand on Ben's coat sleeve to remind anyone who cared to know that he was her husband and therefore she would never go where he wasn't welcome.

'The Marquis of Pemberley's son will find us in as well,' the Duke was forced to admit in the light of all the eyes centred on them as if fascinated, and the even more eagerly pricked ears straining for any hint of a public rift with their only grandchild.

'How fortunate for him,' Ben replied wickedly and pretended not to feel the kick Charlotte strategically aimed at his ankle while outwardly they all pretended to be as serene as gliding swans on a summer lake.

'On other afternoons I attend the Queen, of course,' the Duchess reminded herself rather unnecessarily, and at last the party broke up when the ducal pair spotted another, more predictable marquis to bore.

'Awful people,' Lady Rhys whispered to Charlotte as she finally joined them after declaring any more late-comers could find her and Kate if they wanted to be effused over, 'but it had to be done.'

'I suppose so,' she murmured back, 'not that I care one way or the other any more, I'm thankful to say.'

'Maybe not, but Pemberley does, and will you just look at him, Charlotte, I never saw a prouder father than he looks tonight.'

Charlotte turned to eye the still-handsome marquis as instructed even as a revolutionary idea occurred to her. She slanted a sidelong look at Lady Rhys, then met Kate's amused scrutiny and they smiled at each other conspiratorially and nodded as that inveterate match-maker was sized up and potentially matched herself. That ought to give them something to do this heady Season, other than attend the Regent's extravagant entertainments for the Allied Sovereigns and visit duchesses on Wednesday afternoons. Charlotte doubted Kate had met her match yet, but at least she wouldn't be bored for the rest of the summer.

'Scheming again, my lovely?' Ben asked as he swept his wife on to the dance floor so they could finally open the ball.

'Now did I ever?' she asked half-seriously, desperately hoping he didn't feel she had trapped him now he was actually wedded to her.

'Not nearly enough, or we might have been married nigh on two years ago now,' he informed her mock sternly as they waltzed as perfectly together as gangling Miss Wells had once dreamt they might, although only in her wildest fantasies had she thought it might one day happen.

'It took someone knocking you out of your senses and locking you up under threat of death for you to make love to me, let alone ask me to marry you. You surely don't expect me to believe you'd ever have ventured it without such a pressing reason to do so?' she asked with a limp attempt at gaiety.

'Maybe I like being married to you so well that I regret my stubbornness, though,' he admitted gruffly, 'two years is such a waste when we could have been happy so much sooner.'

'Are you happy, then?' she heard herself ask wistfully and could have kicked herself after all the resolutions she had made to make their marriage easy on him, not to cling or ask more than he was willing to give.

'Blissfully,' he said fervently and then paused. 'Or at least I would be if I thought you might be too.'

'I could be,' she told him cautiously.

'Then perhaps you wouldn't mind telling me how, because I should like to ensure it as soon as possible.'

The dance finally came to an end and she met his eyes with a plea in her own. 'Don't make me say it,

Ben,' she begged as his strong arm came up to hold her unfashionably close, even now the music had stopped.

Among so many people it seemed impossible that they could seem so enclosed in their own private world, but nobody else felt quite real anyway as she accepted a glass of champagne from a footman and let her husband sweep her off to a private corner of the ballroom so similar to the one she'd sat in at Lady Wintergreen's ball.

'Then I'll brave it first after all. I love you, Charlotte,' he told her and the sincerity in his silver-grey gaze allowed no room for doubt as she gazed up at him with such painful hope she hardly dared breathe. 'I knew it even before I saw those damn rogues attack you and carry you off.'

'Then why didn't you tell me so, you stubborn man?' she chided him even as she wondered if she ought to pinch herself in case she was dreaming after all.

'Because I promised my mother I'd never fall in love, and certainly never produce children who might have to watch me pine uselessly for a lover who'd walk away without a backward look as I did her.'

'As if I could ever leave you, and you really mean that she asked that of you?' Charlotte asked incredulously, for if his mother had loved her son as deeply as she thought she had, that was the last promise she would ever have thought her capable of demanding.

'No, I vowed it to myself as she lay dying with my father's name on her lips,' he said bleakly, and her heart bled for that boy, already halfway to manhood after such a truncated childhood as his mother had been able to give him.

'She would never have wanted you to make such a promise. I dare say she'd rather you chopped off your own leg than hold yourself aloof from the world for the rest of your life because of her.'

'I know that now,' he said with a grimace for the folly of devastated ten-year-old boys, and of much older and supposedly wiser men. 'They were too young to manage such a heady passion, don't you think?'

'Yes, I do.'

'And we're altogether older and wiser?'

'About that I'm not quite so sure,' she said ruefully, thinking of those two years and how reluctant they'd both been to admit how strongly they were attracted to each other.

'Then do you, my lovely Angela Charlotte Venetia Louisa Standish Kirkwell-Shaw, really take me, plain Ben Shaw, to love and cherish as long as we both shall live?'

'I do, Ben, and I don't think you're plain at all,' she told him with a flirtatious look from under her eyelashes Miss Wells would have been highly ashamed of, probably.

'How gratifying, but damn it all, woman, do you love me or no?'

'Of course I do, haven't I just said so?'

'Have you?' he asked and then seemed to review their recent conversation in his mind. 'Oh, so you have. But tell me, wife, have you made a promise never to tell a man outright that you love him, or might you consider actually saying so some time before our tenth anniversary?'

'Yes, I've considered it and I still love you, Ben Shaw,' she informed him with a delightful surge of feeling rushing through her just like bubbles through champagne.

'Good, because I love you, my darling, and I can't wait to get you home and have another shot at beginning our ten children.'

'Ten?' Charlotte heard her voice squeak at the very idea. 'You were adamant you'd never have any only a short time ago.'

'That was before you converted me; now I want as many as I can get and, as you're really rather mature to fit them all in if we don't hurry, I feel it's high time we went home and began the enterprise.'

'Stone and Shaw and all their many Sons?' she asked dubiously.

'Always room for another, and if there isn't we'll launch another venture,' he said accommodatingly and grinned at her look of shocked delight. 'The great benefit of being born illegitimate is that I don't have to hand my father's title on to the eldest of them and push the others into the church, the army or the law,' he joked and finally Charlotte snapped out of her bubble of disbelief and into the glory of reality.

If her Ben was able to joke about his own illegitimacy, then miracles really did happen and he truly loved her after all.

'Well, what are we waiting for then, my love?' she invited, parting her lips for his kiss and wriggling scandalously close to her own husband, and in a ballroom of all places.

'For all these people to go home?' he suggested distractedly.

'All what people?'

'You really do love me, don't you, my darling dragon?'

'Yes, I really, really do, and what do you mean by calling me that?'

Seeing the militant, Miss Wells–like glint in her eyes as she asked that question, Ben laughed. 'I never met such a tempting, tantalising, altogether irresistible dragon before I laid eyes on Miss Charlotte Wells, love, and she blew me off my feet the first moment I laid eyes on her.'

'Even if you did think of her as a dragon lady?' she asked wistfully.

'Especially because of that,' he murmured and shocked polite society by picking up his lanky wife in his mighty arms and carrying her out of their own marriage celebrations like some sort of pirate king claiming his woman, without even bothering to make the slightest pretence she'd been taken faint and needed her bed.

'And I think we know exactly where they're bound,' one of the dowagers was heard to say disapprovingly.

'Lucky creature,' her bosom bow replied absently as she observed Mr Shaw's long stride and the play of his mighty muscles as he ran up the stairs with his lady brazenly enjoying them much closer to.

'I know,' the dowager agreed with a wistful look and an envious sigh.

'They think we're scandalous,' Charlotte murmured as Ben finally tumbled her into their carriage and he offered to double the coachman's wages if he got them home in half the usual time.

'Who cares? Anyway, they're right, and now about those ten children…'

'What about them, Mr Shaw?' she murmured, trying to hang on to some semblance of sanity as he set about the row of tiny buttons all down her back as if there wasn't a moment to spare for such a task when he finally got her to bed.

'I expect at least one to be a gorgeous little girl with hair the colour of a bonfire and eyes like the best, darkest chocolate,' he informed her arrogantly.

'I can see why it might take ten of them to guarantee that, then,' she agreed solemnly as she felt cool air on her heated skin as her gown began to fall off her shoulders and joy and love and sheer overwhelming desire coursed through her and she found she didn't care much about propriety either.

'In the end I'm sure you'll manage it; after all, I believe you can do anything, Mrs Shaw, even persuade their idiot of a father that they needed to be born in the first place.'

'One thing at a time, husband,' she cautioned as he jumped out of the carriage and ran up the steps of their new home with her cradled in his arms once more, and both of them were gasping for breath when he finally reached their bedroom, but not solely because of the effort of getting there so quickly.

'I love you, Ben,' Charlotte announced as if she couldn't say it often enough now they'd finally broken the drought.

'And I love you, Angela…Charlotte…Venetia…

Louisa…Shaw,' he replied huskily, punctuating each of her over-supply of names with a kiss to a different part of her as he skilfully stripped her of every stitch she was wearing. 'More than I ever dared dream I could love anyone,' he added, settling beside his naked wife on their bed to watch fascinated as his touch, his kisses, his hot gaze set her creamy skin afire.

'Prove it!' she challenged him boldly when she was finally impatient with such tantalising caresses.

He proved it so effectively that Miss Isabella Charlotte Shaw was born almost nine months after that scandalous marriage ball at Carnwood House, and at her christening three months later her striking resemblance to her flame-headed mama was generally marvelled at.

'You needn't think you've got away with the other nine, though,' her husband informed Charlotte sternly as he 'assisted' her to bed without Jessie's capable help that night.

'But even you must admit it's a good start,' she replied, confident at last that he really did adore her red hair and her long, long limbs and their daughter would never be made to feel awkward or overgrown while she had a father who so clearly loved her *and* her mother to distraction.

'True,' he said pompously, 'but practice makes perfect, Mrs Shaw, practice makes perfect.'

* * * * *